Acclaim For the Work of STEPHEN KING!

"Excellent, psychologically textured…Stephen King is so widely acknowledged as America's master of paranormal terrors that you can forget his real genius is for the everyday."
—*New York Times Book Review*

"King has written…a novel that's as hauntingly touching as it is just plain haunted…one of his freshest and most frightening works to date."
—*Entertainment Weekly*

"Extraordinarily vivid…an impressive tour de force, a sensitive character study that holds the reader rapt."
—*Playboy*

"Stephen King is superb."
—*Time*

"Mr. King makes palpable the longing and regret that arise out of calamity."
—*Wall Street Journal*

"King is a master at crafting a story and creating a sense of place."
—*USA Today*

"Don't start this one on a school night, kids. You'll be up till dawn."
—*People*

Marsden's house came into view. It was like one of those Hollywood Hills mansions you see in the movies: big and jutting out over the drop. The side facing us was all glass.

"The house that heroin built." Liz sounded vicious.

There was one more curve before we came to the paved yard in front of the house. Liz drove around it and I saw a man in front of the double garage where Marsden's fancy cars were. I opened my mouth to say it must be Teddy, the gatekeeper, but then I saw his mouth was gone.

And given the red hole where his mouth had been, he hadn't died a natural death.

Like I said, this is a horror story...

LATER

by **Stephen King**

A HARD CASE CRIME NOVEL

A HARD CASE CRIME BOOK
(HCC-147)
First Hard Case Crime edition: March 2021

Published by

Titan Books
A division of Titan Publishing Group Ltd
144 Southwark Street
London SE1 0UP

in collaboration with Winterfall LLC

Print edition ISBN 978-1-78909-649-1
E-book ISBN 978-1-78909-650-7

Design direction by Max Phillips
www.maxphillips.net

Typeset by Swordsmith Productions

The name "Hard Case Crime" and the Hard Case Crime logo are trademarks of Winterfall LLC. Hard Case Crime books are selected and edited by Charles Ardai.

Printed in the United States of America

Visit us on the web at www.HardCaseCrime.com

For Chris Lotts

"There are only so many tomorrows."

— Michael Landon

LATER

I don't like to start with an apology—there's probably even a rule against it, like never ending a sentence with a preposition —but after reading over the thirty pages I've written so far, I feel like I have to. It's about a certain word I keep using. I learned a lot of four-letter words from my mother and used them from an early age (as you will find out), but this is one with five letters. The word is *later*, as in "Later on" and "Later I found out" and "It was only later that I realized." I know it's repetitive, but I had no choice, because my story starts when I still believed in Santa Claus and the Tooth Fairy (although even at six I had my doubts). I'm twenty-two now, which makes this later, right? I suppose when I'm in my forties—always assuming I make it that far—I'll look back on what I thought I understood at twenty-two and realize there was a lot I didn't get at all. There's always a later, I know that now. At least until we die. Then I guess it's all *before that*.

My name is Jamie Conklin, and once upon a time I drew a Thanksgiving turkey that I thought was the absolute cat's ass. Later—and not much later—I found out it was more like the stuff that comes out of the cat's ass. Sometimes the truth really sucks.

I think this is a horror story. Check it out.

1

I was coming home from school with my mother. She was holding my hand. In the other hand I clutched my turkey, the ones we made in first grade the week before Thanksgiving. I was so proud of mine I was practically shitting nickels. What you did, see, was put your hand on a piece of construction paper and then trace around it with a crayon. That made the tail and body. When it came to the head, you were on your own.

I showed mine to Mom and she's all yeah yeah yeah, right right right, totally great, but I don't think she ever really saw it. She was probably thinking about one of the books she was trying to sell. "Flogging the product," she called it. Mom was a literary agent, see. It used to be her brother, my Uncle Harry, but Mom took over his business a year before the time I'm telling you about. It's a long story and kind of a bummer.

I said, "I used Forest Green because it's my favorite color. You knew that, right?" We were almost to our building by then. It was only three blocks from my school.

She's all yeah yeah yeah. Also, "You play or watch *Barney* and *The Magic Schoolbus* when we get home, kiddo, I've got like a zillion calls to make."

So *I* go yeah yeah yeah, which earned me a poke and a grin. I loved it when I could make my mother grin because even at six I knew that she took the world very serious. Later on I found out part of the reason was me. She thought she might be raising a crazy kid. The day I'm telling you about was the one when she decided for sure I wasn't crazy after all. Which must have been sort of a relief and sort of not.

"You don't talk to anybody about this," she said to me later that day. "Except to me. And maybe not even me, kiddo. Okay?"

I said okay. When you're little and it's your mom, you say okay to everything. Unless she says it's bedtime, of course. Or to finish your broccoli.

We got to our building and the elevator was still broken. You could say things might have been different if it had been working, but I don't think so. I think that people who say life is all about the choices we make and the roads we go down are full of shit. Because check it, stairs or elevator, we still would have come out on the third floor. When the fickle finger of fate points at you, all roads lead to the same place, that's what I think. I may change my mind when I'm older, but I really don't think so.

"Fuck this elevator," Mom said. Then, "You didn't hear that, kiddo."

"Hear what?" I said, which got me another grin. Last grin for her that afternoon, I can tell you. I asked her if she wanted me to carry her bag, which had a manuscript in it like always, that day a big one, looked like a five-hundred-pager (Mom always sat on a bench reading while she waited for me to get out of school, if the weather was nice). She said, "Sweet offer, but what do I always tell you?"

"You have to tote your own burden in life," I said.

"Correctamundo."

"Is it Regis Thomas?" I asked.

"Yes indeed. Good old Regis, who pays our rent."

"Is it about Roanoke?"

"Do you even have to ask, Jamie?" Which made me snicker. *Everything* good old Regis wrote was about Roanoke. That was the burden he toted in life.

We went up the stairs to the third floor, where there were two other apartments plus ours at the end of the hall. Ours was the fanciest one. Mr. and Mrs. Burkett were standing outside 3A, and I knew right away something was wrong because Mr. Burkett was smoking a cigarette, which I hadn't seen him do before and was illegal in our building anyway. His eyes were bloodshot and his hair was all crazied up in gray spikes. I always called him mister, but he was actually Professor Burkett, and taught something smart at NYU. English and European Literature, I later found out. Mrs. Burkett was dressed in a nightgown and her feet were bare. That nightgown was pretty thin. I could see most of her stuff right through it.

My mother said, "Marty, what's wrong?"

Before he could say anything back, I showed him my turkey. Because he looked sad and I wanted to cheer him up, but also because I was so proud of it. "Look, Mr. Burkett! I made a turkey! Look, Mrs. Burkett!" I held it up for her in front of my face because I didn't want her to think I was looking at her stuff.

Mr. Burkett paid no attention. I don't think he even heard me. "Tia, I have some awful news. Mona died this morning."

My mother dropped her bag with the manuscript inside it between her feet and put her hand over her mouth. "Oh, no! Tell me that's not true!"

He began to cry. "She got up in the night and said she wanted a drink of water. I went back to sleep and she was on the couch this morning with a comforter pulled up to her chin and so I tiptoed to the kitchen and put on the coffee because I thought the pleasant smell would w-w-wake... would wake..."

He really broke down then. Mom took him in her arms the way she did me when I hurt myself, even though Mr. Burkett was about a hundred (seventy-four, I found out later).

That was when Mrs. Burkett spoke to me. She was hard to hear, but not as hard as some of them because she was still pretty fresh. She said, "Turkeys aren't green, James."

"Well mine is," I said.

My mother was still holding Mr. Burkett and kind of rocking him. They didn't hear her because they couldn't, and they didn't hear me because they were doing adult things: comforting for Mom, blubbering for Mr. Burkett.

Mr. Burkett said, "I called Dr. Allen and he came and said she probably had a soak." At least that's what I thought he said. He was crying so much it was hard to tell. "He called the funeral parlor. They took her away. I don't know what I'll do without her."

Mrs. Burkett said, "My husband is going to burn your mother's hair with his cigarette if he doesn't look out."

And sure enough, he did. I could smell the singeing hair, a kind of beauty shop smell. Mom was too polite to say anything about it, but she made him let go of her, and then she took the cigarette from him and dropped it on the floor and stepped on it. I thought that was a groady thing to do, extreme litterbugging, but I didn't say anything. I got that it was a special situation.

I also knew that talking to Mrs. Burkett any more would freak him out. Mom, too. Even a little kid knows certain basic things if he's not soft in the attic. You said please, you said thank you, you didn't flap your weenie around in public or chew with your mouth open, and you didn't talk to dead folks when they were standing next to living folks who were just starting to miss them. I only want to say, in my own defense, that when I saw her I didn't know she was dead. Later on I got better at telling the difference, but back then I was just learning. It was her nightgown I could see through, not her. Dead people look just like living people, except they're always wearing the clothes they died in.

Meanwhile, Mr. Burkett was rehashing the whole thing. He told my mother how he sat on the floor beside the couch and held his wife's hand till that doctor guy came and again till the mortician guy came to take her away. "Conveyed her hence" was what he actually said, which I didn't understand until Mom explained it to me. And at first I thought he said *beautician*, maybe because of the smell when he burned Mom's hair. His crying had tapered off, but now it ramped up again. "Her rings are gone," he said through his tears. "Both her wedding ring and her engagement ring, that big diamond. I looked on the night table by her side of the bed, where she puts them when she rubs that awful-smelling arthritis cream into her hands—"

"It does smell bad," Mrs. Burkett admitted. "Lanolin is basically sheep dip, but it really helps."

I nodded to show I understood but didn't say anything.

"—and on the bathroom sink, because sometimes she leaves them there…I've looked *everywhere*."

"They'll turn up," my mother soothed, and now that her hair was safe, she took Mr. Burkett in her arms again. "They'll turn up, Marty, don't you worry about that."

"I miss her so much! I miss her already!"

Mrs. Burkett flapped a hand in front of her face. "I give him six weeks before he's asking Dolores Magowan out to lunch."

Mr. Burkett was blubbing, and my mother was doing her soothing thing like she did to me whenever I scraped my knee or this one time when I tried to make her a cup of tea and slopped hot water on my hand. Lots of noise, in other words, so I took a chance but kept my voice low.

"Where are your rings, Mrs. Burkett? Do you know?"

They have to tell you the truth when they're dead. I didn't know that at the age of six; I just assumed all grownups told the truth, living *or* dead. Of course back then I also believed Goldilocks was a real girl. Call me stupid if you want to. At least I didn't believe the three bears actually talked.

"Top shelf of the hall closet," she said. "Way in the back, behind the scrapbooks."

"Why there?" I asked, and my mother gave me a strange look. As far as she could see, I was talking to the empty doorway…although by then she knew I wasn't quite the same as other kids. After a thing that happened in Central Park, not a nice thing—I'll get to it—I overheard her telling one of her editor friends on the phone that I was "fey." That scared the shit out of me, because I thought she meant she was changing my name to Fay, which is a girl's name.

"I don't have the slightest idea," Mrs. Burkett said. "By then I suppose I was having the stroke. My thoughts would have been drowning in blood."

Thoughts drowning in blood. I never forgot that.

Mom asked Mr. Burkett if he wanted to come down to our apartment for a cup of tea ("or something stronger"), but he said no, he was going to have another hunt for his wife's missing rings. She asked him if he would like us to bring him some Chinese take-out, which my mother was planning for dinner, and he said that would be good, thank you Tia.

My mother said de nada (which she used almost as much as yeah yeah yeah and right right right), then said we'd bring it to his apartment around six, unless he wanted to eat with us in ours, which he was welcome to do. He said no, he'd like to eat in his place but he would like us to eat with him. Except what he actually said was *our* place, like Mrs. Burkett was still alive. Which she wasn't, even though she was there.

"By then you'll have found her rings," Mom said. She took my hand. "Come on, Jamie. We'll see Mr. Burkett later, but for now let's leave him alone."

Mrs. Burkett said, "Turkeys aren't green, Jamie, and that doesn't look like a turkey anyway. It looks like a blob with fingers sticking out of it. You're no Rembrandt."

Dead people have to tell the truth, which is okay when you want to know the answer to a question, but as I said, the truth can really suck. I started to be mad at her, but just then she started to cry and I couldn't be. She turned to Mr. Burkett and said, "Who'll make sure you don't miss the belt loop in the back of your pants now? Dolores Magowan? I should smile and kiss a pig." She kissed his cheek…or kissed *at* it, I couldn't really tell which. "I loved you, Marty. Still do."

Mr. Burkett raised his hand and scratched the spot where her lips had touched him, as if he had an itch. I suppose that's what he thought it was.

2

So yeah, I see dead people. As far as I can remember, I always have. But it's not like in that movie with Bruce Willis. It can be interesting, it can be scary sometimes (the Central Park dude), it can be a pain in the ass, but mostly it just *is*. Like being left-handed, or being able to play classical music when you're like three years old, or getting early-onset Alzheimer's, which is what happened to Uncle Harry when he was only forty-two. At age six, forty-two seemed old to me, but even then I understood it's young to wind up not knowing who you are. Or what the names of things are—for some reason that's what always scared me the most when we went to see Uncle Harry. His thoughts didn't drown in blood from a busted brain vessel, but they drowned, just the same.

Mom and me trucked on down to 3C, and Mom let us in. Which took some time, because there are three locks on the door. She said that's the price you pay for living in style. We had a six-room apartment with a view of the avenue. Mom called it the Palace on Park. We had a cleaning woman who came in twice a week. Mom had a Range Rover in the parking garage on Second Avenue, and sometimes we went up to Uncle Harry's place in Speonk. Thanks to Regis Thomas and a few other writers (but mostly good old Regis), we were living high on the hog. It didn't last, a depressing development I will discuss all too soon. Looking back on it, I sometimes think my life was like a Dickens novel, only with swearing.

Mom tossed her manuscript bag and purse on the sofa and sat down. The sofa made a farting noise that usually made us laugh, but not that day. "Jesus-fuck," Mom said, then raised a hand in a stop gesture. "You—"

"I didn't hear it, nope," I said.

"Good. I need to have an electric shock collar or something that buzzes every time I swear around you. That'd teach me." She stuck out her lower lip and blew back her bangs. "I've got another two hundred pages of Regis's latest to read—"

"What's this one called?" I asked, knowing the title would have *of Roanoke* in it. They always did.

"*Ghost Maiden of Roanoke*," she said. "It's one of his better ones, lots of se…lots of kissing and hugging."

I wrinkled my nose.

"Sorry, kiddo, but the ladies love those pounding hearts and torrid thighs." She looked at the bag with *Ghost Maiden of Roanoke* inside, secured with the usual six or eight rubber bands, one of which always snapped and made Mom give out some of her best swears. Many of which I still use. "Now I feel like I don't want to do anything but have a glass of wine. Maybe the whole bottle. Mona Burkett was a prize pain the ass, he might actually be better off without her, but right now he's gutted. I hope to God he's got relatives, because I don't relish the idea of being Comforter in Chief."

"She loved him, too," I said.

Mom gave me a strange look. "Yeah? You think?"

"I know. She said something mean about my turkey, but then she cried and kissed him on the cheek."

"You imagined that, James," she said, but half-heartedly. She knew better by then, I'm sure she did, but grownups have a tough time believing, and I'll tell you why. When they find out as kids that Santa Claus is a fake and Goldilocks isn't a real girl and the Easter Bunny is bullshit—just three examples, I could give more—it makes a complex and they stop believing anything they can't see for themselves.

"Nope, didn't imagine it. She said I'd never be Rembrandt. Who is that?"

"An artist," she said, and blew her bangs back again. I don't know why she didn't just cut them or wear her hair a different way. Which she could, because she was really pretty.

"When we go down there to eat, don't you dare say anything to Mr. Burkett about what you think you saw."

"I won't," I said, "but she was right. My turkey sucks." I felt bad about that.

I guess it showed, because she held out her arms. "Come here, kiddo."

I came and hugged her.

"Your turkey is beautiful. It's the most beautiful turkey I ever saw. I'm going to put it up on the refrigerator and it will stay there forever."

I hugged as tight as I could and put my face in the hollow of her shoulder so I could smell her perfume. "I love you, Mom."

"I love you too, Jamie, a million bunches. Now go play or watch TV. I need to roll some calls before ordering the Chinese."

"Okay." I started for my room, then stopped. "She put her rings on the top shelf of the hall closet, behind some scrapbooks."

My mother stared at me with her mouth open. "Why would she do that?"

"I asked her and she said she didn't know. She said by then her thoughts were drownding in blood."

"Oh my God," Mom whispered, and put her hand to her neck.

"You should figure out a way to tell him when we have the Chinese. Then he won't worry about it. Can I have General Tso's?"

"Yes," she said. "And brown rice, not white."

"Right right right," I said, and went to play with my Legos. I was making a robot.

3

The Burketts' apartment was smaller than ours, but nice. After dinner, while we were having our fortune cookies (mine said *A feather in the hand is better than a bird in the air*, which makes no sense at all), Mom said, "Have you checked the closets, Marty? For her rings, I mean?"

"Why would she put her rings in a closet?" A sensible enough question.

"Well, if she was having a stroke, she might not have been thinking too clearly."

We were eating at the little round table in the kitchen nook. Mrs. Burkett was sitting on one of the stools at the counter and nodded vigorously when Mom said that.

"Maybe I'll check," Mr. Burkett said. He sounded pretty vague. "Right now I'm too tired and upset."

"You check the bedroom closet when you get around to it," Mom said. "I'll check the one in the hall right now. A little stretching will do me good after all that sweet and sour pork."

Mrs. Burkett said, "Did she think that up all by herself? I didn't know she was that smart." Already she was getting hard to hear. After awhile I wouldn't be able to hear her at all, just see her mouth moving, like she was behind a thick pane of glass. Pretty soon after that she'd be gone.

"My mom's plenty smart," I said.

"Never said she wasn't," Mr. Burkett said, "but if she finds those rings in the front hall closet, I'll eat my hat."

Just then my mother said "Bingo!" and came in with the rings on the palm of one outstretched hand. The wedding ring was pretty ordinary, but the engagement ring was as big as an eyeball. A real sparkler.

"Oh my God!" Mr. Burkett cried. "How in God's name…?"

"I prayed to St. Anthony," Mom said, but cast a quick glance my way. And a smile. " 'Tony, Tony, come around! Something's lost that must be found!' And as you see, it worked."

I thought about asking Mr. Burkett if he wanted salt and pepper on his hat, but didn't. It wasn't the right time to be funny, and besides, it's like my mother always says—nobody loves a smartass.

4

The funeral was three days later. It was my first one, and interesting, but not what you'd call fun. At least my mother didn't have to be Comforter in Chief. Mr. Burkett had a sister and brother to take care of that. They were old, but not as old as he was. Mr. Burkett cried all the way through the service and the sister kept handing him Kleenex. Her purse seemed to be full of them. I'm surprised she had room for anything else.

That night mom and I had pizza from Domino's. She had wine and I had Kool-Aid as a special treat for being good at the funeral. When we were down to the last piece of the pie, she asked me if I thought Mrs. Burkett had been there.

"Yeah. She was sitting on the steps leading up to the place where the minister and her friends talked."

"The pulpit. Could you…" She picked up the last slice, looked at it, then put it down and looked at me. "Could you see through her?"

"Like a movie ghost, you mean?"

"Yes. I suppose that is what I mean."

"Nope. She was all there, but still in her nightgown. I was surprised to see her, because she died three days ago. They don't usually last that long."

"They just disappear?" Like she was trying to get it straight in her mind. I could tell she didn't like talking about it, but I was glad she was. It was a relief.

"Yeah."

"What was she doing, Jamie?"

"Just sitting there. Once or twice she looked at her coffin, but mostly she looked at him."

"At Mr. Burkett. Marty."

"Right. She said something once, but I couldn't hear. Pretty soon after they die, their voices start to fade away, like turning down the music on the car radio. After awhile you can't hear them at all."

"And then they're gone."

"Yes," I said. There was a lump in my throat, so I drank the rest of my Kool-Aid to make it go away. "Gone."

"Help me clean up," she said. "Then we can watch an episode of *Torchwood*, if you want."

"Yeah, cool!" In my opinion *Torchwood* wasn't really cool, but getting to stay up an hour after my usual bedtime was way cool.

"Fine. Just as long as you understand we're not going to make a practice of it. But I need to tell you something first, and it's very serious, so I want you to pay attention. *Close* attention."

"Okay."

She got down on one knee, so our faces were more or less level and took hold of me by the shoulders, gently but firmly. "Never tell anyone about seeing dead people, James. *Never*."

"They wouldn't believe me anyway. You never used to."

"I believed *something*," she said. "Ever since that day in Central Park. Do you remember that?" She blew back her bangs. "Of course you do. How could you forget?"

"I remember." I only wished I didn't.

She was still on her knee, looking into my eyes. "So here it is. People not believing is a good thing. But someday somebody might. And that might get the wrong kind of talk going, or put you in actual danger."

"Why?"

"There's an old saying that dead men tell no tales, Jamie. But they *can* talk to you, can't they? Dead men *and* women. You say they have to answer questions, and give truthful answers. As if dying is like a dose of sodium pentothal."

I had no clue what that was and she must have seen it on my face because she said to never mind that, but to remember what Mrs. Burkett had told me when I asked about her rings.

"So?" I said. I liked being close to my mom, but I didn't like her looking at me in that intense way.

"Those rings were valuable, especially the engagement ring. People die with secrets, Jamie, and there are always people who want to know those secrets. I don't mean to scare you, but sometimes a scare is the only lesson that works."

Like the man in Central Park was a lesson about being careful in traffic and always wearing your helmet when you were on your bike, I thought…but didn't say.

"I won't talk about it," I said.

"Not ever. Except to me. If you need to."

"Okay."

"Good. We have an understanding."

She got up and we went in the living room and watched TV. When the show was over, I brushed my teeth and peed and washed my hands. Mom tucked me in and kissed me and said what she always said: "Sweet dreams, pleasant repose, all the bed and all the clothes."

Most nights that was the last time I saw her until morning. I'd hear the clink of glass as she poured herself a second glass of wine (or a third), then jazz turned way down low as she started reading some manuscript. Only I guess moms must have an extra sense, because that night she came back in and sat on my bed. Or maybe she just heard me crying, although I was trying my best to keep it on the down-low. Because, as she also always said, it's better to be part of the solution instead of part of the problem.

"What's wrong, Jamie?" she asked, brushing back my hair. "Are you thinking about the funeral? Or Mrs. Burkett being there?"

"What would happen to me if you died, Mom? Would I have to go live in an orphanage home?" Because it sure as shit wouldn't be with Uncle Harry.

"Of course not," Mom said, still brushing my hair. "And it's what we call a moot point, Jamie, because I'm not going to die for a long time. I'm thirty-five years old, and that means I still have over half my life ahead of me."

"What if you get what Uncle Harry's got, and have to live in that place with him?" The tears were streaming down my face. Having her stroke my forehead made me feel better, but it also made me cry more, who knows why. "That place smells bad. It smells like *pee!*"

"The chance of that happening is so teensy that if you put it next to an ant, the ant would look like Godzilla," she said. That made me smile and feel better. Now that I'm older I know she was either lying or misinformed, but the gene that triggers what Uncle Harry had—early-onset Alzheimer's—swerved around her, thank God.

"I'm not going to die, *you're* not going to die, and I think there's a good chance that this peculiar ability of yours will fade when you get older. So…are we good?"

"We're good."

"No more tears, Jamie. Just sweet dreams and—"

"Pleasant repose, all the bed and all the clothes," I finished.

"Yeah yeah yeah." She kissed my forehead and left. Leaving the door open a little bit, as she always did.

I didn't want to tell her it wasn't the funeral that had made me cry, and it wasn't Mrs. Burkett, either, because she wasn't scary. Most of them aren't. But the bicycle man in Central Park scared the shit out of me. He was *gooshy*.

5

We were on the 86th Street Transverse, heading for Wave Hill in the Bronx, where one of my preschool friends was having a big birthday party. ("Talk about spoiling a kid rotten," Mom said.) I had my present to give Lily in my lap. We went around a curve and saw a bunch of people standing in the street. The accident must have just happened. A man was lying half on the pavement and half on the sidewalk with a twisted-up bicycle beside him. Someone had put a jacket over his top half. His bottom half was wearing black bike shorts with red stripes up the sides, and a knee brace, and sneakers with blood all over them. It was on his socks and legs, too. We could hear approaching sirens.

Standing next to him was the same man in the same bike shorts and knee brace. He had white hair with blood in it. His face was caved in right down the middle, I think maybe from where he hit the curb. His nose was like in two pieces and so was his mouth.

Cars were stopping and my mother said, "Close your eyes." It was the man lying on the ground she was looking at, of course.

"He's dead!" I started to cry. "That man is dead!"

We stopped. We had to. Because of the other cars in front of us.

"No, he's not," Mom said. "He's asleep, that's all. It's what happens sometimes when someone gets banged hard. He'll be fine. Now close your eyes."

I didn't. The smashed-up man raised a hand and waved at me. They know when I see them. They always do.

"His face is in *two pieces!*"

Mom looked again to be sure, saw the man was covered down to his waist, and said, "Stop scaring yourself, Jamie. Just close your—"

"He's *there!*" I pointed. My finger was trembling. *Everything* was trembling. "Right *there*, standing next to himself!"

That scared her. I could tell by the way her mouth got all tight. She laid on her horn with one hand. With the other she pushed the button that rolled down her window and started waving at the cars ahead of her. *"Go!"* she shouted. *"Move! Stop staring at him, for Christ's sake, this isn't a fucking movie!"*

They did, except for the one right in front of her. That guy was leaning over and taking a picture with his phone. Mom pulled up and bumped his fender. He gave her the bird. My mother backed up and pulled into the other lane to go around. I wish I'd also given him the bird, but I was too freaked out.

Mom barely missed a police car coming the other way and drove for the far side of the park as fast as she could. She was almost there when I unbuckled my seatbelt. Mom yelled at me not to do that but I did it anyway and buzzed down my window and kneeled on the seat and leaned out and blew groceries all down the side of the car. I couldn't help it. When we got to the Central Park West side, Mom pulled over and wiped off my face with the sleeve of her blouse. She might have worn that blouse again, but if she did I don't remember it.

"God, Jamie. You're white as a sheet."

"I couldn't help it," I said. "I never saw anyone like that before. There were *bones* sticking right out of his no-nose—" Then I ralphed again, but managed to get most of that one on the street instead of on our car. Plus there wasn't as much.

She stroked my neck, ignoring someone (maybe the man who gave us the finger) who honked at us and drove around our car. "Honey, that's just your imagination. He was covered up."

"Not the one on the ground, the one standing beside him. He *waved* at me."

She stared at me for a long time, seemed like she was going to say something, then just buckled my seatbelt. "I think maybe we should skip the party. How does that sound to you?"

"Good," I said. "I don't like Lily anyway. She sneaky-pinches me during Story Time."

We went home. Mom asked me if I could keep down a cup of cocoa and I said I could. We drank cocoa together in the living room. I still had Lily's present. It was a little doll in a sailor suit. When I gave it to Lily the next week, instead of sneaky-pinching me, she gave me a kiss right on the mouth. I got teased about that and never minded a bit.

While we were drinking our cocoa (she might have put a little something extra in hers), Mom said, "I promised myself when I was pregnant that I'd never lie to my kid, so here goes. Yeah, that guy was probably dead." She paused. "No, he *was* dead. I don't think even a bike helmet would have saved him, and I didn't see one."

No, he wasn't wearing a helmet. Because if he'd been wearing it when he got hit (it was a taxi that did it, we found out), he would have been wearing it as he stood beside his body. They're always wearing what they had on when they died.

"But you only imagined you saw his face, honey. You couldn't have. Someone covered him up with a jacket. Someone very kind."

"He was wearing a tee-shirt with a lighthouse on it," I said. Then I thought of something else. It was only a little bit cheery, but after something like that, I guess you take what you can get. "At least he was pretty old."

"Why do you say that?" She was looking at me oddly. Looking back on it, I think that was when she started to believe, at least a little bit.

"His hair was white. Except for the parts with the blood in it, that is."

I started to cry again. My mother hugged me and rocked me and I went to sleep while she was doing it. I tell you what, there's nothing like having a mother around when you're thinking of scary shit.

We got the *Times* delivered to our door. My mother usually read it at the table in her bathrobe while we ate breakfast, but the day after the Central Park man she was reading one of her manuscripts instead. When breakfast was over, she told me to get dressed and maybe we'd ride the Circle Line, so it must have been a Saturday. I remember thinking it was the first weekend the Central Park man was dead in. That made it real all over again.

I did what she said, but first I went into her bedroom while she was in the shower. The newspaper was on the bed, open to the page where they put dead folks who are famous enough for the *Times*. The picture of the Central Park man was there. His name was Robert Harrison. At four I was already reading at a third-grade level, my mother was very proud of that, and there were no tough words in the headline of the story, which was all I read: CEO OF LIGHTHOUSE FOUNDATION DIES IN TRAFFIC ACCIDENT.

I saw a few more dead people after that—the saying about how in life we are in death is truer than most people know—and sometimes I said something to Mom, but mostly I didn't because I could see it upset her. It wasn't until Mrs. Burkett died and Mom found her rings in the closet that we really talked about it again.

That night after she left my room I thought I wouldn't be able to sleep, and if I did I would dream about the Central Park man with his split-open face and bones sticking out of his nose, or about my mother in her coffin, but also sitting on the steps to the pulpit, where only I could see her. But so far as I can remember, I didn't dream about anything. I got up the next morning feeling good, and Mom was feeling good, and we joked around like we sometimes did, and she stuck my turkey on the fridge and then put a big smackeroo on it, which made me giggle, and she walked me to school, and Mrs. Tate told us about dinosaurs, and life went on for two years in the good ways it usually did. Until, that is, everything fell apart.

6

When Mom realized how bad things were, I heard her talking to Anne Staley, her editor friend, about Uncle Harry on the phone. Mom said, "He was soft even before he went soft. I realize that now."

At six I wouldn't have had a clue. But by then I was eight going on nine, and I understood, at least partly. She was talking about the mess her brother had gotten himself—and her—into even before the early-onset Alzheimer's carried off his brains like a thief in the night.

I agreed with her, of course; she was my mother, and it was us against the world, a team of two. I hated Uncle Harry for the jam we were in. It wasn't until later, when I was twelve or maybe even fourteen, that I realized my mother was also partly to blame. She might have been able to get out while there was still time, probably could have, but she didn't. Like Uncle Harry, who founded the Conklin Literary Agency, she knew a lot about books but not enough about money.

She even got two warnings. One was from her friend Liz Dutton. Liz was an NYPD detective, and a great fan of Regis Thomas's Roanoke series. Mom met her at a launch party for one of those books, and they clicked. Which turned out to be not so good. I'll get to it, but for now I'll just say that Liz told my mother that the Mackenzie Fund was too good to be true. This might have been around the time Mrs. Burkett died, I'm not sure about that, but I know it was before the fall of 2008, when the economy went belly-up. Including our part of it.

Uncle Harry used to play racquetball at some fancy club near Pier 90, where the big boats dock. One of the friends he played with was a Broadway producer who told him about the Mackenzie Fund. The friend called it a license to coin money, and Uncle Harry took him seriously about that. Why wouldn't he? The friend had produced like a bazillion musicals that ran on Broadway for a bazillion years, plus also all over the country, and the royalties just poured in. (I knew exactly what royalties were—I was a literary agent's kid.)

Uncle Harry checked it out, talked to some big bug who worked for the Fund (although not to James Mackenzie himself, because Uncle Harry was just a small bug in the great scheme of things), and put in a bunch of money. The returns were so good that he put in more. And more. When he got the Alzheimer's—and he went downhill really fast— my mother took over all the accounts, and she not only stuck with the Mackenzie Fund, she put even more money into it.

Monty Grisham, the lawyer who helped with contracts back then, not only told her not to put in more, he told her to get out while the getting was good. That was the other warning she got, and not long after she took over the Conklin Agency. He also said that if a thing looked too good to be true, it probably was.

I'm telling you everything I found out in little driblets and drablets—like that overheard conversation between Mom and her editor pal. I'm sure you get that, and I'm sure you don't need me to tell you that the Mackenzie Fund was actually a big fat Ponzi scheme. The way it worked was Mackenzie and his merry band of thieves took in mega-millions and paid back big percentage returns while skimming off most of the investment dough. They kept it going by roping in new investors, telling each one how special he or she was because only a select few were allowed into the Fund. The select few, it turned out, were thousands, everyone from Broadway producers to wealthy widows who stopped being wealthy almost overnight.

A scheme like that depends on investors being happy with their returns and not only leaving their initial investments in the Fund but putting in more. It worked okay for awhile, but when the economy crashed in 2008, almost everybody in the Fund asked for their money back and the money wasn't there. Mackenzie was a piker compared to Madoff, the king of Ponzi schemes, but he gave old Bern a run for his money;

after taking in over twenty billion dollars, all he had in the Mackenzie accounts was a measly fifteen million. He went to jail, which was satisfying, but as Mom sometimes said, "Grits ain't groceries and revenge don't pay the bills."

"We're okay, we're okay," she told me when Mackenzie started showing up on all the news channels and in the *Times*. "Don't worry, Jamie." But the circles under her eyes said that *she* was plenty worried, and she had plenty of reasons to be.

Here's more of what I found out later: Mom only had about two hundred grand in assets she could put her hands on, and that included the insurance policies on her and me. What she had on the liability side of the ledger, you don't want to know. Just remember our apartment was on Park Avenue, the agency office was on Madison Avenue, and the extended care home where Uncle Harry was living ("If you can call that living," I can hear my mother adding) was in Pound Ridge, which is about as expensive as it sounds.

Closing the office on Madison was Mom's first move. After that she worked out of the Palace on Park, at least for awhile. She paid some rent in advance by cashing in those insurance policies I mentioned, including her brother's, but that would only last eight or ten months. She rented Uncle Harry's place in Speonk. She sold the Range Rover ("We don't really need a car in the city anyway, Jamie," she said) and a bunch of first edition books, including a signed Thomas Wolfe of *Look Homeward, Angel*. She cried over that one and said she didn't get half of what it was worth, because the rare book market was also in the toilet, thanks to a bunch of sellers as desperate for cash as she was. Our Andrew Wyeth painting went, too. And every day she cursed James Mackenzie for the thieving, money-grubbing, motherfucking, cock-sucking, bleeding hemorrhoid on legs that he was. Sometimes she also cursed Uncle Harry, saying he'd be living behind a garbage dumpster by the end of the year and it would serve him right. And, to be fair, later on she cursed herself for not listening to Liz and Monty.

"I feel like the grasshopper who played all summer instead of working," she said to me one night. January or February of 2009, I think. By then Liz was staying over sometimes, but not that night. That might have been the first time I noticed there were threads of gray in my mom's pretty red hair. Or maybe I remember because she started to cry and it was my turn to comfort her, even though I was just a little kid and didn't really know how to do it.

That summer we moved out of the Palace on Park and into a much smaller place on Tenth Avenue. "Not a dump," Mom said, "and the price is right." Also: "I'll be damned if I'll move out of the city. That would be waving the white flag. I'd start losing clients."

The agency moved with us, of course. The office was in what I suppose would have been my bedroom if things hadn't been so fucking dire. My room was an alcove adjacent to the kitchen. It was hot in the summer and cold in the winter, but at least it smelled good. I think it used to be the pantry.

She moved Uncle Harry to a facility in Bayonne. The less said about that place the better. The only good thing about it, I suppose, was that poor old Uncle Harry didn't know where he was, anyway; he would have pissed his pants just as much if he'd been in the Beverly Hilton.

Other things I remember about 2009 and 2010: My mother stopped getting her hair done. She stopped lunching with friends and only lunched with clients of the agency if she really had to (because she was the one who always got stuck with the check). She didn't buy many new clothes, and the ones she did buy were from discount stores. And she started drinking more wine. A lot more. There were nights when she and her friend Liz—the Regis Thomas fan and detective I told you about—would get pretty soused together. The next day Mom would be red-eyed and snappy, puttering around in her office in her pajamas. Sometimes she'd sing, "Crappy days are here again, the skies are fucking drear again." On those days it was a relief to go to school. A *public* school, of course; my private school days were over, thanks to James Mackenzie.

There were a few rays of light in all that gloom. The rare book market might have been in the shithouse, but people were reading regular books again—novels to escape and self-help books because, let's face it, in 2009 and '10, a lot of people needed to help themselves. Mom was always a big mystery reader, and she had been building up that part of the Conklin stable ever since taking over for Uncle Harry. She had ten or maybe even a dozen mystery authors. They weren't big-ticket guys and gals, but their fifteen percent brought in enough to pay the rent and keep the lights on in our new place.

Plus, there was Jane Reynolds, a librarian from North Carolina. Her novel, a mystery titled *Dead Red*, came in over the transom, and Mom just raved about it. There was an auction for who would get to publish it. All the big companies took part, and the rights ended up selling for two million dollars. Three hundred thousand of those scoots were ours, and my mother began to smile again.

"It will be a long time before we get back to Park Avenue," she said, "and we've got a lot of climbing to do before we get out of the hole Uncle Harry dug for us, but we just might make it."

"I don't want to go back to Park Avenue anyway," I said. "I like it here."

She smiled and hugged me. "You're my little love." She held me at arms' length and studied me. "Not so little anymore, either. Do you know what I'm hoping, kiddo?"

I shook my head.

"That Jane Reynolds turns out to be a book-a-year babe. And that the movie of *Dead Red* gets made. Even if neither of those things happen, there's good old Regis Thomas and his Roanoke Saga. He's the jewel in our crown."

Only *Dead Red* turned out to be like a final flash of sunlight before a big storm moves in. The movie never got made, and the publishers who bid on the book got it wrong, as they sometimes do. The book flopped, which didn't hurt us financially—the money was paid—but other stuff happened and that three hundred grand vanished like dust in the wind.

First, Mom's wisdom teeth went to hell and got infected. She had to have them all pulled. That was bad. Then Uncle Harry, troublesome Uncle Harry, still not fifty years old, tripped in the Bayonne care facility and fractured his skull. That was a lot worse.

Mom talked to the lawyer who helped her with book

contracts (and took a healthy bite of our agency fee for his trouble). He recommended another lawyer who specialized in liability and negligence suits. That lawyer said we had a good case, and maybe we did, but before the case got anywhere near a courtroom, the Bayonne facility declared bankruptcy. The only one who made money out of that was the fancy slip-and-fall lawyer, who banked just shy of forty thousand dollars.

"Those billable hours are a bitch," Mom said one night when she and Liz Dutton were well into their second bottle of wine. Liz laughed because it wasn't her forty thousand. Mom laughed because she was squiffed. I was the only one who didn't see the humor in it, because it wasn't just the lawyer's bills. We were on the hook for Uncle Harry's medical bills as well.

Worst of all, the IRS came after Mom for back taxes Uncle Harry owed. He had been putting off that other uncle—Sam—so he could dump more money into the Mackenzie Fund. Which left Regis Thomas.

The jewel in our crown.

7

Now check this out.

It's the fall of 2009. Obama is president, and the economy is slowly getting better. For us, not so much. I'm in the third grade, and Ms. Pierce has me doing a fractions problem on the board because I'm good at shit like that. I mean I was doing percentages when I was seven—literary agent's kid, remember. The kids behind me are restless because it's that funny little stretch of school between Thanksgiving and Christmas. The problem is as easy as soft butter on toast, and I'm just finishing when Mr. Hernandez, the assistant principal, sticks his head in. He and Ms. Pierce have a brief murmured conversation, and then Ms. Pierce asks me to step out into the hall.

My mother is waiting out there, and she's as pale as a glass of milk. *Skim* milk. My first thought is that Uncle Harry, who now has a steel plate in his skull to protect his useless brain, has died. Which in a gruesome way would actually be good, because it would cut down on expenses. But when I ask, she says Uncle Harry—by then living in a third-rate care home in Piscataway (he kept moving further west, like some fucked-up brain-dead pioneer)—is fine.

Mom hustles me down the hall and out the door before I can ask any more questions. Parked at the yellow curb where parents drop off their kids and pick them up in the afternoon is a Ford sedan with a bubble light on the dash. Standing beside it in a blue parka with NYPD on the breast is Liz Dutton.

Mom is rushing me toward the car, but I dig in my heels and make her stop. "What is it?" I ask. "Tell me!" I'm not crying, but the tears are close. There's been a lot of bad news since we found out about the Mackenzie Fund, and I don't think I can stand any more, but I get some. Regis Thomas is dead.

The jewel just fell out of our crown.

8

I have to stop here and tell you about Regis Thomas. My mother used to say that most writers are as weird as turds that glow in the dark, and Mr. Thomas was a case in point.

The Roanoke Saga—that's what he called it—consisted of nine books when he died, each one as thick as a brick. "Old Regis always serves up a heaping helping," Mom said once. When I was eight, I snitched a copy of the first one, *Death Swamp of Roanoke*, off one of the office shelves and read it. No problem there. I was as good at reading as I was at math and seeing dead folks (it's not bragging if it's true). Plus *Death Swamp* wasn't exactly *Finnegans Wake*.

I'm not saying it was badly written, don't get that idea; the man could tell a tale. There was plenty of adventure, lots of scary scenes (especially in the Death Swamp), a search for buried treasure, and a big hot helping of good old S-E-X. I learned more about the true meaning of sixty-nine in that book than a kid of eight should probably know. I learned something else as well, although I only made a conscious connection later. It was about all those nights Mom's friend Liz stayed over.

I'd say there was a sex scene every fifty pages or so in *Death Swamp*, including one in a tree while hungry alligators crawled around beneath. We're talking *Fifty Shades of Roanoke*. In my early teens Regis Thomas taught me to jack off, and if that's too much information, deal with it.

The books really were a saga, in that they told one continuing story with a cast of continuing characters. They were
strong men with fair hair and laughing eyes, untrustworthy
men with shifty eyes, noble Indians (who in later books became noble Native Americans), and gorgeous women with
firm, high breasts. Everyone—the good, the bad, the firm-
breasted—was randy all the time.

The heart of the series, what kept the readers coming
back (other than the duels, murders, and sex, that is) was the
titanic secret that had caused all the Roanoke settlers to disappear. Had it been the fault of George Threadgill, the chief
villain? Were the settlers dead? Was there really an ancient
city beneath Roanoke full of ancient wisdom? What did
Martin Betancourt mean when he said "Time is the key"
before expiring? What did that cryptic word *croatoan*, found
carved on a palisade of the abandoned community, really
mean? Millions of readers slavered to know the answers to
those questions. To anyone far in the future finding that
hard to believe, I'd simply tell you to hunt up something by
Judith Krantz or Harold Robbins. Millions of people read
their stuff, too.

Regis Thomas's characters were classic projection. Or
maybe I mean wish fulfillment. He was a little wizened dude
whose author photo was routinely altered to make his face
look a little less like a lady's leather purse. He didn't come to
New York City because he couldn't. The guy who wrote
about fearless men hacking their way through pestilent
swamps, fighting duels, and having athletic sex under the
stars was an agoraphobe bachelor who lived alone. He was
also incredibly paranoid (so said my mother) about his work.

No one saw it until it was done, and after the first two volumes were such rip-roaring successes, staying at the top of the bestseller lists for months, that included a copyeditor. He insisted that they be published as he wrote them, word for golden word.

He wasn't a book-a-year author (that literary agent's El Dorado), but he was dependable; a book with *of Roanoke* in the title would appear every two or three years. The first four came during Uncle Harry's tenure, the next five in Mom's. That included *Ghost Maiden of Roanoke*, which Thomas announced was the penultimate volume. The last book in the series, he promised, would answer all the questions his loyal readers had been asking ever since those first expeditions into the Death Swamp. It would also be the longest book in the series, maybe seven hundred pages. (Which would allow the publisher to tack an extra buck or two onto the purchase price.) And once Roanoke and all its mysteries were put to rest, he had confided to my mother on one of her visits to his upstate New York compound, he intended to begin a multi-volume series focused on the *Mary Celeste*.

It all sounded good until he dropped dead at his desk with only thirty or so pages of his magnum opus completed. He had been paid a cool three million in advance, but with no book, the advance would have to be paid back, including our share. Only our share was either gone or spoken for. This, as you may have guessed, was where I came in.

Okay, back to the story.

9

As we approached the unmarked police car (I knew what it was, I'd seen it lots of times, parked in front of our building with the sign reading POLICE OFFICER ON CALL on the dash), Liz held open the side of her parka to show me her empty shoulder holster. This was a kind of joke between us. No guns around my son, that was Mom's hard and fast rule. Liz always showed me the empty holster when she was wearing it, and I'd seen it plenty of times on the coffee table in our living room. Also on the night table on the side of the bed my mother didn't use, and by the age of nine, I had a pretty good idea of what that meant. *Death Swamp of Roanoke* included some steamy stuff going on between Laura Good-hugh and Purity Betancourt, the widow of Martin Betancourt (pure she wasn't).

"What's *she* doing here?" I asked Mom when we got to the car. Liz was right there, so I guess it was an impolite thing to say, if not downright rude, but I had just been jerked out of class and been told before we even got outside that our meal ticket had been revoked.

"Get in, Champ," Liz said. She always called me Champ. "Time's a-wasting."

"I don't want to. We're having fish sticks for lunch."

"Nope," Liz said, "we're having Whoppers and fries. I'm buying."

"Get in," my mother said. "Please, Jamie."

So I got in the back. There were a couple of Taco Bell wrappers on the floor and a smell that might have been microwave popcorn. There was also another smell, one I associated with our visits to Uncle Harry in his various care homes, but at least there was no metal grill between the back and the front, like I'd seen on some of the police shows Mom watched (she was partial to *The Wire*).

Mom got in front and Liz pulled out, pausing at the first red light to turn on the dashboard flasher. It went *blip-blip-blip*, and even without any siren, cars moved out of her way and we were on the FDR lickety-split.

My mother turned around and looked at me from between the seats with an expression that scared me. She looked desperate. "Could he be at his house, Jamie? I'm sure they've taken his body away to the morgue or the funeral parlor, but could he still be there?"

The answer to that was I didn't know, but I didn't say that or anything else at first. I was too amazed. And hurt. Maybe even mad, I don't remember for sure about that, but the amazement and hurt I remember very well. She had told me never to tell anybody about seeing dead people, and I never had, but then *she* did. She told Liz. That was why Liz was here, and would soon be using her blipping dashboard light to shift traffic out of our way on the Sprain Brook Parkway.

At last I said, "How long has she known?"

I saw Liz wink at me in the rearview mirror, the kind of wink that said *we've got a secret*. I didn't like it. It was Mom and me who were supposed to have the secret.

Mom reached over the seat and grasped me by the wrist.

Her hand was cold. "Never mind that, Jamie, just tell me if he could still be there."

"Yeah, I guess. If that's where he died."

Mom let go of me and told Liz to go faster, but Liz shook her head.

"Not a good idea. We might pick up a police escort, and they'd want to know what the big deal was. Am I supposed to tell them we need to talk to a dead guy before he disappears?" I could tell by the way she said it that she didn't believe a word of what Mom had told her, she was just humoring her. Joshing her along. That was okay with me. As for Mom, I don't think she cared what Liz thought, as long as she got us to Croton-on-Hudson.

"As fast as you can, then."

"Roger that, Tee-Tee." I never liked her calling Mom that, it's what some kids in my class called having to go to the bathroom, but Mom didn't seem to mind. On that day she wouldn't have cared if Liz called her Bonnie Boobsalot. Probably wouldn't even have noticed.

"Some people can keep secrets and some people can't," I said. I couldn't help myself. So I guess I was mad.

"Stop it," my mother said. "I can't afford to have you sulking."

"I'm not sulking," I said sulkily.

I knew she and Liz were tight, but she and I were supposed to be even tighter. She could have at least asked me what I thought about the idea before spilling our greatest secret some night when she and Liz were in bed after climbing what Regis Thomas called "the ladder of passion."

"I can see you're upset, and you can be pissed off at me later, but right now I need you, kiddo." It was like she had forgotten Liz was there, but I could see Liz's eyes in the rearview mirror and knew she was listening to every word.

"Okay." She was scaring me a little. "Chill, Mom."

She ran her hand through her hair and gave her bangs a yank for good measure. "This is so unfair. Everything that's happened to us…that's still happening…is so fucking fucked up!" She ruffled my hair. "You didn't hear that."

"Yes I did," I said. Because I was still mad, but she was right. Remember what I said about being in a Dickens novel, only with swears? You know why people read books like that? Because they're so happy that fucked-up shit isn't happening to them.

"I've been juggling bills for two years now and never dropped a single one. Sometimes I had to let the little ones go to pay the big ones, sometimes I let the big ones go to pay a bunch of little ones, but the lights stayed on and we never missed a meal. Right?"

"Yeah yeah yeah," I said, thinking it might raise a smile. It didn't.

"But now…" She gave her bangs another yank, leaving them all clumpy. "*Now* half a dozen things have come due at once, with goddam Infernal Revenue leading the pack. I'm drowning in a sea of red ink and I was expecting Regis to save me. Then the son of a bitch dies! At the age of fifty-nine! Who dies at fifty-nine if they're not a hundred pounds overweight or using drugs?"

"People with cancer?" I said.

Mom gave a watery snort and yanked her poor bangs.

"Easy, Tee," Liz murmured. She laid her palm against the side of Mom's neck, but I don't think Mom felt it.

"The book could save us. The book, the whole book, and

nothing but the book." She gave a wild laugh that scared me even more. "I know he only had a couple of chapters done, but nobody else knows it, because he didn't talk to anybody but my brother before Harry got sick and now me. He didn't outline or keep notes, Jamie, because he said it straitjacketed the creative process. Also because he didn't have to. He always knew where he was going."

She took my wrist again and squeezed so hard she left bruises. I saw them later that night.

"He *still* might know."

10

We did the drive-thru at the Tarrytown Burger King, and I got a Whopper, as promised. Also a chocolate shake. Mom didn't want to stop, but Liz insisted. "He's a growing boy, Tee. He needs chow even if you don't."

I liked her for that, and there were other things I liked her for, but there were also things I didn't like. Big things. I'll get to that, I'll have to, but for now let's just say my feelings about Elizabeth Dutton, Detective 2nd Grade, NYPD, were complicated.

She said one other thing before we got to Croton-on-Hudson, and I need to mention it. She was just making conversation, but it turned out to be important later (I know, that word again). Liz said Thumper had finally killed someone.

The man who called himself Thumper had been on the local news every now and then over the last few years, especially on NY1, which Mom watched most nights while she was making supper (and sometimes while we were eating, if it had been an interesting news day). Thumper's "reign of terror"—thanks, NY1—had actually been going on even before I was born, and he was sort of an urban legend. You know, like Slender Man or The Hook, only with explosives.

"Who?" I said. "Who did he kill?"

"How long until we get there?" Mom asked. She had no interest in Thumper; she had her own fish to fry.

"A guy who made the mistake of trying to use one of Manhattan's few remaining phone booths," Liz said, ignoring my mother. "Bomb Squad thinks it went off the second he lifted the receiver. Two sticks of dynamite—"

"Do we have to talk about this?" Mom asked. "And why is every goddam light *red*?"

"Two sticks of dynamite taped under the little ledge where people can put their change," Liz went on, undeterred. "Thumper's a resourceful SOB, got to give him that. They're going to crank up another task force—this will be the third since 1996—and I'm going to try for it. I was on the last one, so I've got a shot, and I can use the OT."

"Light's green," Mom said. "Go."

Liz went.

11

I was still eating a few last French fries (cold by then, but I didn't mind) when we turned onto a little dead-end street called Cobblestone Lane. There might have been cobble-stones on it once, but now it was just smooth tar. The house at the end of it was Cobblestone Cottage. It was a big stone house with fancy carved shutters and moss on the roof. You heard me, moss. Crazy, right? There was a gate, but it was open. There were signs on the gateposts, which were the same gray stone as the house. One said DO NOT TRESPASS, WE ARE TIRED OF HIDING THE BODIES. The other showed a snarling German Shepherd and said BEWARE ATTACK DOG.

Liz stopped and looked at my mother, eyebrows raised.

"The only body Regis ever buried was his pet parakeet, Francis," Mom said. "Named after Francis Drake, the explorer. And he never had a dog."

"Allergies," I said from the back seat.

Liz drove up to the house, stopped, and turned off the blippy dashboard light. "Garage doors are shut and I see no cars. Who's here?"

"Nobody," Mom said. "The housekeeper found him. Mrs. Quayle. Davina. She and a part-time gardener were the whole staff. Nice woman. She called me right after she called for an ambulance. *Ambulance* made me wonder if she was sure he was really dead, and she said she was, because she worked in a nursing home before coming to work for Regis, but he still had to go to the hospital first. I told her to go home as soon as the body was removed. She was pretty freaked out. She asked about Frank Wilcox, he's Regis's business manager, and I said I'd get in touch with him. In time I will, but the last time I spoke to Regis, he told me Frank and his wife were in Greece."

"Press?" Liz asked. "He was a bestselling writer."

"Jesus-God, I don't know." Mom looked around wildly, as

if expecting to see reporters hiding in the bushes. "I don't see any."

"They may not even know yet," Liz said. "If they do, if they heard it on a scanner, they'll go after the cops and EMTs first. The body's not here so the story's not here. We've got some time, so calm down."

"I'm staring bankruptcy in the face, I've got a brother who may live in a home for the next thirty years, and a boy who might like to go to college someday, so don't tell me to calm down. Jamie, do you see him? You know what he looks like, right? Tell me you see him."

"I know what he looks like, but I don't see him," I said.

Mom groaned and slapped the heel of her palm against her poor clumped-up bangs.

I grabbed for the door handle, and surprise surprise, there wasn't one. I told Liz to let me out and she did. We all got out.

"Knock on the door," Liz said. "If no one answers, we'll go around and boost Jamie up so he can look in the windows."

We could do that because the shutters—with fancy little ornamental doodads carved into them—were all open. My mother ran to try the door, and for the moment Liz and I were alone.

"You don't really think you can see dead people like the kid in that movie, do you, Champ?"

I didn't care if she believed me or not, but something about her tone—as if this was all a big joke—pissed me off. "Mom told you about Mrs. Burkett's rings, didn't she?"

Liz shrugged. "That might have been a lucky guess. You didn't happen to see any dead folks on the way here, did you?"

I said no, but it can be hard to tell unless you talk to them…or they talk to you. Once when me and Mom were on the bus I saw a girl with cuts in her wrists so deep they looked like red bracelets, and I was pretty sure *she* was dead, although she was nowhere near as gooshy as the Central Park man. And just that day, as we drove out of the city, I spotted an old woman in a pink bathrobe standing on the corner of Eighth Avenue. When the sign turned to WALK, she just stood there, looking around like a tourist. She had those roller things in her hair. She might have been dead, but she also might have been a live person just wandering around, the way Mom said Uncle Harry used to do sometimes before she had to put him in that first care home. Mom told me that when Uncle Harry started doing that, sometimes in his pj's, she gave up thinking he might get better.

"Fortune tellers guess lucky all the time," Liz said. "And there's an old saying about how even a stopped clock is right twice a day."

"So you think my mother's crazy and I'm helping her be crazy?"

She laughed. "That's called *enabling*, Champ, and no, I don't think that. What I think is she's upset and grasping at straws. Do you know what that means?"

"Yeah. That she's crazy."

Liz shook her head again, more emphatically this time. "She's under a lot of stress. I totally get it. But making things up won't help her. I hope *you* get *that*."

Mom came back. "No answer, and the door's locked. I tried it."

"Okay," Liz said. "Let's go window-peeking."

We walked around the house. I could look in the dining room windows, because they went all the way to the ground, but I was too short for most of the other ones. Liz made a hand-step so I could look into those. I saw a big living room with a wide-screen TV and lots of fancy furniture. I saw a dining room with a table long enough to seat the starting team of the Mets, plus maybe their bullpen pitchers. Which was crazy for a guy who hated company. I saw a room that Mom called the small parlor, and around back was the kitchen. Mr. Thomas wasn't in any of the rooms.

"Maybe he's upstairs. I've never been up there, but if he died in bed…or in the bathroom…he might still be…"

"I doubt if died on the throne, like Elvis, but I suppose it's possible."

That made me laugh, calling the toilet the throne always made me laugh, but I stopped when I saw Mom's face. This was serious business, and she was losing hope. There was a kitchen door, and she tried the knob, but it was locked, just like the front door.

She turned to Liz. "Maybe we could…"

"Don't even think about it," Liz said. "No way are we breaking in, Tee. I've got enough problems at the Department without setting off a recently deceased bestselling author's security system and trying to explain what we're doing here when the guys from Brinks or ADT show up. Or the local cops. And speaking of the cops…he died alone, right? The housekeeper found him?"

"Yes, Mrs. Quayle. She called me, I told you that—"

"The cops will want to ask her some questions. Probably

doing it right now. Or maybe the medical examiner. I don't know how they do things in Westchester County."

"Because he's famous? Because they think someone might have *murdered* him?"

"Because it's routine. And yeah, because he's famous, I suppose. The point is, I'd like for us to be gone when they show up."

Mom's shoulders slumped. "Nothing, Jamie? No sign of him?"

I shook my head.

Mom sighed and looked at Liz. "Maybe we should check the garage?"

Liz gave her a shrug that said *it's your party*.

"Jamie? What do you think?"

I couldn't imagine why Mr. Thomas would be hanging out in his garage, but I guessed it was possible. Maybe he had a favorite car. "I guess we should. As long as we're here."

We started for the garage, but then I stopped. There was a gravel path beyond Mr. Thomas's swimming pool, which had been drained. The path was lined with trees, but because it was late in the season and most of the leaves were gone, I could see a little green building. I pointed to it. "What's that?"

Mom gave her forehead another slap. I was starting to worry she might give herself a brain tumor, or something. "Oh my God, *La Petite Maison dans le Bois*! Why didn't I think of it first?"

"What's that?" I asked.

"His study! Where he writes! If he's anywhere, it would there! Come on!"

She grabbed my hand and ran me around the shallow end of the pool, but when we got to where the gravel path started, I set my feet and stopped. Mom kept going, and if Liz hadn't grabbed me by the shoulder, I probably would have face-planted.

"Mom? *Mom!*"

She turned around, looking impatient. Except that's not the right word. She looked halfway to crazy. "Come on! I'm telling you if he's anywhere *here*, it will be *there*!"

"You need to calm down, Tee," Liz said. "We'll check out his writing cabin, and then I think we should go."

"*Mom!*"

My mother ignored me. She was starting to cry, which she hardly ever did. She didn't do it even when she found out how much the IRS wanted, that day she just pounded her fists on her desk and called them a bunch of bloodsucking bastards, but she was crying now. "You go if you want, but we're staying here until Jamie's sure it's a bust. This might be just a pleasure jaunt for you, humoring the crazy lady—"

"That's unfair!"

"—but this is my *life* we're talking about—"

"I know that—"

"—and Jamie's life, and—"

"*MOM!*"

One of the worst things about being a kid, maybe the very worst, is how grownups ignore you when they get going on their shit. "*MOM! LIZ! BOTH OF YOU! STOP!*"

They stopped. They looked at me. There we stood, two women and a little boy in a New York Mets hoodie, beside a drained pool on an overcast November day.

I pointed to the gravel path leading to the little house in the woods where Mr. Thomas wrote his Roanoke books.

"He's right there," I said.

12

He came walking toward us, which didn't surprise me. Most of them, not all but most, are attracted to living people for awhile, like bugs to a bug-light. That's kind of a horrible way to put it, but it's all I can think of. I would have known he was dead even if I didn't *know* he was dead, because of what he was wearing. It was a chilly day, but he was dressed in a plain white tee, baggy shorts, and those strappy sandals Mom calls Jesus shoes. Plus there was something else, something weird: a yellow sash with a blue ribbon pinned to it.

Liz was saying something to my mother about how there was no one there and I was just pretending, but I paid no attention. I pulled free of Mom's hand and walked toward Mr. Thomas. He stopped.

"Hello, Mr. Thomas," I said. "I'm Jamie Conklin. Tia's son. I've never met you."

"Oh, come on," Liz said from behind me.

"Be quiet," Mom said, but some of Liz's skepticism must have gotten through, because she asked me if I was sure Mr. Thomas was really there.

I ignored this, too. I was curious about the sash he was wearing. Had been wearing when he died.

"I was at my desk," he said. "I always wear my sash when I'm writing. It's my good luck charm."

"What's the blue ribbon for?"

"The Regional Spelling Bee I won when I was in the sixth

grade. Spelled down kids from twenty other schools. I lost in the state competition, but I got this blue ribbon for the Regional. My mother made the sash and pinned the ribbon on it."

In my opinion I thought that was sort of a weird thing to still be wearing, since sixth grade must have been a zillion years ago for Mr. Thomas, but he said it without any embarrassment or self-consciousness. Some dead people can feel love—remember me telling you about Mrs. Burkett kissing Mr. Burkett's cheek?—and they can feel hate (something I found out in due time), but most of the other emotions seem to leave when they die. Even the love never seemed all that strong to me. I don't like to tell you this, but hate stays stronger and lasts longer. I think when people see ghosts (as opposed to dead people), it's because they are hateful. People think ghosts are scary because they *are*.

I turned back to Mom and Liz. "Mom, did you know Mr. Thomas wears a sash when he writes?"

Her eyes widened. "That was in the *Salon* interview he did five or six years ago. He's wearing it now?"

"Yeah. It's got a blue ribbon on it. From—"

"The spelling bee he won! In the interview, he laughed and called it 'my silly affectation.'"

"Maybe so," Mr. Thomas said, "but most writers have silly affectations and superstitions. We're like baseball players that way, Jimmy. And who can argue with nine straight *New York Times* bestsellers?"

"I'm Jamie," I said.

Liz said, "You told Champ there about the interview, Tee.

Must have. Or he read it himself. He's a hell of a good reader. He knew, that's all, and he—"

"*Be quiet*," my mother said fiercely. Liz raised her hands, like surrendering.

Mom stepped up beside me, looking at what to her was just a gravel path with nobody on it. Mr. Thomas was standing right in front of her with his hands in the pockets of his shorts. They were loose, and I hoped he wouldn't push down on his pockets too hard, because it looked to me like he wasn't wearing any undies.

"Tell him what I told you to tell him!"

What Mom wanted me to tell him was that he had to help us or the thin financial ice we'd been walking on for a year or more was going to break and we'd drown in a sea of debt. Also that the agency had begun to bleed clients because some of her writers knew we were in trouble and might be forced to close. Rats deserting a sinking ship was what she called them one night when Liz wasn't there and Mom was into her fourth glass of wine.

I didn't bother with all that blah-de-blah, though. Dead people have to answer your questions—at least until they disappear—and they have to tell the truth. So I just cut to the chase.

"Mom wants to know what *The Secret of Roanoke* is about. She wants to know the whole story. Do you *know* the whole story, Mr. Thomas?"

"Of course." He shoved his hands deeper into his pockets, and now I could see a little line of hair running down the middle of his stomach from below his navel. I didn't want to see that, but I did. "I always have *everything* before I write *anything*."

"And keep it all in your head?"

"I have to. Otherwise someone might steal it. Put it on the Internet. Spoil the surprises."

If he'd been alive, that might have come out sounding paranoid. Dead, he was just stating a fact, or what he believed was a fact. And hey, I thought he had a point. Computer trolls were always spilling stuff on the Net, everything from boring shit like political secrets to the really important things, like what was going to happen in the season finale of *Fringe*.

Liz walked away from me and Mom, sat on one of the benches beside the pool, crossed her legs, and lit a cigarette. She had apparently decided to let the lunatics run the asylum. That was okay with me. Liz had her good points, but that morning she was basically in the way.

"Mom wants you to tell me everything," I said to Mr. Thomas. "I'll tell her, and she'll write the last *Roanoke* book. She'll say you sent her almost all of it before you died, along with notes about how to finish the last couple of chapters."

Alive, he would have howled at the idea of someone else finishing his book; his work was the most important thing in his life and he was very possessive of it. But now the rest of him was lying on a mortician's table somewhere, dressed in the khaki shorts and the yellow sash he'd been wearing as he wrote his last few sentences. The version of him talking to me was no longer jealous or possessive of his secrets.

"Can she do that?" was all he asked.

Mom had assured me (and Liz) on the way out to Cobblestone Cottage that she really could do that. Regis Thomas insisted that no copyeditor should sully a single one of his precious words, but in fact Mom had been copyediting his books for years without telling him—even back when Uncle Harry was still in his right mind and running the business. Some of the changes were pretty big, but he never knew… or at least never said anything. If anyone in the world could copy Mr. Thomas's style, it was my mother. But style wasn't the problem. The problem was *story*.

"She can," I said, because it was simpler than telling him all of that.

"Who is that other woman?" Mr. Thomas asked, pointing at Liz.

"That's my mother's friend. Her name is Liz Dutton." Liz looked up briefly, then lit another cigarette.

"Are she and your mother fucking?" Mr. Thomas asked.

"Pretty sure, yeah."

"I thought so. It's how they look at each other."

"What did he say?" Mom asked anxiously.

"He asked if you and Liz were close friends," I said. Kind of lame, but all I could think of on the spur of the moment. "So will you tell us *The Secret of Roanoke*?" I asked Mr. Thomas. "I mean the whole book, not just the secret part."

"Yes."

"He says yes," I told Mom, and she took both her phone and a little tape recorder out of her bag. She didn't want to miss a single word.

"Tell him to be as detailed as he can."

"Mom says to be—"

"I heard her," Mr. Thomas said. "I'm dead, not deaf." His shorts were lower than ever.

"Cool," I said. "Listen, maybe you better pull up your shorts, Mr. Thomas, or your willy's gonna get chilly."

He pulled up his shorts so they hung off his bony hips. "Is it chilly? It doesn't feel that way to me." Then, with no change in tone: "Tia is starting to look old, Jimmy."

I didn't bother to tell him again that my name was Jamie. Instead I looked at my mother and holy God, she *did* look old. Was starting to, anyway. When had that happened?

"Tell us the story," I said. "Begin at the beginning."

"Where else?" Mr. Thomas said.

13

It took an hour and a half, and by the time we were done, I was exhausted and I think Mom was, too. Mr. Thomas looked just the same at the end as when we started, standing there with that somehow sorry yellow sash falling down over his poochy belly and low-slung shorts. Liz parked her car between the gateposts with the dashboard light blipping, which was probably a good idea, because the news of Mr. Thomas's death had begun to spread, and people were showing up out front to snap pictures of Cobblestone Cottage. Once she came back to ask how much longer we'd be and Mom just waved her off, told her to inspect the grounds or something, but mostly Liz hung in.

It was stressful as well as exhausting, because our future depended on Mr. Thomas's book. It wasn't fair for me to have to bear the weight of that responsibility, not at nine, but there was no choice. I had to repeat everything Mr. Thomas said to Mom—or rather to Mom's recording devices—and Mr. Thomas had plenty to say. When he told me he was able to keep everything in his head, he wasn't just blowing smoke. And Mom kept asking questions, mostly for clarification. Mr. Thomas didn't seem to mind (didn't seem to care one way or the other, actually), but the way Mom was dragging things out started bugging the shit out of me. Also, my mouth got wickedly dry. When Liz brought me her leftover Coke from Burger King, I gulped down the few swallows that were left and gave her a hug.

"Thank you," I said, handing back the paper cup. "I needed that."

"Very welcome." Liz had stopped looking bored. Now she looked thoughtful. She couldn't see Mr. Thomas, and I don't think she still totally believed he was there, but she knew *something* was going on, because she'd heard a nine-year-old boy spieling out a complicated plot featuring half a dozen major characters and at least two dozen minor ones. Oh, and a threesome (under the influence of bulbous canary grass supplied by a helpful Native American of the Nottoway People) consisting of George Threadgill, Purity Betancourt, and Laura Goodhugh. Who ended up getting pregnant. Poor Laura always got the shitty end of the stick.

At the end of Mr. Thomas's summary, the big secret came out, and it was a dilly. I'm not going to tell you what it was. Read the book and find out for yourself. If you haven't read it already, that is.

"Now I'll tell you the last sentence," Mr. Thomas said. He seemed as fresh as ever…although "fresh" is probably the wrong word to use with a dead person. His voice had started to fade, though. Just a little. "Because I always write that first. It's the beacon I row to."

"Last sentence coming up," I told Mom.

"Thank God," she said.

Mr. Thomas raised one finger, like an old-time actor getting ready to give his big speech. " 'On that day, a red sun went down over the deserted settlement, and the carved word that would puzzle generations glowed as if limned in blood: CROATOAN.' Tell her *croatoan* in capital letters, Jimmy."

I told her (although I didn't know exactly what "limbed in blood" meant), then asked Mr. Thomas if we were done. Just as he said we were, I heard a brief siren from out front—two whoops and a blat.

"Oh God," Liz said, but not in a panicky way; more like she had been expecting it. "Here we go."

She had her badge clipped to her belt and unzipped her parka so it would show. Then she went out front and came back with two cops. They were also wearing parkas, with Westchester County Police patches on them.

"Cheese it, the cops," Mr. Thomas said, which I didn't understand at all. Later, when I asked Mom, she told me it was slang from the olden days of the 1950s.

"This is Ms. Conklin," Liz said. "She's my friend and was Mr. Thomas's agent. She asked me to run her up here, because she was concerned someone might take the opportunity to steal souvenirs."

"Or manuscripts," my mother added. The little tape recorder was safe in her bag and her phone was in the back pocket of her jeans. "One in particular, the last book in a cycle of novels Mr. Thomas was writing."

Liz gave her a look that said *enough, already*, but my mother continued.

"He just finished it, and millions of people will want to read it. I felt it my duty to make sure they get the chance."

The cops didn't seem all that interested; they were here to look at the room where Mr. Thomas had died. Also to make sure the people who had been observed on the grounds had a good reason to be there.

"I believe he died in his study," Mom said, and pointed toward *La Petite Maison*.

"Uh-huh," one of the cops said. "That's what we heard. We'll check it out." He had to bend down with his hands on his knees to get face time with me; I was pretty shrimpy in those days. "What's your name, son?"

"James Conklin." I gave Mr. Thomas a pointed look. "*Jamie*. This is my mother." I took her hand.

"Are you playing hooky today, Jamie?"

Before I could answer, Mom cut in, smooth as silk. "I usually pick him up when he gets out of school, but I thought I might not get back in time today, so we swung by to get him. Didn't we, Liz?"

"Roger that," Liz said. "Officers, we didn't check the study, so I can't tell you if it's locked or not."

"Housekeeper left it open with the body inside," the one who'd talked to me said. "But she gave me her keys and we'll lock up after we have a quick look around."

"You might tell them there was no foul play," Mr. Thomas said. "I had a heart attack. Hurt like the devil."

I was going to tell them no such thing. I was only nine, but that didn't make me stupid.

"Is there also a key to the gate?" Liz asked. She was being all pro now. "Because it was open when we arrived."

"There is, and we'll lock it when we leave," the second cop said. "Good move parking your car there, detective."

Liz spread her hands, as if to say it was all in a day's work. "If you're set, we'll get out of your way."

The cop who had spoken to me said, "We should know what that valuable manuscript looks like so we can make sure it's safe."

This was a ball my mother could carry. "He sent the original to me just last week. On a thumb drive. I don't think there's another copy. He was pretty paranoid."

"I was," Mr. Thomas admitted. His shorts were sinking again.

"Glad you were here to keep an eye out," the second cop said. He and the other one shook hands with Mom and Liz, also with me. Then they started down the gravel path to the little green building where Mr. Thomas had died. Later on I found out a whole lot of writers died at their desks. Must be a Type A occupation.

"Let's go, Champ," Liz said. She tried to take my hand, but I wouldn't let her.

"Go stand over by the swimming pool for a minute," I said. "Both of you."

"Why?" Mom asked.

I looked at my mother in a way I don't think I ever had before—as if she was stupid. And right then, I thought she *was* being stupid. Both of them were. Not to mention rude as fuck.

"Because you got what you wanted and I need to say thank you."

"Oh my God," Mom said, and slapped her brow again. "What was I thinking? Thank you, Regis. So much."

Mom was directing her thank-you to a flower bed, so I took her arm and turned her. "He's over here, Mom."

She said another thank you, to which Mr. Thomas didn't respond. He didn't seem to care. Then she walked over to where Liz was standing by the empty pool, lighting another cigarette.

I didn't really need to say thank you, by then I knew that dead people don't give much of a shit about things like that, but I said thanks anyway. It was only polite, and besides, I wanted something else.

"My mom's friend," I said. "Liz?"

Mr. Thomas didn't reply, but he looked at her.

"She still mostly thinks I'm making it up about seeing you. I mean, she knows something weird happened, because no kid could make up that whole story—by the way, I loved what happened to George Threadgill—"

"Thank you. He deserved no better."

"But she'll work it around in her head so in the end she's got it the way she wants it."

"She will rationalize."

"If that's what you call it."

"It is."

"Well, is there any way you can show her you're here?" I was thinking about how Mr. Burkett scratched his cheek when his wife kissed him.

"I don't know. Jimmy, do you have any idea what comes next for me?"

"I'm sorry, Mr. Thomas. I don't."

"I suppose I will find out for myself."

He walked toward the pool where he'd never swim again. Someone might fill it when warm weather returned, but by then he would be long gone. Mom and Liz were talking quietly and sharing Liz's cigarette. One of the things I didn't like about Liz was how she'd gotten my mother smoking again. Only a little, and only with her, but still.

Mr. Thomas stood in front of Liz, drew in a deep breath, and blew it out. Liz didn't have bangs to blow on, her hair was pulled back tight and tied in a ponytail, but she still slitted her eyes the way you will when the wind gusts in your face, and recoiled. She would have fallen into the pool, I think, if Mom hadn't grabbed her.

I said, "Did you feel that?" Stupid question, of course she had. "That was Mr. Thomas."

Who was now walking away from us, back toward his study.

"Thanks again, Mr. Thomas!" I called. He didn't turn, but raised a hand to me before putting it back in the pocket of his shorts. I was getting an excellent view of his plumber's crack (that's what Mom called it when she spotted a guy wearing low-riding jeans), and if that's also too much information for you, too bad. We made him tell us—in one hour!—everything it had taken him months of thinking to come up with. He couldn't say no, and maybe that gave him the right to show us his ass.

Of course I was the only one who could see it.

14

It's time to talk about Liz Dutton, so check it out. Check *her* out.

She was about five-six, my mom's height, with shoulder-length black hair (when it wasn't yanked back in her cop-approved ponytail, that was), and she had what some of the boys in my fourth grade class would call—as if they had any idea what they were talking about—a "smokin' hot bod." She had a great smile and gray eyes that were usually warm. Unless she was mad, that is. When she was mad, those gray eyes could turn as cold as a sleety day in November.

I liked her because she could be kind, like when my mouth and throat were so dry and she gave me what was left in that Burger King Coke without me having to ask her (my mother was just fixated on getting the ins and outs of Mr. Thomas's unwritten last book). Also, she would sometimes bring me a Matchbox car to add to my growing collection and once in awhile would get right down on the floor beside me and we'd play together. Sometimes she'd give me a hug and ruffle my hair. Sometimes she'd tickle me until I screamed for her to stop or I'd pee myself…which she called "watering my Jockeys."

I *didn't* like her because sometimes, especially after our trip to Cobblestone Cottage, I'd look up and catch her studying me like I was a bug on a slide. There was no warmth in her gray eyes then. Or she'd tell me my room was a mess, which in fairness it usually was, although my mom didn't seem to mind. "It hurts my eyes," Liz would say. Or, "Are you going to live that way all your life, Jamie?" She also thought I was too old for a nightlight, but my mother put an end to *that* discussion, just saying "Leave him alone, Liz. He'll give it up when he's ready."

The biggest thing? She stole a lot of my mother's attention and affection that I used to get. Much later, when I read some of Freud's theories in a sophomore psych class, it occurred to me that as a kid I'd had a classic mother fixation, seeing Liz as a rival.

Well, duh.

Of *course* I was jealous, and I had good reason to be. I had no father, didn't even know who the fuck he was because my mother wouldn't talk about him. Later I found out she had good reason for *that*, but at the time all I knew was that it was "You and me against the world, Jamie." Until Liz came along, that was. And remember this, I didn't have a whole lot of Mom even *before* Liz, because Mom was too busy trying to save the agency after she and Uncle Harry got fucked by James Mackenzie (I hated that he and I had the same first name). Mom was always mining for gold in the slush pile, hoping to come across another Jane Reynolds.

I would have to say that liking and disliking were pretty evenly balanced on the day we went to Cobblestone Cottage, with liking slightly ahead for at least four reasons: Matchbox cars and trucks were not to be sneezed at; sitting between them on the sofa and watching *The Big Bang Theory* was fun and cozy; I wanted to like who my mother liked; Liz made her happy. Later (there it is again), not so much.

That Christmas was excellent. I got cool presents from both of them, and we had an early lunch at Chinese Tuxedo before Liz had to go to work. Because, she said, "Crime never takes a holiday." So Mom and me went to the old place on Park Avenue.

Mom stayed in touch with Mr. Burkett after we moved, and sometimes the three of us hung out. "Because he's lonely," Mom said, "but also because why, Jamie?"

"Because we like him," I said, and that was true.

We had Christmas dinner in his apartment (actually turkey sandwiches with cranberry sauce from Zabar's) because his daughter was on the west coast and couldn't come back. I found out more about that later.

And yes, because we liked him.

As I may have told you, Mr. Burkett was actually *Professor* Burkett, now Emeritus, which I understood to mean that he was retired but still allowed to hang around NYU and teach the occasional class in his super-smart specialty, which happened to be E and E—English and European Literature. I once made this mistake of calling it Lit and he corrected me, saying *lit* was either for lights or being drunk.

Anyway, even with no stuffing and only carrots for veg, it was a nice little meal, and we had more presents after. I gave Mr. Burkett a snow globe for his collection. I later found out it had been his wife's collection, but he admired it, thanked me, and put it on the mantel with the others. Mom gave him a big book called *The New Annotated Sherlock Holmes*, because back when he was working full time, he'd taught a course called Mystery and Gothic in English Fiction.

He gave Mom a locket that he said had belonged to his

wife. Mom protested and said he should save it for his daughter. Mr. Burkett said that Siobhan had gotten all the good pieces of Mona's jewelry, and besides, "If you snooze, you lose." Meaning, I guess, that if his daughter (from the sound of it, I thought her name was *Shivonn*) couldn't bother to come east, she could go whistle. I sort of agreed with that, because who knew how many more Christmases she might have her father around? He was older than God. Besides, I had a soft spot for fathers, not having one myself. I know they say you can't miss what you've never had, and there's some truth to that, but I knew I was missing *something*.

My present from Mr. Burkett was also a book. It was called *Twenty Unexpurgated Fairy Tales*.

"Do you know what *unexpurgated* means, Jamie?" Once a professor, always a professor, I guess.

I shook my head.

"What do you reckon?" He was leaning forward with his big gnarly hands between his skinny thighs, smiling. "Can you guess from the context of the title?"

"Uncensored? Like R-rated?"

"Nailed it," he said. "Well done."

"I hope there's not a lot of sex in them," Mom said. "He reads at high school level, but he's only nine."

"No sex, just good old violence," Mr. Burkett said (I never called him *professor* in those days, because it seemed stuck-up somehow). "For instance, in the original tale of Cinderella, which you'll find here, the wicked stepsisters—"

Mom turned to me and stage-whispered, "Spoiler alert."

Mr. Burkett was not to be deterred. He was in full teaching mode. I didn't mind, it was interesting.

"In the original, the wicked stepsisters cut off their toes in their efforts to make the glass slipper fit."

"Eww!" I said this in a way that meant *gross, tell me more*.

"And the glass slipper wasn't glass at all, Jamie. That seems to have been a translation error which has been immortalized by Walt Disney, that homogenizer of fairy tales. The slipper was actually made of squirrel fur."

"Wow," I said. Not as interesting as the stepsisters cutting off their toes, but I wanted to keep him rolling.

"In the original story of the Frog King, the princess doesn't kiss the frog. Instead, she—"

"No more," Mom said. "Let him read the stories and find out for himself."

"Always best," Mr. Burkett agreed. "And perhaps we'll discuss them, Jamie."

You mean you'll *discuss them while I listen*, I thought, but that would be okay.

"Should we have hot chocolate?" Mom asked. "It's also from Zabar's, and they make the best. I can reheat it in a jiff."

"Lay on, Macduff," Mr. Burkett said, "and damn'd be him that first cries, 'Hold, enough!' " Which meant yes, and we had it with whipped cream.

In my memory that's the best Christmas I had as a kid, from the Santa pancakes Liz made in the morning to the hot chocolate in Mr. Burkett's apartment, just down the hall from where Mom and I used to live. New Year's Eve was also fine, although I fell asleep on the couch between Mom and Liz before the ball dropped. All good. But in 2010, the arguments started.

Before that, Liz and my mother used to have what Mom called "spirited discussions," mostly about books. They liked many of the same writers (they bonded over Regis Thomas, remember) and the same movies, but Liz thought my mother was too focused on things like sales and advances and various writers' track records instead of the stories. And she actually laughed at the works of a couple of Mom's clients, calling them "subliterate." To which my mother responded that those subliterate writers paid the rent and kept the lights on. (Kept them *lit*.) Not to mention paying for the care home where Uncle Harry was marinating in his own pee.

Then the arguments began to move away from the more or less safe ground of books and films and get more heated. Some were about politics. Liz loved this Congress guy, John Boehner. My mother called him John Boner, which is what some kids of my acquaintance called a stiffy. Or maybe she meant to pull a boner, but I don't really think so. Mom thought Nancy Pelosi (another politician, which you probably know as she's still around) was a brave woman working in "a boys' club." Liz thought she was your basic liberal dingleberry.

The biggest fight they ever had about politics was when Liz said she didn't completely believe Obama had been born in America. Mom called her stupid and racist. They were in the bedroom with the door shut—that was where most of their arguments happened—but their voices were raised and I could hear every word from the living room. A few minutes later, Liz left, slamming the door on her way out, and didn't come back for almost a week. When she did, they made up. In the bedroom. With the door closed. I heard that, too, because the making-up part was pretty noisy. Groans and laughter and squeaky bedsprings.

They argued about police tactics, too, and this was still a few years before Black Lives Matter. That was a sore point with Liz, as you might guess. Mom decried what she called "racial profiling," and Liz said you can only draw a profile if the features are clear. (Didn't get that then, don't get it now.) Mom said when black people and white people were sentenced for the same type of crime, it was the black people who got hit with the heaviest sentences, and sometimes the white people didn't do time at all. Liz countered by saying, "You show me a Martin Luther King Boulevard in any city, and I'll show you a high crime area."

The arguments started to come closer together, and even at my tender age I knew one big reason why—they were drinking too much. Hot breakfasts, which my mother used to make twice or even three times a week, pretty much ceased. I'd come out in the morning and they'd be sitting there in their matching bathrobes, hunched over mugs of coffee, their faces pale and their eyes red. There'd be three, sometimes four, empty bottles of wine in the trash with cigarette butts in them.

My mother would say, "Get some juice and cereal for yourself while I get dressed, Jamie." And Liz would tell me not to make a lot of noise because the aspirin hadn't kicked in yet, her head was splitting, and she either had roll-call or was on stakeout for some case or other. Not the Thumper task force, though; she didn't get on that.

I'd drink my juice and eat my cereal quiet as a mouse on those mornings. By the time Mom was dressed and ready to walk me to school (ignoring Liz's comment that I was now big enough to make that walk by myself), she was starting to come around.

All of this seemed normal to me. I don't think the world starts to come into focus until you're fifteen or sixteen; up until then you just take what you've got and roll with it. Those two hungover women hunched over their coffee was just how I started my day on some mornings that eventually became lots of mornings. I didn't even notice the smell of wine that began to permeate everything. Only part of me must have noticed, because years later, in college, when my roomie spilled a bottle of Zinfandel in the living room of our little apartment, it all came back and it was like getting hit in the face with a plank. Liz's snarly hair. My mother's hollow eyes. How I knew to close the cupboard where we kept the cereal *slowly* and *quietly*.

I told my roomie I was going down to the 7-Eleven to get a pack of cigarettes (yes, I eventually picked up that particular bad habit), but basically I just had to get away from that smell. Given a choice between seeing dead folks—yes, I still see them—and the memories brought on by the smell of spilled wine, I'd pick the dead folks.

Any day of the fucking week.

15

My mother spent four months writing *The Secret of Roanoke* with her trusty tape recorder always by her side. I asked her once if writing Mr. Thomas's book was like painting a picture. She thought about it and said it was more like one of those Paint by Numbers kits, where you just followed the

directions and ended up with something that was suppos-
edly "suitable for framing."

She hired an assistant so she could work on it pretty much
full time. She told me on one of our walks home from school
—which was just about the only fresh air she ever got during
the winter of 2009 and 2010—that she couldn't afford to
hire an assistant and couldn't afford not to. Barbara Means
was fresh out of the English program at Vassar, and was
willing to toil in the agency at bargain-basement wages for
the experience, and she was actually pretty good, which was
a big help. I liked her big green eyes, which I thought were
beautiful.

Mom wrote, Mom rewrote, Mom read the *Roanoke* books
and little else during those months, wanting to immerse herself in Regis Thomas's style. She listened to my voice. She
rewound and fast forwarded. She filled in the picture. One
night, deep into their second bottle of wine, I heard her tell
Liz that if she had to write another sentence containing a
phrase such as "firm thrusting breasts tipped with rosy nip-
ples," she might lose her mind. She also had to field calls
from the trades—and once from Page Six of the *New York
Post*—about the state of the final Thomas book, because all
sorts of rumors were flying around. (All this came back to
me, and vividly, when Sue Grafton died without writing the
final book of her alphabet series of mysteries.) Mom said she
hated the lying.

"Ah, but you're so good at it," I remember Liz saying, which
earned her one of the cold looks I saw from my mother more
and more in the final year of their relationship.

She lied to Regis's editor as well, telling her Regis had

instructed her not long before he died that the manuscript of *Secret* should be withheld from everyone (except Mom, of course) until 2010, "in order to build reader interest." Liz said she thought that was a little bit shaky, but Mom said it would fly. "Fiona never edited him, anyway," she said. Meaning Fiona Yarbrough, who worked for Doubleday, Mr. Thomas's publisher. "Her only job was writing Regis a letter after she got each new manuscript, telling him that he'd outdone himself this time."

Once the book was finally turned in, Mom spent a week pacing and snapping at everyone (I was not excluded from said snappery), waiting for Fiona to call and say *Regis didn't write this book, it doesn't sound a bit like him, I think* you *wrote it, Tia*. But in the end it was fine. Either Fiona never guessed or didn't care. Certainly the reviewers never guessed when the book was crashed into production and appeared in the fall of 2010.

Publishers Weekly: "Thomas saved the best for last!"

Kirkus Reviews: "Fans of sweet-savage historical fiction will once more be in bodice-ripping clover."

Dwight Garner, in *The New York Times*: "The trudging, flavorless prose is typical Thomas: the rough equivalent of a heaping plate of food from an all-you-can-eat buffet in a dubious roadside restaurant."

Mom didn't care about the reviews; she cared about the huge advance and the refreshed royalties from the previous *Roanoke* volumes. She bitched mightily about only getting fifteen percent when she had written the whole thing, but got a small measure of revenge by dedicating it to herself. "Because I deserve it," she said.

"I'm not so sure," Liz said. "When you think about it, Tee, you were just the secretary. Maybe you should have dedicated it to Jamie."

This earned Liz another of my mom's cold looks, but I thought Liz had something there. Although when you *really* thought about it, I was also just the secretary. It was still Mr. Thomas's book, dead or not.

16

Now check this out: I told you at least some of the reasons why I liked Liz, and there were probably a few more. I told you all the reasons I *didn't* like Liz, and there were probably a few more of those, too. What I never considered until later (yup, there's that word again) was the possibility that she didn't like *me*. Why would I? I was used to being loved, almost blasé about it. I was loved by my mother and my teachers, especially Mrs. Wilcox, my third-grade teacher, who hugged me and said she'd miss me on the day school let out. I was loved by my best friends Frankie Ryder and Scott Abramowitz (although of course we didn't talk or even think about it that way). And don't forget Lily Rhinehart, who once put a big smackeroo on my mouth. She also gave me a Hallmark card before I changed schools. It had a sad-looking puppy on the front and inside it said *I'LL MISS YOU EVERY DAY YOU'RE AWAY*. She signed it with a little heart over the *i* in her name. Also x's and o's.

Liz at least *liked* me, at least for awhile, I'm sure of it. But that began to change after Cobblestone Cottage. That was when she started to see me as a freak of nature. I think—no, I *know*—that was when Liz started to be scared of me, and it's hard to like what you're scared of. Maybe impossible.

Although she thought nine was old enough for me to walk home from school by myself, Liz sometimes came for me instead of Mom if Liz was working what she called "the swing shift," which started at four in the morning and ended at noon. It was a shift detectives tried to avoid, but Liz got it quite a bit. That was another thing that I never wondered about then, but later (there it is again, yeah yeah yeah, right right right) I realized that she wasn't exactly liked by her bosses. Or trusted. It didn't have anything to do with the relationship she had with my mother; when it came to sex, the NYPD was slowly moving into the 21st century. It wasn't the drinking, either, because she wasn't the only cop who liked to put it away. But certain people she worked with had begun to suspect that Liz was a dirty cop. And—spoiler alert!—they were right.

17

I need to tell you about two particular times Liz got me after school. On both occasions she was in her car—not the one we took out to Cobblestone Cottage, but the one she called her personal. The first time was in 2011, while she and Mom were still a thing. The second was in 2013, a year or so after they stopped being a thing. I'll get to that, but first things first.

I came out of school that day in March with my backpack

slung over just one shoulder (which was how the cool sixth-grade boys did it) and Liz was waiting for me at the curb in her Honda Civic. On the yellow part of the curb, as a matter of fact, which was for handicapped people, but she had her little POLICE OFFICER ON CALL sign for that…which, you could argue, should have told me something about her character even at the tender age of eleven.

I got in, trying not to wrinkle my nose at the smell of stale cigarette smoke that not even the little pine tree air-freshener hanging from the rearview mirror could hide. By then, thanks to *The Secret of Roanoke*, we had our own apartment and didn't have to live in the agency anymore, so I was expecting a ride home, but Liz turned toward downtown instead.

"Where are we going?" I asked.

"Little field trip, Champ," she said. "You'll see."

The field trip was to Woodlawn Cemetery, in the Bronx, final resting place of Duke Ellington, Herman Melville, and Bartholomew "Bat" Masterson, among others. I know about them because I looked it up, and later wrote a report about Woodlawn for school. Liz drove in from Webster Avenue and then just started cruising up and down the lanes. It was nice, but it was also a little scary.

"Do you know how many people are planted here?" she asked, and when I shook my head: "Three hundred thousand. Less than the population of Tampa, but not by much. I checked it out on Wikipedia."

"Why are we here? Because it's interesting, but I've got homework." This wasn't a lie, but I only had, like, a half-hour's worth. It was a bright sunshiny day and she seemed normal enough—just Liz, my mom's friend—but still, this was sort of a freaky field trip.

She totally ignored the homework gambit. "People are being buried here all the time. Look to your left." She pointed and slowed from twenty-five or so to a bare creep. Where she was pointing, people were standing around a coffin placed over an open grave. Some kind of minister was standing at the head of the grave with an open book in his hand. I knew he wasn't a rabbi, because he wasn't wearing a beanie.

Liz stopped the car. Nobody at the service paid any attention. They were absorbed in whatever the minister was saying.

"You see dead people," she said. "I accept that now. Hard not to, after what happened at Thomas's place. Do you see any here?"

"No," I said, more uneasy than ever. Not because of Liz, but because I'd just gotten the news that we were currently surrounded by 300,000 dead bodies. Even though I knew the dead went away after a few days—a week at most—I almost expected to see them standing beside their graves or right on top of them. Then maybe converging on us, like in a fucking zombie movie.

"Are you sure?"

I looked at the funeral (or graveside service, or whatever you call it). The minister must have started a prayer, because all the mourners had bowed their heads. All except one, that was. He was just standing there and looking unconcernedly up at the sky.

"That guy in the blue suit," I said finally. "The one who's

not wearing a tie. He might be dead, but I can't be sure. If there's nothing wrong with them when they die, nothing that *shows*, they look pretty much like anyone else."

"I don't see a man without a tie," she said.

"Well okay then, he's dead."

"Do they always come to their burials?" Liz asked.

"How should I know? This is my first graveyard, Liz. I saw Mrs. Burkett at her funeral, but I don't know about the graveyard, because me and Mom didn't go to that part. We just went home."

"But you see *him*." She was staring at the funeral party like she was in a trance. "You could go over there and talk to him, the way you talked to Regis Thomas that day."

"I'm not going over there!" I don't like to say I squawked this, but I pretty much did. "In front of all his friends? In front of his wife and kids? You can't make me!"

"Mellow out, Champ," she said, and ruffled my hair. "I'm just trying to get it straight in my mind. How did he get here, do you think? Because he sure didn't take an Uber."

"I don't know. I want to go home."

"Pretty soon," she said, and we continued our cruise of the cemetery, passing tombs and monuments and about a billion regular gravestones. We passed three more graveside ceremonies in progress, two small like the first one, where the star of the show was attending sight unseen, and one humungous one, where about two hundred people were gathered on a hillside and the guy in charge (beanie, check— plus a cool-looking shawl) was using a microphone. Each time Liz asked me if I could see the dead person and each time I told her I didn't have a clue.

"You probably wouldn't tell me if you did," she said. "I can tell you're in a pissy mood."

"I'm not in a pissy mood."

"You are, though, and if you tell Tee I brought you out here, we'll probably have a fight. I don't suppose you could tell her we went for ice cream, could you?"

We were almost back to Webster Avenue by then and I was feeling a little better. Telling myself Liz had a right to be curious, that anyone would be. "Maybe if you actually bought me one."

"Bribery! That's a Class B felony!" She laughed, gave my hair a ruffle, and we were pretty much all right again.

We left the cemetery and I saw a young woman in a black dress sitting on a bench and waiting for her bus. A little girl in a white dress and shiny black shoes was sitting beside her. The girl had golden hair and rosy cheeks and a hole in her throat. I waved to her. Liz didn't see me do it; she was waiting for a break in traffic so she could make her turn. I didn't tell her what I saw. That night Liz left after dinner to either go to work or go back to her own place, and I almost told my mother. In the end I didn't. In the end I kept the little girl with the golden hair to myself. Later I would think that the hole in her throat was from the little girl choking on food and they cut into her throat so she could breathe but it was too late. She was sitting there beside her mother and her mother didn't know. But I knew. I saw. When I waved to her, she waved back.

18

While we were eating our ice cream at Lickety Split (Liz phoned my mother to tell her where we were and what we were up to), Liz said, "It must be so strange, what you can do. So *weird*. Doesn't it freak you out?"

I thought of asking her if it freaked her out to look up at night and see the stars and know they go on forever and ever, but didn't bother. I just said no. You get used to marvelous things. You take them for granted. You can try not to, but you do. There's too much wonder, that's all. It's everywhere.

19

I'll tell you about the other time Liz picked me up from school very soon, but first I have to tell you about the day they broke up. That was a scary morning, believe me.

I woke up that day even before my alarm clock went off, because Mom was yelling. I'd heard her mad before, but never *that* mad.

"You brought it into the apartment? Where I live with my *son*?"

Liz answered something, but it was little more than a mumble and I couldn't hear.

"Do you think that matters to me?" Mom shouted. "On

the cop shows that's what they call *serious weight*! I could go to jail as an accessory!"

"Don't be dramatic," Liz said. Louder now. "There was never any chance of—"

"*That doesn't matter!*" Mom yelled. "It was here! It still *is* here! On the fucking table beside the fucking sugar bowl! You brought drugs into my house! *Serious weight!*"

"Would you stop saying that? This isn't an episode of *Law and Order*." Now Liz was also getting loud. Getting mad. I stood with one ear pressed against my bedroom door, barefoot and dressed in my pajamas, my heart starting to pound. This wasn't a discussion or even an argument. This was more. Worse. "If you hadn't been going through my pockets—"

"Searching your stuff, is that what you think? I was trying to do you a *favor*! I was going to take your extra uniform coat to the cleaners along with my wool skirt. How long has it been there?"

"Only a little while. The guy it belongs to is out of town. He's going to be back tomor—"

"*How long?*"

Liz's reply was again too low for me to hear.

"Then why bring it here? I don't understand that. Why not put it in the gun safe at your place?"

"I don't…" She stopped.

"Don't what?"

"Don't actually *have* a gun safe. And there have been break-ins in my building. Besides, I was going to be here. We were going to spend the week together. I thought it would save me a trip."

"*Save you a trip?*"

To this Liz made no reply.

"No gun safe in your apartment. How many other things have you been lying to me about?" Mom didn't sound mad anymore. At least not right then. She sounded hurt. Like she wanted to cry. I felt like going out and telling Liz to leave my mother alone, even if my mother had started it by finding whatever she'd found—the *serious weight*. But I just stood there, listening. Trembling, too.

Liz mumbled some more.

"Is this why you're in trouble at the Department? Are you using as well as…I don't know *couriering* the stuff? *Distributing* the stuff?"

"I'm not using and I'm not distributing!"

"Well, you're passing it on!" Mom's voice was rising again. "That sounds like distributing to me." Then she went back to what was really troubling her. Well, not the only thing, but the one that was troubling her the most. "You brought it into my *apartment*. Where my *son* is. You lock your gun in your car, I always insisted on that, but now I find *two pounds of cocaine* in your spare jacket." She actually laughed, but not the way people do when something is funny. "Your spare *police* jacket!"

"It's not two pounds." Sounding sulky.

"I grew up weighing meat in my father's market," Mom said. "I know two pounds when I've got it in my hand."

"I'll get it out," she said. "Right now."

"You do that, Liz. Posthaste. And you can come back to get your things. By appointment. When I'm here and Jamie's not. Otherwise never."

"You don't mean that," Liz said, but even through the

door I could tell she didn't believe what she was saying.

"I absolutely do. I'm going to do you a favor and not report what I found to your watch captain, but if you ever show your face here again—except for that one time to pick up your shit—I will. That's a promise."

"You're throwing me out? Really?"

"Really. Take your dope and fuck off."

Liz started to cry. That was horrible. Then, after she was gone, Mom started to cry and that was even worse. I went out into the kitchen and hugged her.

"How much of that did you hear?" Mom asked, and before I could answer: "All of it, I imagine. I'm not going to lie to you, Jamie. Or gloss it over. She had dope, a lot of dope, and I never want you to say a word about it, okay?"

"Was it really cocaine?" I had also been crying, but didn't realize it until I heard my voice come out all husky.

"It was. And since you already know so much, I might as well tell you I tried it in college, just a couple of times. I tasted what was in the Baggie I found, and my tongue went numb. It was coke, all right."

"But it's gone. She took it."

Moms know what kids are scared of, if they're good moms. A critic might call that a romantic notion, but I think it's just a practical fact. "She did and we're fine. It was a nasty way to start the day, but it's over. We'll draw a line under it and move on."

"Okay, but…is Liz really not your friend anymore?"

Mom used a dishtowel to wipe her face. "I don't think she's been my friend for quite awhile now. I just didn't know it. Now get ready for school."

That night while I was doing my homework, I heard a *glug-glug-glug* coming from the kitchen and smelled wine. The smell was a lot stronger than usual, even on nights when Mom and Liz put away a lot of vino. I came out of my room to see if she'd spilled a bottle (although there had been no crash of glass) and saw Mom standing over the sink with a jug of red wine in one hand and a jug of white in the other. She was pouring it down the drain.

"Why are you throwing it away? Did it go bad?"

"In a manner of speaking," she said. "I think it started to go bad about eight months ago. It's time to stop."

I found out later that my mother went to AA for awhile after she broke up with Liz, then decided she didn't need it. ("Old men pissing and moaning about a drink they took thirty years ago," she said.) And I don't think she quit completely, because once or twice I thought I smelled wine on her breath when she kissed me goodnight. Maybe from dinner with a client. If she kept a bottle in the apartment, I never knew where she stashed it (not that I looked very hard). What I do know is that in the years that followed, I never saw her drunk and I never saw her hungover. That was good enough for me.

20

I didn't see Liz Dutton for a long time after that, a year or maybe a little more. I missed her at first, but that didn't last long. When the feeling came, I just reminded myself she screwed my mom over, and bigtime. I kept waiting for Mom to have another sleepover friend, but she didn't. Like ever. I asked her once, and she said, "Once burned, twice shy. We're okay, that's the important thing."

And we were. Thanks to Regis Thomas—27 weeks on the *New York Times* bestseller list—and a couple new clients (one of them discovered by Barbara Means, who was by then full-time and actually ended up getting her name on the door in 2017), the agency was back on a firm footing. Uncle Harry returned to the care home in Bayonne (same facility, new management), which wasn't great but better than it had been. Mom was no longer cross in the morning and she got some new clothes. "Have to," she told me once that year. "I've lost fifteen pounds of wine-weight."

I was in middle school by then, which sucked in some respects, was okay in others, and came with one excellent perk: student athletes with no class during the last period of the day could go to the gym, the art room, the music room, or sign out. I only played JV basketball, and the season was over, but I still qualified. Some days I checked out the art room, because this foxy chick named Marie O'Malley occasionally hung out there. If she wasn't working on one of her watercolors, I just went home. Walked if it was nice (on my own, it should go without saying), took the bus if it was nasty.

On the day Liz Dutton came back into my life, I didn't even bother looking for Marie, because I'd gotten a new Xbox for my birthday and I wanted to hit it. I was all the way down the walk and shouldering my backpack (no more one-armed tote for me; sixth grade was in the prehistoric past) when she called to me.

"Hey, Champ, what the haps, bambino?"

She was leaning against her personal, legs crossed at the ankles, wearing jeans and a low-cut blouse. It was a blazer over the blouse instead of a parka, but it still had NYPD on the breast and she flapped it open in the old way to show me her shoulder holster. Only this time it wasn't empty.

"Hi, Liz," I mumbled. I looked down at my shoes and made a right turn onto the street.

"Hold on, I need to talk to you."

I stopped, but I didn't turn back to her. Like she was Medusa and one look at her snaky head would turn me to stone. "I don't think I should. Mom would be mad."

"She doesn't need to know. Turn around, Jamie. Please. Looking at nothing but your back is just about killing me."

She sounded like she really felt bad, and that made me feel bad. I turned around. The blazer was closed again, but I could see the bulge of her gun just the same.

"I want you to take a ride with me."

"Not a good idea," I said. I was thinking of this girl named Ramona Sheinberg. She was in a couple of my classes at the beginning of the year, but then she was gone and my friend Scott Abramowitz told me her father snatched her during a custody suit and took her to someplace where there was no extradition. Scott said he hoped it was at least a place with palm trees.

"I need what you can do, Champ," she said. "I really do."

I didn't reply to that, but she must have seen I was wavering, because she gave me a smile. It was a nice one that lit up those gray eyes of hers. They weren't a bit sleety that day. "Maybe it will come to nothing, but I want to try. I want *you* to try."

"Try what?"

She didn't answer, not then, just held out a hand to me. "I helped your mother when Regis Thomas died. Won't you help me now?"

Technically, I was the one who helped my mother that day, Liz just gave us a quick ride up the Sprain Brook Parkway, but she *had* stopped to buy me a Whopper when Mom just wanted to push on. And she gave me the rest of her Coke when my mouth was so dry from talking. So I got in the car. I didn't feel good about it, but I did it. Adults have power, especially when they beg, and that's what Liz was doing.

I asked Liz where we were going, and she said Central Park to start with. Maybe a couple of other places after that. I said if I didn't get home by five, Mom would be worried. Liz told me she'd try to get me back before then, but this was very important.

That's when she told me what it was about.

21

The guy who called himself Thumper set his first bomb in Eastport, a Long Island town not all that far from Speonk, one-time home of Uncle Harry's Cabin (literary joke). This was in 1996. Thumper dropped a stick of dynamite hooked up to a timer in a trash can outside the restrooms of the King Kullen Supermarket. The timer was nothing but a cheap alarm clock, but it worked. The dynamite went off at 9 PM, just as the supermarket was closing. Three people were hurt, all store employees. Two of them suffered only superficial injuries, but the third guy was coming out of the men's when the bomb blew. He lost an eye and his right arm up to the elbow. Two days later, a note came in to the Suffolk County Police Department. It was typed on an IBM Selectric. It said, *How do you like my work so far? More to come! THUMPER*.

Thumper set nineteen bombs before he actually killed anybody. *"Nineteen!"* Liz exclaimed. "And it wasn't as if he wasn't trying. He set them all over the five boroughs, and a couple in New Jersey—Jersey City and Fort Lee—for good measure. All dynamite, Canadian manufacture."

But the score of the maimed and wounded was high. It had been closing in on fifty when he finally killed the man who picked the wrong Lexington Avenue pay phone. Every kaboom was followed by a note to the police responsible for the area where said kaboom occurred, and the notes were always the same: *How do you like my work so far? More to come! THUMPER*.

Before Richard Scalise (that was the pay phone man's name), a long period of time went by before each new explosion. The two closest were six weeks apart. The longest delay was close to a year. But after Scalise, Thumper sped up. The bombs became bigger and the timers more sophisticated. Nineteen explosions between 1996 and 2009—twenty, counting the pay phone bomb. Between 2010 and the pretty May day in 2013 when Liz came back into my life, he set ten more, wounding twenty and killing three. By then, Thumper wasn't just an urban legend, or an NY1 staple; by then he was nationwide.

He was good at avoiding security cameras, and those he couldn't avoid just showed a guy in a coat, sunglasses, and a

Yankees cap pulled down low. He kept his head low, too. Some white hair showed around the sides and back of the cap, but that could have been a wig. Over the seventeen years of his "reign of terror," three different task forces were organized to catch him. The first one disbanded during a long break in his "reign," when the police assumed he was finished. The second disbanded after a big shakeup in the department. The third started in 2011, when it became clear Thumper had gone into overdrive. Liz didn't tell me all this on our way to Central Park; I found it out later, as I did so many other things.

Finally, two days ago, they got the break in the case they'd been waiting and hoping for. Son of Sam was caught by a parking ticket. Ted Bundy got caught because he forgot to put his headlights on. Thumper—real name Kenneth Alan Therriault—was nailed because a building super had a minor accident on trash day. He was wheeling a dolly loaded with garbage cans down an alley to the pickup point out front. He hit a pothole and one of the cans spilled. When he went to clean up the mess, he found a bundle of wires and a yellow scrap of paper with CANACO printed on it. He might not have called the police if that had been all, but it wasn't. Attached to one of the wires was a Dyno Nobel blasting cap.

We got to Central Park and parked with a bunch of regular cop cars (another thing I found out later is that Central Park has its own precinct, the 22nd). Liz put her little cop sign on the dashboard and we walked down 86th Street for a little while before turning onto a path that led to the Alexander Hamilton Monument. That's one thing I didn't find out later; I just read the fucking sign. Or plaque. Whatever.

"The super took a picture of the wires, the scrap of paper, and the blasting cap with his phone, but the task force didn't get it until the next day."

"Yesterday," I said.

"Right. As soon as we saw it, we knew we had our guy."

"Sure, because of the blasting cap."

"Yeah, but not just that. The scrap of paper? Canaco is a Canadian company that manufactures dynamite. We got a list of all the building's tenants, and eliminated most of them without any fieldwork, because we knew we were looking for a male, probably single, and probably white. There were only six tenants who checked all those boxes, and only one guy who'd ever worked in Canada."

"Googled 'em, right?" I was getting interested.

"Right you are. Among other things, we found Kenneth Therriault has dual citizenship, U.S. and Canada. He worked all sorts of construction jobs up there in the great white north, plus fracking and oil shale sites. He was Thumper, pretty much had to be."

I only got a quick look at Alexander Hamilton, just enough to read the sign and note his fancy pants. Liz had me by the hand and was leading me toward a path a little way beyond the statue. Pulling me, actually.

"We went in with a SWAT team, but his crib was empty. Well, not *empty* empty, all his stuff was there, but he was gone. The super didn't keep his big discovery to himself, unfortunately, although he was told to. He blabbed to some of the residents, and the word spread. One of the things we found in the apartment was an IBM Selectric."

"That's a typewriter?"

She nodded. "Those babies used to come with different type elements for different fonts. The one in the machine matched Thumper's notes."

Before we get to the path and the bench that wasn't there, I need to tell you some other stuff I found out later. She was telling the truth about how Therriault finally tripped over his dick, but she kept talking about *we*. *We* this and *we* that, but Liz wasn't a part of the Thumper task force. She *had* been part of the second task force, the one that ended in the big departmental shakeup when everybody was running around like chickens with their heads cut off, but by 2013 all Liz Dutton had left in the NYPD was a toehold, and only that much because cops have a kickass union. The rest of her was already out the door. Internal Affairs was circling like buzzards around fresh roadkill, and on the day she picked me up from school, she wouldn't have been put on a task force dedicated to catching serial litterbugs. She needed a miracle, and I was supposed to be it.

"By today," she went on, "every cop in the boroughs had Kenneth Therriault's name and description. Every way out of the city was being monitored by human eyeballs as well as cameras—and as I'm sure you know, there's plenty of cameras. Nailing this guy, dead or alive, became our number one priority, because we were afraid he might decide to go out in a blaze of glory. Maybe setting off a bomb in front of Saks Fifth Avenue, or in Grand Central. Only he did us a favor."

She stopped and pointed at a spot beside the path. I noticed the grass was beaten down, as if a lot of people had been standing there.

"He came into the park, he sat down on a bench, and he blew his brains out with a Ruger .45 ACP."

I looked at the spot, awestruck.

"The bench is at the NYPD Forensics Lab in Jamaica, but this is where he did it. So here's the big question. Do you see him? Is he here?"

I looked around. I had no clue what Kenneth Alan Therriault looked like, but if he'd blown his brains out, I didn't think I could miss him. I saw some kids throwing a Frisbee for their dog to chase (the dog was off his leash, a Central Park no-no), I saw a couple of lady runners, a couple of 'boarders, and a couple of old guys further down the path reading newspapers, but I didn't see any guy with a hole in his head, and I told her that.

"Fuck," Liz said. "Well, all right. We've got two more chances, at least that I can see. He worked as an orderly at City of Angels Hospital on 70th—quite a comedown from his construction days, but he was in his seventies—and the apartment building where he lived is in Queens. Which do you think, Champ?"

"I think I want to go home. He might be anyplace."

"Really? Didn't you say they hang around places where they spent time when they were alive? Before they, I don't know, pop off for good?"

I couldn't remember if I'd said that to her, exactly, but it was true. Still, I was feeling more and more like Ramona Sheinberg. Kidnapped, in other words. "Why bother? He's dead, right? Case closed."

"Not quite." She bent down to look me in the eye. She didn't have to bend so far in 2013, because I was getting taller.

Nowhere near the six feet I am now, but a couple of inches. "There was a note pinned to his shirt. It said, *There's one more, and it is a big one. Fuck you and see you in hell.* It was signed *THUMPER*."

Well, that kind of changed things.

22

We went to City of Angels first, because it was closer. There was no guy with a hole in his head out front, just some smokers, so we went in through the Emergency Room entrance. A lot of people were sitting around in there, and one guy was bleeding from the head. The wound looked like a laceration to me rather than a bullet hole, and he was younger than Liz said Kenneth Therriault was, but I asked Liz if she could see him, just to be sure. She said she could.

We went to the desk, where Liz showed her badge and identified herself as an NYPD detective. She asked if there was a room where the custodians put their stuff and changed their clothes for their shifts. The lady at the desk said there was, but the other police had already been there and cleaned out Therriault's locker. Liz asked if they were still there and the lady said no, the last of them left hours ago.

"I'd like to grab a quick peek, anyway," Liz said. "Tell me how to get there."

The lady said to take the elevator down to B level and turn right. Then she smiled at me and said, "Are you helping your mom in her investigations today, young man?"

I thought of saying *Well, she's not my mom, but I guess I*

am helping because she hopes that if Mr. Therriault is still hanging around, I'll see him. Of course that wouldn't fly, so I was stuck.

Liz wasn't. She explained that the school nurse thought I might have mono, so this seemed like a chance to get me checked out and visit Therriault's place of work at the same time. Two birds with one stone type of deal.

"You'd probably do better with your own doctor," the desk lady said. "This place is a madhouse today. You'll wait for hours."

"That's probably best," Liz agreed. I thought how natural she sounded, and what a smooth liar she was. I couldn't decide if I was grossed out or admiring. I guess a little of both.

The desk lady leaned forward. I was fascinated by how her extremely large bazams shoved her papers forward. It made me think of an icebreaker boat I'd seen in a movie. She lowered her voice. "Everyone was shocked, let me tell you. Ken was the oldest of all the orderlies, and the nicest. Hardworking and willing to please. If someone asked him to do something, he was always happy to do it. And with a smile. To think we were working with a *killer*! Do you know what it proves?"

Liz shook her head, clearly impatient for us to be on our way.

"That you never know," the desk lady said. She spoke like someone who's imparting a great truth. "You just never know!"

"He was good at covering up, all right," Liz said, and I thought, *It takes one to know one.*

In the elevator, I asked, "If you're on a task force, how come you're not *with* the task force?"

"Don't be dumb, Champ. Was I supposed to take *you* to the task force? Having to make up a story about you at the desk was bad enough." The elevator stopped. "If anyone asks about you, remember why you're here."

"Mono."

"Right."

But there was no one to ask. The custodian's room was empty. It had yellow tape saying POLICE INVESTIGATION KEEP OUT across the door. Liz and I ducked under it, her holding my hand. There were benches, a few chairs, and about two dozen lockers. Also a fridge, a microwave, and a toaster oven. There was an open box of Pop Tarts by the toaster oven, and I thought I wouldn't have minded a Pop Tart just then. But there was no Kenneth Therriault.

The lockers had names stuck to them in DymoTape. Liz opened Therriault's, using a handkerchief because of the leftover fingerprint powder. She did it slowly, like she expected him to be hiding inside like the boogeyman in a kid's closet. Therriault was sort of a boogeyman, but he wasn't in there. It was empty. The cops took everything.

Liz said fuck again. I looked at my phone to check the time. It was twenty past three.

"I know, I know," she said. Her shoulders were slumped, and although I resented the way she'd just scooped me up and taken me away, I couldn't help feeling a little sorry for her. I remembered Mr. Thomas saying my mom looked older, and now I thought my mom's lost friend looked older, too. Thinner. And I had to admit I also felt some admiration, because she was trying to do the right thing and save lives. She was like the hero of a movie, the lone wolf who means to solve the case on her own. Maybe she did care about the innocent people who might be vaporized in Thumper's last bomb. Probably she did. But I know now she was also concerned with saving her job. I don't like to think it was her major concern, but in light of what happened later—I'll get to it—I have to think it was.

"Okay, one more shot. And stop looking at your dumb phone, Champ. I know what time it is, and no matter how much trouble you're in if I don't get you home before your mother shows up, I'll be in more."

"She'll probably take Barbara out for a drink before she goes home, anyway. Barbara works for the agency now." I don't know why I said that, exactly. Because I also wanted to save innocent lives, I suppose, although that seemed rather academic to me, because I didn't think we were going to find Kenneth Therriault. I think it was because Liz looked so beaten down. So backed into a corner.

"Well, that's a lucky break," Liz said. "All we need is one more."

23

The Frederick Arms was twelve or fourteen stories high, gray brick, with bars on the windows of the first- and second-floor apartments. To a kid who grew up in the Palace on Park, it looked more like that *Shawshank Redemption* prison than an apartment building. And Liz knew right away that we were never going to get inside, let alone to Kenneth Therriault's apartment. The place was swarming with cops. Lookie-loos were standing in the middle of the street, as close to the police sawhorse barricades as they could get, snapping photos. TV news vans were parked on both sides of the block with their antennas up and cables snaking everywhere. There was even a Channel 4 helicopter hovering overhead.

"Look," I said. "Stacy-Anne Conway! She's on NY1!"

"Ask me if I give a shit," Liz said.

I didn't.

We had been lucky not to run into reporters at Central Park or City of Angels, and I realized the only reason we hadn't was because they were all here. I looked at Liz and saw a tear trickling down one of her cheeks. "Maybe we can go to his funeral," I said. "Maybe he'll be there."

"He'll probably be cremated. Privately, at the city's expense. No relatives. He outlived them all. I'll take you home, Champ. Sorry to drag you all this way."

"That's okay," I said, and patted her hand. I knew Mom wouldn't like me doing that, but Mom wasn't there.

Liz pulled a U-turn and headed back toward the Queensboro bridge. A block away from the Frederick Arms, I glanced at a little grocery on my side and said, "Oh my God. There he is."

She snapped a wide-eyed glance at me. "Are you sure? Are you *sure*, Jamie?"

I leaned forward and vomited between my sneakers. That was all the answer she needed.

24

I can't really say if he was as bad as the Central Park man, that was a long time ago. He could have been worse. Once you've seen what can happen to a human body that's suffered an act of violence—accident, suicide, murder—maybe it doesn't even matter. Kenneth Therriault, alias Thumper, was bad, okay? Really bad.

There were benches on either side of the grocery's door, so people could eat the snacks they bought, I suppose. Therriault was sitting on one of them with his hands on the thighs of his khaki pants. People were passing by, headed for whatever they were headed for. A black kid with a skateboard under his arm went into the store. A lady came out with a steaming paper cup of coffee. Neither of them glanced at the bench where Therriault was sitting.

He must have been right-handed, because that side of his head didn't look too bad. There was a hole in his temple, maybe the size of a dime, maybe a little smaller, surrounded by a dark corona that was either bruising or gunpowder. Probably gunpowder. I doubt if his body had time to muster enough blood to make a bruise.

The real damage was on the left, where the bullet exited. The hole on that side was almost as big as a dessert plate and surrounded by irregular fangs of bone. The flesh on his head was swelled, like from a gigantic infection. His left eye had been yanked sideways and bulged from its socket. Worst of all, gray stuff had dripped down his cheek. That was his brain.

"Don't stop," I said. "Just keep going." The smell of puke was strong in my nose and the taste of it was in my mouth, all slimy. "Please, Liz, I can't."

She swerved to the curb in front of a fire hydrant near the end of the block instead. "You have to. And I have to. Sorry, Champ, but we have to know. Now pull yourself together so people don't stare at us and think I've been abusing you."

But you are, I thought. *And you won't stop until you get what you want.*

The taste in my mouth was the ravioli I'd eaten in the school caff. As soon as I realized that I opened the door, leaned out, and puked some more. Like on the day of the Central Park man, when I never made it to Lily's birthday party at fancy-shmancy Wave Hill. That was *déjà vu* I could have done without.

"Champ? *Champ!*"

I turned to her and she was holding out a wad of Kleenex (show me a woman without Kleenex in her purse and I'll show you no one at all). "Wipe your mouth and then get out of the car. Try to look normal. Let's get this done."

I could see she meant it—we weren't going to leave until she had what she wanted. *Man up*, I thought. *I can do this. I have to, because lives are at stake.*

I wiped my mouth and got out. Liz put her little sign on the dashboard—the police version of Get Out of Jail Free—and came around to where I was standing on the sidewalk, staring into a laundromat at a woman folding clothes. That wasn't very interesting, but at least it kept me from looking

at the ruined man up the street. For the time being, anyway.
Soon I'd have to. Worse—oh God—I'd have to talk to him.
If he even *could* talk.

I held out my hand without thinking. Thirteen was probably too old to be holding hands with a woman the people
passing by would assume was my mother (if they bothered
thinking about us at all), but when she took it, I was glad.
Glad as hell.

We started back to the store. I wished we'd had miles to
walk, but it was only half a block.

"Where is he, exactly?" she asked in a low voice.

I risked a look to make sure he hadn't moved. Nope, he
was still on the bench, and now I could look directly into the
crater where there had once been thoughts. His ear was still
on, but it was crooked and I found myself remembering a
Mr. Potato Head I'd had when I was four or five. My stomach
clenched again.

"Get it together, Champ."

"Don't call me that anymore," I managed to say. "I hate it."

"Duly noted. Where is he?"

"Sitting on the bench."

"The one on this side of the door, or—"

"This side, yeah."

I was looking at him again, we were close now so I couldn't
help it, and I saw an interesting thing. A man came out of
the store with a newspaper under his arm and a hot dog in
one hand. The hot dog was in one of those foil bags that's
supposed to keep them hot (believe that and you'll believe
the moon is made of green cheese). He started to sit down
on the other bench, already pulling his hot dog out of the
bag. Then he stopped, looked either at me and Liz or the

other bench, and walked on down the block to eat his pup somewhere else. He didn't see Therriault—he would have run if he had, most likely screaming his head off—but I think he *felt* him. No, I don't just think it, I know it. I wish I'd paid more attention at the time, but I was upset, as I'm sure you understand. If you don't, you're an idiot.

Therriault turned his head. It was a relief because the move hid the worst of the exit wound. It wasn't a relief because his face was normal on one side and all bloated out of shape on the other, like that guy Two-Face in the Batman comics. Worst of all, now he was looking at me.

I see them and they know I do. It's always been that way.

"Ask him where the bomb is," Liz said. She was speaking from the corner of her mouth, like a spy in a comedy.

A woman with a baby in a Papoose carrier came up the sidewalk. She gave me a distrustful glance, maybe because I looked funny or maybe because I smelled of puke. Maybe both. I was past the point of caring. All I wanted was to do what Liz Dutton had brought me here to do, then get the fuck out. I waited until the woman with the baby went inside.

"Where's the bomb, Mr. Therriault? The last bomb?"

At first he didn't reply and I was thinking *okay, his brains are blown out, he's here but he can't talk, end of story.* Then he spoke up. The words didn't exactly match the movements of his mouth and it came to me that he was talking from somewhere else. Like on a time-delay from hell. That scared the shit out of me. If I'd known that was when something awful came into him and took him over, it would have been even worse. But *do* I know that? Like for sure? No, but I almost know it.

"I don't want to tell you."

That stunned me to silence. I had never gotten such a reply from a dead person before. True, my experience was limited, but up until then I would have said they had to tell you the truth first time, every time.

"What did he say?" Liz asked. Still talking from the corner of her mouth.

I ignored her and spoke to Therriault again. Since there was no one around, I spoke louder, enunciating every word the way you would for a person who was deaf or only had a shaky grasp on English. "Where…is…the last…bomb?"

I also would have said that the dead can't feel pain, that they are beyond it, and Therriault certainly did not seem to be suffering from the cataclysmic self-inflicted wound in his head, but now his half-bloated face twisted as if I were burning him or stabbing him in the belly instead of just asking him a question.

"Don't want to *tell* you!"

"What did he—" Liz began again, but then the lady with the baby came back out. She had a lottery ticket. The baby in the Papoose had a Kit-Kat finger which he was smearing all over his face. Then he looked at the bench where Therriault was sitting and started crying. The mom must have thought her kid was looking at me, because she gave me another glance, *mega* distrustful this time, and hurried on her way.

"Champ…Jamie, I mean…"

"Shut up," I said. Then, because my mother would have hated me talking to any grownup like that, "Please."

I looked back to Therriault. His grimace of pain made his ruined face look more ruined than ever, and all at once I decided I didn't care. He had maimed enough people to fill a hospital ward, he had killed people, and if the note he'd pinned to his shirt wasn't a lie, he had died trying to kill even more. I decided I *hoped* he was suffering.

"Where…is it…you…motherfucker?"

He clasped his hands around his middle, bent over like he had cramps, groaned. Then he gave it up. "King Kullen. The King Kullen Supermarket in Eastport."

"Why?"

"Seemed right to finish where I started," he said, and drew a circle in the air with one finger. "Complete the circle."

"No, why do it at all? Why set all those bombs?"

He smiled, and the way it kind of squelched the bloated side of his face? I still see that, and I'll never be able to un-see it.

"Because," he said.

"Because what?"

"Because I felt like it," he said.

25

When I told Liz everything Therriault had said, she was excited and nothing else. I could understand that, she wasn't the one looking at a man who'd pretty much blown off one whole side of his head. She told me she had to go into the store and get some stuff.

"And leave me here with *him*?"

"No, go back down the street. Wait by the car. I'll only be a minute."

Therriault was sitting there looking at me with the eye

that was more or less regular and the one that was all stretched out. I could feel his gaze. It made me think of the time I went to camp and got fleas and had to have this special stinky shampoo like five times before they were all gone.

Shampoo wouldn't fix the way Therriault made me feel, only getting away from him would do that, so I did what Liz said. I walked as far as the laundromat and looked in at the woman who was still folding clothes. She saw me and gave me a wave. That brought back the little girl with the hole in her throat, and how *she* had waved to me, and for one horrible moment I thought the laundromat lady was also dead. Only a dead person wouldn't be folding clothes, they only stood around. Or sat around, like Therriault. So I gave her a return wave. I even tried to smile.

Then I turned back to the store. I told myself it was to see if Liz was coming out yet, but that wasn't why. I was looking to see if Therriault was still looking at me. He was. He raised one hand, palm up, three fingers tucked into his palm, one finger pointing. He curled it once, then twice. Very slowly. *Come here, boy*.

I walked back, my legs seeming to move of their own accord. I didn't want to, but couldn't seem to help myself.

"She doesn't care about you," Kenneth Therriault said. "Not a fig. Not one single *fig*. She's using you, boy."

"Fuck you, we're saving lives." There was no one passing by, but even if somebody had been, he or she wouldn't have heard me. He had stolen all of my voice but a whisper.

"What she's saving is her job."

"You don't know that, you're just some random psycho." Still only a whisper, and I felt on the verge of peeing myself.

He didn't say anything, only grinned. That was his answer.

Liz came out. She had one of those cheap plastic bags they gave you in stores like that back then. She looked at the bench, where the ruined man she couldn't see was sitting, and then at me. "What are you doing here, Cha…Jamie? I told you to go to the car." And before I could answer, quick and harsh, like I was a perp in a TV cop show interrogation room: "Did he tell you something else?"

That you only care about saving your job, I thought of saying. *But maybe I already knew that.*

"No," I said. "I want to go home, Liz."

"We will. We will. As soon as I do one more thing. Two, actually, I've also got to get your mess out of my car." She put an arm around my shoulders (like a good mom would) and walked me up past the laundromat. I would have waved to the clothes-folding lady again, but her back was turned.

"I set something up. I didn't really think I'd have a chance to use it, but thanks to you…"

When we were next to her car, she took a flip-phone out of the store bag. It was still in its blister pack. I leaned against the window of a shoe repair place and watched her fiddle with it until she got it working. It was now quarter past four. If Mom went for a drink with Barbara, we could still get back before she came home…but could I keep the afternoon's adventures to myself? I didn't know, and right then it didn't seem that important. I wished Liz could at least have driven around the corner, I thought she could have smelled my puke for that long after what I'd done for her, but she was too wound up. Plus, there was the bomb to consider. I thought of all the movies I'd seen where the clock is counting down to nothing and the hero is wondering whether to cut the red wire or the blue one.

Now she was calling.

"Colton? Yes, this is m...shut up, just listen. It's time to do your thing. You owe me a favor, a big one, and this is it. I'm going to tell you exactly what to say. Record it, then...*shut up, I said!*"

She sounded so vicious that I took a step back. I'd never heard Liz like that, and realized that I was seeing her for the first time in her other life. The police life where she dealt with scumbuckets.

"Record it, then write it down, then call me back. Do it right away." She waited. I snuck a look back at the store. Both benches were empty. That should have been a relief, but somehow I didn't feel relieved.

"Ready? Okay." Liz closed her eyes, shutting out everything but what she wanted to say. She spoke slowly and carefully. " 'If Ken Therriault was really Thumper...' I'll break in there and say I want to record this. You wait until I say 'Go ahead, start again.' Got that?" She listened until Colton—whoever he was—said he got it. You say, 'If Ken Therriault was really Thumper, he was always talking about finishing where he started. I'm calling you because we talked in 2008. I kept your card.' You got that?" Another pause. Liz nodding. "Good. I'll say who is this, and you hang up. Do it right away, this is time-sensitive. Screw it up and I'll fuck you bigtime. You know I can."

She ended the call. She paced around on the sidewalk. I snuck another look at the benches. Empty. Maybe Therriault —whatever remained of him—was heading back home to check out the scene at the good old Frederick Arms.

The drumbeat intro to "Rumor Has It" came from the pocket of Liz's blazer. She took out her real phone and said hello. She listened, then said, "Hold on, I want to record this." She did that, then said, "Go ahead, start again."

Once the script was played out, she ended the call and put her phone away. "It's not as strong as I'd like," she said. "But will they care?"

"Probably not, once they find the bomb," I said. Liz gave a little start, and I realized she had been talking to herself. Now that I'd done what she wanted, I was just baggage.

She had a roll of paper towels and a can of air freshener in the bag. She cleaned up my puke, dropped it in the gutter (hundred-dollar fine for littering, I found out later), and then sprayed the car with something that smelled like flowers.

"Get in," she told me.

I'd been turned away so I didn't have to look at what remained of my lunchtime ravioli (as far as cleaning up the mess went, I thought she owed me that), but when I turned back to get in the car, I saw Kenneth Therriault standing by the trunk. Close enough to reach out and touch me, and still grinning. I might have screamed, but when I saw him I was between breaths and my chest wouldn't seem to expand and grab another one. It was as if all the muscles had gone to sleep.

"I'll be seeing you," Therriault said. The grin widened and I could see a cake of dead blood between his teeth and cheek. *"Champ."*

26

We only drove three blocks before she stopped again. She took out her phone (her real one, not the burner), then looked at me and saw I was shaking. I maybe could have used a hug then, but all I got was a pat on the shoulder, presumably sympathetic. "Delayed reaction, kiddo. Know all about it. It'll pass."

Then she made a call, identified herself as Detective Dutton, and asked for Gordon Bishop. She must have been told he was on the job, because Liz said, "I don't care if he's on Mars, patch me through. This is Priority One."

She waited, tapping the fingers of her free hand on the steering wheel. Then she straightened up. "It's Dutton, Gordo…no, I know I'm not, but you need to hear this. I just got a tip about Therriault from someone I interviewed when I *was* on it…no, I don't know who. You need to check out the King Kullen in Eastport…where he started, right. It makes a degree of sense if you think about it." Listening. Then: "Are you kidding? How many people did we interview back then? A hundred? Two hundred? Listen, I'll play you the message. I recorded it, assuming my phone worked."

She knew it had; she'd checked it on our short three-block drive. She played it for him and when it was done, she said, "Gordo? Did you…shit." She ended the call. "He hung up." Liz gave me a grim smile. "He hates my guts, but he'll check. He knows it'll be on him if he doesn't."

Detective Bishop did check, because by then they'd had time to start digging into Kenneth Therriault's past, and they'd found a nugget that stood out in light of Liz's "anonymous tip." Long before his career in construction and his post-retirement career as an orderly at City of Angels, Therriault had grown up in the town of Westport, which is, natch, next door to Eastport. As a high school senior, he'd worked as a bag boy and shelf stocker at King Kullen. Where he was caught shoplifting. The first time he did it, Therriault was warned. The second time he got canned. But stealing, it seemed, was a hard habit to break. Later in life he moved on to dynamite and blasting caps. A good supply of both was later found in a Queens storage locker. All of it old, all of it from Canada. I guess the border searches were a lot less thorough in those days.

"Can we go home now?" I asked Liz. "Please?"

"Yes. Are you going to tell your mother about this?"

"I don't know."

She smiled. "It was a rhetorical question. Of course you will. And that's okay, doesn't bother me in the slightest. Do you know why?"

"Because nobody would believe it."

She patted my hand. "That's right, Champ. Hole in one."

27

Liz dropped me off on the corner and sped away. I walked down to our building. My mother and Barbara hadn't gone for that drink after all, Barb had a cold and said she was going home right after work. Mom was on the steps with her phone in her hand.

She flew down the steps when she saw me coming and grabbed me in a panicky hug that squeezed the breath out of me. "Where the fuck were you, James?" She only called me that when she was super-pissed, which you might have already guessed. "How could you be so thoughtless? I've been calling *everyone*, I was starting to think you'd been kidnapped, I even thought of calling…"

She quit hugging and held me at arms' length. I could see she had been crying and was starting to again and that made me feel really bad, even though none of it had been my fault. I think only your mother can truly make you feel lower than whale shit.

"Was it Liz?" And without waiting for an answer: "It was." Then, in a low and deadly voice: "That *bitch*."

"I had to go with her, Mom," I said. "I really had to."

Then I started to cry, too.

28

We went upstairs. Mom made coffee and gave me a cup. My first, and I've been a fool for the stuff ever since. I told her almost everything. How Liz had been waiting outside school. How she told me lives depended on finding Thumper's last bomb. How we went to the hospital, and to Therriault's building. I even told her how awful Therriault looked with half his head blown out of shape on one side. What I didn't tell her was how I'd turned around to see him standing behind Liz's car, close enough to grab my arm…if dead people *can* grab, a thing I never wanted to find out one way or the other. And I didn't tell her what he'd said, but that night when I went to bed it clanged in my head like a cracked bell: "I'll be seeing you...*Champ*."

Mom kept saying *okay* and *I understand*, all the time looking more distressed. But she had to know what was happening on Long Island, and so did I. She turned on the TV and we sat on the couch to watch. Lewis Dodley of NY1 was doing a stand-up on a street with police sawhorses blocking it off. "Police appear to be taking this tip very seriously," he was saying. "According to a source in the Suffolk County Police Department—"

I remembered the news helicopter flying over the Frederick Arms and figured it must have had enough time to chopper out to Long Island, so I grabbed the remote from my mother's lap and flipped over to Channel 4. And there, sure enough, was the roof of the King Kullen supermarket. The parking lot was full of police cars. Parked by the main doors was a big van that just about had to belong to the Bomb Squad. I saw two helmeted cops with a pair of dogs on harnesses going inside. The chopper was too high to see if the Bomb Squad cops were wearing bulletproof vests and flak jackets as well as helmets, but I'm sure they were. Not the dogs, though. If Thumper's bomb went off while they were inside, the dogs would be blown to mush.

The reporter in the chopper was saying, "We've been told that all customers and store personnel have been safely evacuated. Although it's possible this is just another false alarm, there have been many during Thumper's reign of terror—" (Yup, he actually said that) "—taking these things seriously is always the wisest course. All we know now is that this was the site of Thumper's first bomb, and that no bomb has been found yet. Let's send it back to the studio."

The chromo behind the news anchors had a picture of Therriault, maybe his City of Angels ID, because he looked pretty old. He was no movie star, but he looked a hell of a lot better than he had sitting on that bench. Liz's manufactured tip might not have been taken so seriously had it not caused one of the older detectives in the department to recall a case from his childhood, that of George Metesky, dubbed the Mad Bomber by the press. Metesky planted thirty-three pipe bombs during his own reign of terror, which lasted from 1940 to 1956, and the seed was a similar grudge, in his case against Consolidated Edison.

Some quick researcher in the news department had also made the connection, and Metesky's face came up next on the chromo behind the anchors, but Mom didn't bother looking at the old guy…who, I thought, looked weirdly like Therriault in his orderly's uniform. She had grabbed her phone, then went muttering into her bedroom for her address book, presumably having deleted Liz's number after their argument about the *serious weight*.

A commercial for some pill came on, so I crept to her bedroom door to listen. If I'd waited I wouldn't have heard jack shit, because that call didn't last long. "It's Tia, Liz. Listen to me and don't say a word. I'm going to keep this to myself, for reasons that should be obvious to you. But if you ever bother my son again, if he even *sees* you, I will burn your life to the ground. You know I can do it. All it would take is one single push. *Stay away from Jamie.*"

I scurried back to the couch and pretended to be absorbed

in the next commercial. Which turned out to be as useless as tits on a bull.

"You heard that?"

Her eyes were burning, telling me not to lie. I nodded.

"Good. If you see her again, you run like hell. Home. And tell me. Do you understand?"

I nodded again.

"Okay, right right right. I'm ordering take-out. Do you want pizza or Chinese?"

29

The cops found and defused Thumper's last bomb that Wednesday night, around eight o'clock. Mom and me were watching *Person of Interest* on TV when the station broke in with a special bulletin. The sniffer dogs had made lots of passes without finding anything, and their Bomb Squad handlers were about to take them out when one of them alerted in the housewares aisle. They'd been in that one several times before and there was no place on the shelves to hide a bomb, but one of the cops happened to look up and saw a ceiling panel just slightly out of place. That's where the bomb was, between the ceiling and the roof. It was tied to a girder with stretchy orange cord, like the kind bungee jumpers use.

Therriault really blew his wad on that one—sixteen sticks of dynamite and a dozen blasting caps. He'd moved far beyond alarm clocks; the bomb was hooked up to a digital timer very much like the ones in those movies I'd been thinking about (one of the cops took a picture after it was disarmed, and it was in the next day's *New York Times*). It was set to go off at 5 PM on Friday, when the store was always busiest. The next day on NY1 (we were back to Mom's fave) one of the Bomb Squad guys said it would have brought the whole roof down. When asked how many people might have been killed in such a blast, he only shook his head.

That Thursday night as we ate dinner, my mother said, "You did a good thing, Jamie. A *fine* thing. Liz did too, whatever her reasons might have been. It makes me think of something Marty said once." She meant Mr. Burkett, actually Professor Burkett, still Emeritus and still hanging in.

"What did he say?"

"'Sometimes God uses a broken tool.' It was from one of the old English writers he used to teach."

"He always asks me what I'm learning in school," I said, "and he always shakes his head like he's thinking I'm getting a bad education."

Mom laughed. "There's a man who's *stuffed* with education, and he's still totally sharp and in focus. Remember when we had Christmas dinner with him?"

"Sure, turkey sandwiches with cranberry dressing, the best! Plus hot chocolate!"

"Yes, that was a good night. It will be a shame when he passes on. Eat up, there's apple crisp for dessert. Barbara made it. And Jamie?"

I looked at her.

"Could we not talk about this anymore. Just kind of…put it behind us?"

I thought she wasn't just talking about Liz, or even

Therriault; she was also talking about how I could see dead folks. It was what our computer teacher might have called *a global request*, and it was all right with me. More than all right, actually. "Sure."

Right then, sitting in our brightly lit kitchen nook and eating pizza, I really thought we could put it behind us. Only I was wrong. I didn't see Liz Dutton for another two years, and hardly ever thought about her, but I saw Ken Therriault again that very night.

As I said at the beginning, this is a horror story.

30

I was almost asleep when two cats started yowling their heads off and I jerked fully awake. We were on the fifth floor and I might not have heard it—and the clatter of a trashcan that followed—if my window hadn't been cracked to let in some fresh air. I got up to shut it and froze with my hands on the sash. Therriault was standing across the street in the spreading glow of a streetlamp, and I knew right away that the cats hadn't been yowling because they were fighting. They had been yowling because they were scared. The baby in the Papoose carrier had seen him; so had those cats. He scared them on purpose. He knew I would come to the window, just as he knew Liz called me Champ.

He grinned from his half-destroyed head.

He beckoned.

I closed the window and thought about going into my mother's room to get in bed with her, only I was too big for that, and there would be questions. So I pulled the shade instead. I went back to my own bed and lay there, looking up into the dark. Nothing like this had ever happened to me before. No dead person had ever followed me home like a fucking stray dog.

Never mind, I thought. *In three or four days, he'll be gone like all of them are gone. A week at most. And it's not like he* can *hurt* you.

But could I be sure of that? Lying there in the dark, I realized I didn't. *Seeing* dead folks didn't mean *knowing* dead folks.

At last I went back to the window and peeked around the shade, sure he'd still be there. Maybe he'd even beckon again. One finger pointing…and then curling. *Come here. Come to me,* Champ.

No one was under the streetlight. He was gone. I went back to bed, but it took me a long time to go to sleep.

31

I saw him again on Friday, outside of school. There were quite a few parents waiting for their kids—there always are on Fridays, probably because they're going somewhere for the weekend—and they didn't see Therriault, but they must have felt him, because they gave the place where he was standing a wide berth. No one was pushing a baby in a carriage, but if someone had been, I knew that baby would be looking at the empty spot on the sidewalk and bawling its head off.

I went back inside and looked at some posters outside the

office, wondering what to do. I supposed I'd have to talk to him, find out what he wanted, and I made up my mind to do it right then, while there were people around. I didn't think he could hurt me, but I didn't *know*.

I used the boys' room first because all at once I really had to pee, but when I was standing at the urinal, I couldn't squeeze out even a single drop. So I went out, holding my backpack by the strap instead of wearing it. I had never been touched by a dead person, not once, I didn't know if they *could* touch, but if Therriault tried to touch me—or grab me—I intended to hit him with a sackful of books.

Only he was gone.

A week went by, then two. I relaxed, figuring he had to be past his sell-by date.

I was on the YMCA junior swim team, and on a Saturday in late May we had our final practice for an upcoming meet in Brooklyn, which would take place the following weekend. Mom gave me ten dollars for something to eat afterwards and told me—as she always did—to make sure I locked my locker so no one would steal the money or my watch (although why anyone would want to steal a lousy Timex I have no idea). I asked her if she was coming to the meet. She looked up from the manuscript she was reading and said, "For the fourth time, Jamie, *yes*. I'm coming to the meet. It's on my calendar."

It was only the second time I'd asked (or maybe the third), but I didn't tell her that, only kissed her on the cheek and headed down the hall to the elevator. When the doors opened, Therriault was in there, grinning his grin and staring at me from his good eye and the stretched-out one. There was a piece of paper pinned to his shirt. The suicide note was on it.

The note was always on it and the blood spattered across it was always fresh.

"Your mother has cancer, Champ. From the cigarettes. She'll be dead in six months."

I was frozen in place with my mouth hanging open.

The elevator doors rolled shut. I made some kind of sound —a squeak, a moan, I don't know—and leaned back against the wall so I wouldn't fall down.

They have to tell you the truth, I thought. *My mother is going to die.*

But then my head cleared a little and a better thought came. I grasped it like a drowning man clutching at a floating piece of wood. *But maybe they only have to tell the truth if you ask them questions. Otherwise, maybe they can tell you any kind of fake shit they want.*

I didn't want to go to swim practice after that, but if I didn't Coach might call Mom to ask where I'd been. Then *she* would want to know where I had been, and what was I going to tell her? That I was afraid that Thumper would be waiting for me on the corner? Or in the lobby of the Y? Or (somehow this was the most horrible) in the shower room, unseen by naked boys rinsing off the chlorine?

Was I going to tell her she had fucking *cancer*?

So I went, and as you might guess, I swam for shit. Coach told me to get my head on straight, and I had to pinch my armpit to keep from bursting into tears. I had to pinch it really hard.

When I got home, Mom was still deep in her manuscript. I hadn't seen her smoking since Liz left, but I knew she sometimes drank when I wasn't there—with her authors and various editors—so I sniffed at her when I kissed her, and didn't smell anything but a little perfume. Or maybe face cream, since it was Saturday. Some kind of lady stuff, anyway.

"Are you coming down with a cold, Jamie? You dried off well after swimming, didn't you?"

"Yeah. Mom, you're not smoking anymore, are you?"

"So *that's* it." She put aside the manuscript and stretched. "No, I haven't had one since Liz left."

Since you kicked her out, I thought.

"Have you been to the doctor lately? To get a checkup?"

She looked at me quizzically. "What's this about? You've got that crease between your brows."

"Well," I said, "you're the only parent I've got. If something happened to you, I couldn't exactly go live with Uncle Harry, could I?"

She made a funny face at that, then laughed and hugged me. "I'm fine, kiddo. Had the old annual checkup two months ago, as a matter of fact. Passed with flying colors."

And she looked okay. In the pink, as the saying goes. Hadn't lost any more weight that I could see, and wasn't coughing her brains out. Although cancer didn't just have to be in a person's throat or lungs, I knew that.

"Well...that's good. I'm glad."

"That makes two of us. Now make your mom a cup of coffee and let me finish this manuscript."

"Is it a good one?"

"As a matter of fact, it is."

"Better than Mr. Thomas's *Roanoke* books?"

"Much better, but not as commercial, alas."

"Can I have a cup of coffee?"

She sighed. "Half a cup. Now let me read."

32

During my last test in math that year, I looked out the window and saw Kenneth Therriault standing on the basketball court. He did his grinning-and-beckoning thing. I looked back at my paper, then looked up again. Still there, and closer. He turned his head so I could get a good look at the purple-black crater, plus the bone-fangs sticking up all around it. I looked down at my paper again, and when I looked up the third time, he was gone. But I knew he'd be back. He wasn't like the others. He was *nothing* like the others.

By the time Mr. Laghari told us to turn in our papers, I still hadn't solved the last five problems. I got a D- on the test, and there was a note at the top: *This is disappointing, Jamie. You must do better. What do I say at least once in every class?* What he said was that if you fell behind in math, you could never catch up.

Math wasn't so special that way, although Mr. Laghari might think so. It was true for most classes. As if to underline the point, I bricked a history test later that day. Not because Therriault was standing at the blackboard or anything, but because I couldn't stop thinking he *might* be standing at the blackboard.

I got the idea he *wanted* me to do badly in my courses. You could laugh at that, but there's another old saying that goes it's not paranoid if it's true. A few lousy tests weren't going to stop me from passing everything, not that late in the year, and then it would be summer vacation, but what about next year, if he was still hanging around?

Also, what if he was getting stronger? I didn't want to believe that, but just the fact that he was still there suggested it might be true. That it probably was true.

Telling somebody might help, and Mom was the logical choice, she'd believe me, but I didn't want to scare her. She'd already been scared enough, when she thought the agency was going to go under and she wouldn't be able to take care of me and her brother. That I'd helped her out of that pickle might make her blame herself for the one I was in now. That made no sense to me, but it might to her. Besides, she wanted to put the whole seeing-dead-folks stuff behind her. And here's the thing: what could she do, even if I *did* tell her? Blame Liz for putting me with Therriault in the first place, but that was all.

I thought briefly of talking to Ms. Peterson, who was the school's guidance counselor, but she'd assume I was having hallucinations, maybe a nervous breakdown. She'd tell my mother. I even thought of going to Liz, but what could Liz do? Pull out her gun and shoot him? Good luck there, since he was already dead. Besides, I was done with Liz, or so I thought. I was on my own, and that was a lonely, scary place to be.

My mother came to the swim meet where I swam like shit in every event. On the way home she gave me a hug and told me everyone had an off day and I'd do better next time. I almost blurted everything out right then, ending with my fear—which I now felt was reasonably justified—that Kenneth Therriault was trying to ruin my life for screwing up his last and biggest bomb. If we hadn't been in a taxi, I really might have. Since we were, I just put my head on her shoulder as I had when I was small and thought my hand-turkey was the greatest work of art since the *Mona Lisa*. Tell you what, the worst part of growing up is how it shuts you up.

33

When I headed out of our apartment on the last day of school, Therriault was once again in the elevator. Grinning and beckoning. He probably expected me to cringe back like I had the first time I saw him in there, but I didn't. I was scared, all right, but not *as* scared, because I was getting used to him, the way you might get used to a growth or a birthmark on your face, even if it was ugly. This time I was more angry than scared, because he wouldn't leave me the fuck alone.

Instead of cringing, I lunged forward and put my arm out to stop the elevator doors. I wasn't going to get in with him—Christ, no!—but I wasn't going to let the doors close until I got a few answers.

"Does my mother really have cancer?"

Once again his face twisted like I was hurting him, and once again I hoped I was.

"*Does my mother have cancer?*"

"I don't know." The way he was staring at me...you know that old saying about if looks could kill?

"Then why did you say that?"

He was at the back of the car now, with his hands pressed

to his chest, as if *I* was scaring *him*. He turned his head, showing me that enormous exit wound, but if he thought that was going to make me let go of the door and step back, he was wrong. Horrible as it was, I'd gotten used to it.

"*Why did you say that?*"

"Because I hate you," Therriault said, and bared his teeth.

"Why are you still here? How *can* you be?"

"I don't know."

"Go away."

He said nothing.

"Go *away*!"

"I'm not going away. I'm never going away."

That scared the hell out of me and my arm flopped down to my side as if it had gained weight.

"Be seeing you, *Champ*."

The elevator doors rolled shut, but the car didn't go anywhere because there was no one to push any of the inside buttons. When I pushed the one on my side, the doors rolled open on an empty car, but I took the stairs anyway.

I'll get used to him, I thought. *I got used to the hole in his head and I'll get used to him. It's not like he can hurt me.*

But in some ways he'd hurt me already: the D- on my math test and screwing the pooch at the swim meet were just two examples. I was sleeping badly (Mom had already commented on the pouches under my eyes), and little noises, even a dropped book in study hall, made me jump. I kept thinking I'd open my closet to get a shirt and he'd be in there, my own personal boogeyman. Or under the bed, and what if he grabbed my wrist or my dangling foot while I was sleeping? I didn't think he could grab, but I wasn't sure of that, either, especially if he was getting stronger.

What if I woke up and he was lying in bed with me? Maybe even grabbing at my junk?

That was an idea that, once thought, couldn't be *un*thought.

And something else, something even worse. What if he was still haunting me—because that's what this was, all right—when I was twenty? Or forty? What if he was there when I died at eighty-nine, waiting to welcome me into the afterlife, where he would go on haunting me even after I was dead?

If this is what a good deed gets you, I thought one night, looking out my window and watching Thumper across the street under his streetlight, *I never want to do another one*.

34

In late June, Mom and I made our monthly visit to see Uncle Harry. He didn't talk much anymore and hardly ever went into the common room. Although he still wasn't fifty, his hair had gone snow white.

Mom said, "Jamie brought you rugelach from Zabar's, Harry. Would you like some?"

I held the bag up from my place in the doorway (I didn't really want to go all the way in), smiling and feeling a little like one of the models on *The Price is Right*.

Uncle Harry said *yig*.

"Does that mean yes?" Mom asked.

Uncle Harry said *ng*, and waved both hands at me. Which you didn't have to be a mind reader to know meant *no fucking cookies*.

"Would you like to go out? It's beautiful."

I wasn't sure Uncle Harry even knew what *out* was these days.

"I'll help you up," Mom said, and took his arm.

"No!" Uncle Harry said. Not *ng*, not *yig*, not *ug*, no. As clear as a bell. His eyes had gotten big and were starting to water. Then, also as clear as a bell, "Who's that?"

"It's Jamie. You know Jamie, Harry."

Only he didn't know me, not anymore, and it wasn't me he was looking at. He was looking over my shoulder. I didn't need to turn around to know what I was going to see there, but I did, anyway.

"What he's got is hereditary," Therriault said, "and it runs in the male line. You'll be like him, Champ. You'll be like him before you know it."

"Jamie?" Mom asked. "Are you okay?"

"Fine," I said, looking at Therriault. "I'm just fine."

But I wasn't, and Therriault's grin said he knew it, too.

"Go away!" Uncle Harry said. "Go away, go away, go away!"

So we did.

All three of us.

35

I had just about decided to tell my mother everything—I needed to let it out, even if it scared her and made her unhappy—when fate, as the saying is, took a hand. This was in July of 2013, about three weeks after our trip to see Uncle Harry.

My mother got a call early one morning, while she was

getting ready to go to the office. I was sitting at the kitchen table, scarfing up Cheerios with one eye open. She came out of her bedroom, zipping her skirt. "Marty Burkett had a little accident last night. Tripped over something—going to the toilet, I imagine—and strained his hip. He says he's fine, and maybe he is, but maybe he's just trying to be macho."

"Yeah," I said, mostly because it's always safer to agree with my mom when she's rushing around and trying to do like three different things at once. Privately I was thinking that Mr. Burkett was a little old to be a macho man, although it was amusing to think of him starring in a movie like *Terminator: The Retirement Years*. Waving his cane and proclaiming "I'll be back." I picked up my bowl and started to slurp the milk.

"Jamie, how many times have I told you not to do that?"

I couldn't remember if she ever had, because quite a few parental edicts, especially those concerning table manners, had a tendency to slide by me. "How else am I supposed to get it all?"

She sighed. "Never mind. I made a casserole for our supper, but we could have burgers. If, that is, you could interrupt your busy schedule of watching TV and playing games on your phone long enough to take it to Marty. I can't, full schedule. I don't suppose you'd be willing to do that? And then call and tell me how he's doing?"

At first I didn't answer. I felt like I'd just been hit on the head with a hammer. Some ideas are like that. Also, I felt like a total dumbo. Why had I never thought of Mr. Burkett before?

"Jamie? Earth to Jamie."

"Sure," I said. "Happy to do it."

"Really?"

"Really."

"Are you sick? Do you have a fever?"

"Ha-ha," I said. "Funny as a rubber crutch."

She grabbed her purse. "I'll give you cab fare—"

"Nah, just put the casserole thing in a carry-bag. I'll walk."

"Really?" she said again, looking surprised. "All the way to Park?"

"Sure. I can use the exercise." Not strictly true. What I needed was time to be sure my idea was a good idea, and how to tell my story if it was.

36

At this point I'm going to start calling Mr. Burkett Professor Burkett, because he taught me that day. He taught me a lot. But before the teaching, he *listened*. I've already said I knew I had to talk to somebody, but I didn't know what a relief it would be to unburden myself until I actually did it.

He came to the door hobbling on not just one cane, which I'd seen him use before, but two. His face lit up when he saw me, so I guess he was glad to get company. Kids are pretty self-involved (as I'm sure you know if you've ever been one yourself, ha-ha), and I only realized later that he must have been a lonely, lonely man in the years after Mona died. He had that daughter on the west coast, but if she came to visit, I never saw her; see statement above about kids and self-involvement.

"Jamie! You come bearing gifts!"

"Just a casserole," I said. "I think it's a Swedish pie."

"You may mean *shepherd's* pie. I'm sure it's delicious. Would you be kind enough to put it in the icebox for me? I've got these…" He lifted the canes off the floor and for one scary moment I thought he was going to face-plant right in front of me, but he got them braced again in time.

"Sure," I said, and went into the kitchen. I got a kick out of how he called the fridge the icebox and cars autos. He was totally old school. Oh, and he also called the telephone the telefungus. I liked that one so much I started using it myself. Still do.

Getting Mom's casserole into the icebox was no problem, because he had almost nothing in there. He stumped in after me and asked how I was doing. I shut the icebox door, turned to him, and said, "Not so well."

He raised his shaggy eyebrows. "No? What's the problem?"

"It's a pretty long story," I said, "and you'll probably think I'm crazy, but I have to tell somebody, and I guess you're elected."

"Is it about Mona's rings?"

My mouth dropped open.

Professor Burkett smiled. "I never quite believed that your mother just happened to find them in the closet. Too fortuitous. *Far* too fortuitous. It crossed my mind to think she put them there herself, but every human action is predicated on motive and opportunity, and your mother had neither. Also, I was too upset to really think about it that afternoon."

"Because you'd just lost your wife."

"Indeed." He raised one cane enough to touch the heel of his palm to his chest, where his heart was. That made me feel bad for him. "So what happened, Jamie? I suppose it's all water under the bridge at this point, but as a lifetime reader of detective stories, I like to know the answers to such questions."

"Your wife told me," I said.

He stared at me across the kitchen.

"I see the dead," I said.

He didn't reply for so long I got scared. Then he said, "I think I need something with caffeine. I think we both do. Then you can tell me everything that's on your mind. I long to hear it."

37

Professor Burkett was so old school that he didn't have tea bags, just loose tea in a cannister. While I waited for his hot pot to boil, he showed me where to find what he called a "tea ball" and instructed me on how much of the loose tea to put in. Brewing tea was an interesting process. I will always prefer coffee, but sometimes a pot of tea is just the thing. Making it feels *formal*, somehow.

Professor Burkett told me the tea had to steep for five minutes in freshly boiled water—no more and no less. He set the timer, showed me where the cups were, and then stumped into the living room. I heard his sigh of relief when he sat down in his favorite chair. Also a fart. Not a trumpet blast, more of an oboe.

I made two cups of tea and put them on a tray along with the sugar bowl and the Half and Half from the icebox (which neither of us used, probably a good thing since it was a month past its sell-by date). Professor Burkett took his black and smacked his lips over the first sip. "Kudos, Jamie. Perfect on your first try."

"Thanks." I sugared mine up liberally. My mom would have screamed at that third heaping spoonful, but Professor Burkett never said boo.

"Now tell me your tale. I've nothing but time."

"Do you believe me? About the rings?"

"Well," he said, "I believe that you believe. And I *know* that the rings were found; they're in my bank safety deposit box. Tell me, Jamie, if I asked your mother, would she corroborate your story?"

"Yes, but please don't do that. I decided to talk to you because I don't want to talk to her. It would upset her."

He sipped his tea with a hand that shook slightly, then put it down and looked at me. Or maybe even *into* me. I can still see those bright blue eyes peering out from beneath his shaggy every-whichway brows. "Then talk to me. Convince me."

Having rehearsed my story on my crosstown walk, I was able to keep it in a pretty straight line. I started with Robert Harrison—you know, the Central Park man—and moved on to seeing Mrs. Burkett, then all the rest. It took quite awhile. When I finished, my tea was down to just lukewarm (maybe even a little less), but I drank a bunch of it anyway, because my throat was dry.

Professor Burkett considered, then said, "Will you go into

my bedroom, Jamie, and bring me my iPad? It's on the night table."

His bedroom smelled sort of like Uncle Harry's room in the care home, plus some sharp aroma that I guessed was liniment for his strained hip. I got his iPad and brought it back. He didn't have an iPhone, just the landline telefungus that hung on the kitchen wall like something in an old movie, but he loved his pad. He opened it when I gave it to him (the start-up screen was a picture of a young couple in wedding outfits that I assumed was him and Mrs. Burkett) and started poking away at once.

"Are you looking up Therriault?"

He shook his head without looking up. "Your Central Park man. You say you were in preschool when you saw him?"

"Yes."

"So this would have been 2003…possibly 2004…ah, here it is." He read, bent over the pad and occasionally brushing his hair out of his eyes (he had a lot of it). At last he looked up and said, "You saw him lying there dead and also standing beside himself. Your mother would also confirm *that*?"

"She knew I wasn't lying because I knew what the guy was wearing on top, even though that part of him was covered up. But I really don't want—"

"Understood, totally understood. Now concerning Regis Thomas's last book. It was unwritten—"

"Yeah, except for the first couple of chapters. I think."

"But your mother was able to glean enough details to write the rest of it herself, using you as her medium?"

I hadn't thought of myself as a medium, but in a way he was right. "I guess. Like in *The Conjuring*." And off his puzzled expression: "It's a movie. Mr. Burkett...*Professor*...do you think I'm crazy?" I almost didn't care, because the relief of getting it all out there was so great.

"No," he said, but something—probably my expression of relief—caused him to raise a warning finger. "This is not to say I believe your story, at least not without corroboration from your mother, which I have agreed not to ask for. But I will go this far: I don't necessarily *disbelieve*. Mostly because of the rings, but also because that last Thomas book does indeed exist. Not that I've read it." He made a little face at that. "You say your mother's friend—*ex*-friend—could also corroborate the last and most colorful part of your story."

"Yes, but—"

He raised his hand, like he must have done a thousand times to babbling students in class. "You don't want me to speak to her, either, and I quite understand. I only met her once, and I didn't care for her. Did she really bring drugs into your home?"

"I didn't see them myself, but if my mom said she did, she did."

He put his pad aside and fondled his go-to cane, which had a big white knob on the top. "Then Tia is well rid of her. And this Therriault, who you say is haunting you. Is he here now?"

"No." But I looked around to be sure.

"You want to be rid of him, of course."

"Yes, but I don't know how to do it."

He sipped his tea, brooded over the cup, then set it down and fixed me with those blue eyes again. He was old; they weren't. "An interesting problem, especially for an elderly gentleman who's encountered all sorts of supernatural creatures in his reading life. The gothics are full of them, Frankenstein's monster and Count Dracula being just the pair who show up most frequently on movie marquees. There are many more in European literature and folk-tales. Let's presume, at least for the moment, that this Therriault isn't just in your head. Let's presume he actually exists."

I kept myself from protesting that he *did* exist. The professor already knew what I believed, he'd said so himself.

"Let us go a step further. Based on what you've told me about your other sightings of dead people—including my wife—all of them go away after a few days. Disappear to…" He waved his hand. "…to wherever. But not this Therriault. He's still around. In fact, you think he may be getting stronger."

"I'm pretty sure he is."

"If so, perhaps he's not really Kenneth Therriault at all anymore. Perhaps what remained of Therriault after death has been infested—that's the correct word, not possessed—by a demon." He must have seen my expression because he hastened to add, "We're just speculating here, Jamie. I'm going to speak frankly and say I think it far more likely that you're suffering from a localized fugue state that has caused hallucinations."

"In other words, crazy." At that point I was still glad I'd told him, but his conclusion was maximo depressing, even though I'd been more or less expecting it.

He waved a hand. "Bosh. I don't think that at all. You're obviously operating in the real world as well as ever. And I must admit your story is full of things that are hard to explain in strictly rational terms. I don't doubt that you accompanied Tia and her ex-friend to the deceased Mr. Thomas's home. Nor do I doubt that Detective Dutton took you to Therriault's place of employment and his apartment building. If she did those things—I am channeling Ellery Queen here, one of my favorite apostles of deduction—*she* must have believed in your mediumistic talents. Which in turn leads us back to Mr. Thomas's home, where Detective Dutton must have seen something to convince her of that in the first place."

"You lost me," I said.

"Never mind." He leaned forward. "All I'm saying is that although I lean toward the rational, the known, and the empiric—having never seen a ghost, or had a flash of precognition—I must admit there are elements of your story I can't dismiss out of hand. So let us say that Therriault, or something nasty that has inhabited what remains of Therriault, actually exists. The question then becomes: can you get rid of him?"

Now I was leaning forward, thinking of the book he'd given me, the one full of fairy tales that were really horror stories with very few happy endings. The stepsisters cut off their toes, the princess threw the frog against a wall—*splat!*—instead of kissing him, Red Riding Hood actually *encouraged* the big bad wolf to eat Grandma, so she could inherit Grandma's property.

"*Can* I? You've read all those books, there must be a way in at least one of them! Or…" A new idea struck me. "Exorcism! What about that?"

"Probably a nonstarter," Professor Burkett said. "I think a

priest would be more apt to send you to a child psychiatrist than an exorcist. If your Therriault exists, Jamie, you may be stuck with him."

I stared at him with dismay.

"But maybe that's all right."

"All right? How can it be all right?"

He lifted his cup, sipped, and set it down.

"Have you ever heard of the Ritual of Chüd?"

38

Now I'm twenty-two—almost twenty-three, in fact—and living in the land of later. I can vote, I can drive, I can buy booze and cigarettes (which I plan to quit soon). I understand that I'm still very young, and I'm sure that when I look back I'll be amazed (hopefully not disgusted) by how naïve and wet behind the ears I was. Still, twenty-two is light years from thirteen. I know more now, but I believe less. Professor Burkett would never have been able to work the same magic on me now that he did back then. Not that I'm complaining! Kenneth Therriault—I don't know what he really was, so let's stick with that for now—was trying to destroy my sanity. The professor's magic saved it. It may even have saved my life.

Later, when I researched the subject for an anthropology paper in college (NYU, of course), I discovered half of what he told me that day was actually true. The other half was bullshit. I have to give him credit for invention, though (full marks, Mom's British romance writer Philippa Stephens would have said). Check this out, and dig the irony: my

Uncle Harry wasn't even fifty and totally gaga, while Martin Burkett, although in his eighties, could still be creative on the fly…and all in service of a troubled boy who turned up uninvited, bearing a casserole and a weird story.

The Ritual of Chüd, the professor said, was practiced by a sect of Tibetan and Nepalese Buddhists. (True.)

They did it to achieve a sense of perfect nothingness and the resulting state of serenity and spiritual clarity. (True.)

It was also considered useful in combating demons, both those in the mind and the supernatural ones who invaded from the outside. (A gray area.)

"Which makes it perfect for you, Jamie, because it covers all the bases."

"You mean it can work even if Therriault's really not there, and I'm just crazypants."

He gave me a look combining reproach and impatience that he probably perfected in his teaching career. "Stop talking and try listening, if you don't mind."

"Sorry." I was on my second cup of tea, and feeling wired.

With the groundwork laid, Professor Burkett now moved into the land of make-believe…not that I knew the difference. He said that chüd was especially useful when one of these high-country Buddhists encountered a yeti, also known as the abominable snowman.

"Are those things real?" I asked.

"As with your Mr. Therriault, I can't say with any surety. But—also as with you and your Mr. Therriault—I *can* say that the Tibetans believe they are."

The professor went on to say that a person unfortunate enough to meet a yeti would be haunted by it for the rest of his life. Unless, that was, it could be engaged and bested in the Ritual of Chüd.

If you're following this, you know that if bullshit was an event in the Olympics, the judges would have given Professor Burkett all 10s for that one, but I was only thirteen and in a bad place. Which is to say I swallowed it whole. If part of me had an idea of what Professor Burkett was up to—I can't really remember—I shut it down. You have to remember how desperate I was. The idea of being followed around by Kenneth Therriault, aka Thumper, for the rest of my life— *haunted* by him, to use the professor's word—was the most horrible thing I could imagine.

"How does it work?" I asked.

"Ah, you'll like this. It's like one of the uncensored fairy tales in the book I gave you. According to the stories, you and the demon bind yourselves together by biting into each other's tongues."

He said this with a certain relish, and I thought, *Like it? Why would I like it?*

"Once this union has been accomplished, you and the demon have a battle of wills. This would occur telepathically, I assume, since it would be hard to talk while engaged in a…mmm…mutual tongue-bite. The first to withdraw loses all power over the winner."

I stared at him, my mouth open. I had been raised to be polite, especially around my mother's clients and acquaintances, but I was too grossed out to consider the social niceties. "If you think I'm going to—what?—french-kiss that guy, you're out of your mind! For one thing, he's *dead*, did you not get that?"

"Yes, Jamie, I believe I did."

"Besides, how would I even get him to do it? What would I say, come on over here, Ken honey, and slip me some tongue?"

"Are you finished?" Professor Burkett asked mildly, once again making me feel like the most clueless student in class. "I think the tongue-biting aspect is meant to be symbolic. The way chunks of Wonder Bread and little thimbles of wine are meant to be symbolic of Jesus's last supper with his disciples."

I didn't get that, not being much of a churchgoer, so I kept my mouth shut.

"Listen to me, Jamie. Listen very carefully."

I listened as if my life depended on it. Because I thought it did.

39

As I was preparing to leave (politeness had resurfaced and I didn't neglect to tell him thank you), the professor asked me if his wife had said anything else. Besides about where the rings were, that was.

By the time you're thirteen I think you've forgotten most of the things that have happened to you when you're six—I mean, that's more than half your life ago!—but I didn't have any trouble remembering that day. I could have told him how Mrs. Burkett threw shade about my green turkey but figured that wouldn't interest him. He wanted to know if she'd said anything about *him*, not what she'd said to me.

"You were hugging my mom and she said you were going to burn her hair with your cigarette. And you did. Guess you quit smoking, huh?"

"I allow myself three a day. I suppose I could have more, I'm not going to be cut down in my youth, but three is all I seem to want. Did she say anything else?"

"Um, that you'd be having lunch with some woman in a month or two. Her name might have been Debbie or Diana, something like that—"

"Dolores? Was it Dolores Magowan?" He was looking at me with new eyes, and all at once I wished we'd had this part of our conversation to start with. It would have gone a long way toward establishing my credibility.

"It might have been."

He shook his head. "Mona always thought I had eyes for that woman, God knows why."

"She said something about rubbing sheep-dip into her hands—"

"Lanolin," he said. "For her swollen joints. I'll be damned."

"There was one other thing, too. About how you always missed the back loop on your pants. I think she said 'Who'll do that now?' "

"My God," he said softly. "Oh my God. Jamie."

"Oh, and she kissed you. On the cheek."

It was just a little kiss, and years ago, but that sealed the deal. Because he also wanted to believe, I guess. If not in everything, in her. In that kiss. That she had been there.

I left while I was ahead.

40

I kept an eye out for Therriault on my way home—that was second nature to me by then—but didn't see him. Which was great, but I'd given up hoping that he was gone for good. He was a bad penny, and he'd turn up. I only hoped I would be ready for him when he did.

That night I got an email from Professor Burkett. *I did a little research with interesting results*, it said. *I thought you also might be interested*. There were three attachments, all three reviews of Regis Thomas's last book. The professor had highlighted the lines he had found interesting, leaving me to draw my own conclusions. Which I did.

From the Sunday *Times Book Review*: "Regis Thomas's swan song is the usual farrago of sex and swamp-tromping adventure, but the prose is sharper than usual; here and there one finds glimmers of actual writing."

From the *Guardian*: "Although the long-bruited Mystery of Roanoke won't be much of a surprise to readers of the series (who surely saw it coming), Thomas's narrative voice is livelier than one might expect from the previous volumes, where turgid exposition alternated with fervid and sometimes comical sexual encounters."

From the *Miami Herald*: "The dialogue snaps, the pacing is crisp, and for once the lesbian liaison between Laura Goodhugh and Purity Betancourt feels real and touching, rather than like a prurient joke or a stroke fantasy. It's a great wind-up."

I couldn't show those reviews to my mother—they would have raised too many questions—but I was pretty sure she must have seen them herself, and I guessed they had made her as happy as they made me. Not only had she gotten away with it, she had put a shine on Regis Thomas's sadly tarnished reputation.

There were many nights in the weeks and months following my first encounter with Kenneth Therriault when I went to bed feeling unhappy and afraid. That night wasn't one of them.

41

I'm not sure how many times I saw him the rest of that summer, which should tell you something. If it doesn't, here it is in plain English: I was getting used to him. I never would have believed it on the day when I turned around and saw him standing by the trunk of Liz Dutton's car, close enough to touch me. I never would have believed it on the day when the elevator opened and he was in there, telling me my mother had cancer and grinning like it was the happiest news ever. But familiarity breeds contempt, so they say, and in this case the saying was true.

It no doubt helped that he never did show up in my closet or under my bed (which would have been worse, because when I was little I was sure that was where the monster was waiting to grab a dangling foot or arm). That summer I read *Dracula*—okay, not the actual book, but a kick-ass graphic novel I bought at Forbidden Planet—and in it Van Helsing said that a vampire couldn't come in unless you invited him.

If it was true of vampires, it stood to reason (at least to thirteen-year-old me it did) that it was true of other supernatural beings. Like the one inside of Therriault, keeping him from disappearing after a few days like all the other dead people. I checked Wikipedia to see if Mr. Stoker just made that up, but he didn't. It was in lots of the vampire legends. Now (later!) I can see it makes symbolic sense. If we have free will, then you have to invite evil in.

Here's something else. He had mostly stopped crooking that finger at me. For most of that summer he just stood at a distance, staring. The only time I *did* see him beckoning was kind of funny. If, that is, you can say anything about that undead motherfucker was funny.

Mom got us tickets to see the Mets play the Tigers on the last Sunday in August. The Mets lost big, but I didn't care, because Mom bagged a pair of awesome seats from one of her publisher friends (contrary to popular belief, literary agents *do* have friends). They were on the third base side, just two rows up from the field. It was during the seventh inning stretch, while the Mets were still keeping it close, that I saw Therriault. I looked around for the hotdog man, and when I looked back, my pal Thumper was standing near the third base coach's box. Same khaki pants. Same shirt with blood all down the left side and spattering the suicide note. Head blown open like somebody lit off a cherry bomb in there. Grinning. And yes, beckoning.

The Tigers infield was throwing the ball around, and just after I saw Therriault, a chuck from the shortstop to the third basemen went way wild. The crowd whooped and jeered the usual stuff—*nice throw busher, my grandmother can do better than that*—but I just sat there with my hands clamped so tight the nails were biting into my palms. The shortstop hadn't seen Therriault (he would have run into the outfield screaming if he had), but he *felt* him. I know he did.

And here's something else: the third base coach went to retrieve the ball, then backed off and let it roll into the dugout. Shagging it would have brought him right next to the thing only I could see. Did the guy feel a cold spot, like in a ghost movie? I don't think so. I think he felt, just for a second or two, that the world was trembling around him. Vibrating like a guitar string. I have reasons to think that.

Mom said, "Okay, Jamie? You're not getting sunstroke on me, are you?"

"I'm fine," I said, and clenched hands or not, I mostly was. "Do you see the hotdog man?"

She craned around and waved to the nearest vendor. Which gave me a chance to give Kenneth Therriault the finger. His grin turned into a snarl that showed all his teeth. Then he walked into the visitors' dugout, where the players who weren't on the field no doubt shuffled around on the bench to give him room, without any idea why they were doing it.

I sat back with a smile. I wasn't ready to think that I'd vanquished him—not with a cross or holy water but by flipping him the bird—but the idea did kind of tiptoe in.

People started to leave in the top of the ninth, after the Tigers scored seven and put the game out of reach. Mom asked me if I wanted to stay and watch the Mr. Met Dash and I shook my head. The Dash was strictly for little kids. I had done it once, back before Liz, back before that fucker James Mackenzie stole our money in his Ponzi scheme, even before the day Mona Burkett told me turkeys weren't green. Back when I was a little kid and the world was my oyster.

That seemed so long ago.

42

You may be asking yourself a question I never asked myself back then: *Why me? Why Jamie Conklin?* I have asked myself since, and I don't know. I can only guess. I think it was because I was different, and it—the it inside the shell of Therriault—hated me for it and wanted to hurt me, even destroy me if it could. I think, call me crazy if you want, I *offended* it somehow. And maybe there was something else. I think maybe—just maybe—the Ritual of Chüd had already begun.

I think that once it started fucking with me it couldn't stop.

As I said, just guessing here. Its reasons might have been something else entirely, as unknowable as it was to me. And as monstrous. As I said, this is a horror story.

43

I was still scared of Therriault, but I no longer thought that I might chicken out if an opportunity came to put Professor Burkett's ritual into practice. I only needed to be ready. For Therriault to get close, in other words, not just be across the street or standing near third base at Citi Field.

My chance came on a Saturday in October. I was going down to Grover Park to play touch football with a bunch of kids from my school. Mom left me a note that said she'd stayed up late reading Philippa Stephens's latest opus and was going to sleep in. I was to get my breakfast quietly, and no more than half a cup of coffee. I was to have a good time with my friends and not come home with a concussion or a broken arm. I was to be back by two at the very latest. She left me lunch money, which I folded carefully into my pocket. There was a PS: *Would it be a waste of time to ask you to eat something green, even a scrap of lettuce on a hamburger?*

Probably, Mom, probably, I thought as I poured myself a bowl of Cheerios and ate them (quietly).

When I left the apartment, Therriault wasn't on my mind. He spent less and less time there, and I used some of the newly available space to think about other things, mostly girls. I was dwelling on Valeria Gomez in particular as I walked down the hall to the elevator. Did Therriault decide to get close that day because he had a kind of window into my head, and knew he was far from my thoughts? Sort of a low-grade telepathy? I don't know that either.

I pushed the call button, wondering if Valeria would come to the game. It was quite possible because her brother Pablo played. I was deep in a daydream of how I caught a pass, evaded all would-be touchers, and sped into the end zone with the ball held high, but I still stepped back when the elevator arrived—that had become second nature to me. It was empty. I pushed for the lobby. The elevator went down and the door opened. There was a short stub of hallway, and then a door, locked from the inside, which gave on a little foyer. The door to the outside wasn't locked, so the mailman could come in and put the mail in the boxes. If Therriault had been out there, in the foyer, I couldn't have done what I did. But he wasn't in the foyer. He was inside, at the end of the hall, grinning away like doing so was going to be outlawed the day after tomorrow.

He started to say something, maybe one of his bullshit prophecies, and if I'd been thinking of him instead of Valeria, I probably would have either frozen in place or stumbled back into the elevator car, whamming on the DOOR CLOSE button for all I was worth. But I was being pissed at him for intruding on my fantasy and all I remember thinking was what Professor Burkett told me on the day I brought him the casserole.

"The tongue-biting in the Ritual of Chüd is only one ceremony before meeting an enemy," he said. "There are many. The Maoris do a war-cry dance as they face their opponents. Kamikaze pilots toasted each other and photographs of their targets with what they believed was magical saké. In ancient Egypt, members of warring houses struck each other on the forehead before getting out the knives and spears and bows. Sumo wrestlers clap each other on the shoulders. All come down to the same thing: *I meet you in combat, where one of us will best the other*. In other words, Jamie, don't bother sticking out your tongue. Just grab your demon and hold on for dear life."

Instead of freezing or cringing, I bolted thoughtlessly forward with my arms out, like I was about to embrace a long absent friend. I screamed, but I think only in my head, because nobody looked out from one of the ground-floor apartments to see what was going on. Therriault's grin—the one that always showed that lump of dead blood between his teeth and cheek—disappeared, and I saw an amazing, wonderful thing: he was afraid of me. He cringed back against the door to the foyer, but it opened the other way and he was pinned. I grabbed him.

I can't describe how it went down. I don't think a much more gifted writer than I am could, but I'll do the best I can. Remember what I said about the world trembling, or vibrating like a guitar string? That was what it was like on the outside of Therriault, and all around him. I could feel it shaking my teeth and jittering my eyeballs. Only there was something else, on the *inside* of Therriault. It was something that was using him as a vessel and keeping him from moving on to wherever dead people go when their connection to our world rots away.

It was a very bad thing, and it was yelling at me to let it go. Or to let Therriault go. Maybe there was no difference. It was furious with me, and scared, but mostly it was surprised. Being grabbed was the last thing it had expected.

It struggled and would have gotten away if Therriault hadn't been pinned against the door, I'm sure of that. I was a skinny kid, Therriault was easily five inches taller and would have outweighed me by at least a hundred pounds if he'd been alive, but he wasn't. The thing inside him *was* alive, and I was pretty sure it had come in when I was forcing Therriault to answer my questions outside that little store.

The vibration got worse. It was coming up through the floor. It was coming down from the ceiling. The overhead light was shaking and throwing liquid shadows. The walls seemed to be crawling first one way and then the other.

"Let me go," Therriault said, and even his voice was vibrating. It sounded like when you put waxed paper over a comb and blow on it. His arms flew out to either side, then closed in and clapped me on the back. It immediately became hard to breathe. "Let me go and I'll let you go."

"No," I said, and hugged him tighter. *This is it*, I remember thinking. *This is Chüd. I'm in mortal combat with a demon right here in the front hall of my New York apartment building*.

"I'll strangle the breath out of you," it said.

"You can't," I said, hoping I was right about that. I could still breathe, but they were mighty short breaths. I began to think I could see *into* Therriault. Maybe it was a hallucination brought on by the vibration and the sense that the world was on the verge of exploding like a delicate wine glass, but I don't think so. It wasn't his guts I was looking at but a light. It was bright and dark at the same time. It was something from outside the world. It was horrible.

How long did we stand there hugging each other? It could have been five hours or only ninety seconds. You could say five hours was impossible, someone would have come, but I think…I almost *know*…that we were outside of time. One thing I can say for sure is that the elevator doors didn't close as they are supposed to five seconds or so after the passengers get out. I could see the elevator's reflection over Therriault's shoulder and the doors stayed open the whole time.

At last it said, "Let me go and I'll never come back."

That was an extremely tasty idea, as I'm sure you'll understand, and I might have done it if the professor hadn't prepared me for this, as well.

It will try to bargain, he said. *Don't let it*. And then he told me what to do, probably thinking that the only thing I had to confront was some neurosis or complex or whatever psychological thing you want to call it.

"Not good enough," I said, and went on hugging.

I could see more and more into Therriault, and realized he really *was* a ghost. Probably all dead people are and I just saw them as solid. The more insubstantial he became, the brighter that darklight—that deadlight—shone. I don't have any idea what it was. I only knew I had caught it, and there's an old saying that goes *he who takes a tiger by the tail dare not let go*.

The thing inside Therriault was worse than any tiger.

"What do you want?" Gasping it. There was no breath in him, I surely would have felt it on my cheek and neck if there had been, but he was gasping just the same. In worse shape than I was, maybe.

"It's not enough for you to stop haunting me." I took a deep breath and said what Professor Burkett had told me to say, if I was able to engage my nemesis in the Ritual of Chüd. And even though the world was shivering around me, even though this thing had me in a death grip, it gave me pleasure to say it. Great pleasure. *Warrior's* pleasure.

"Now I'll haunt *you*."

"No!" Its grip tightened.

I was squeezed against Therriault even though Therriault was now nothing but a supernatural hologram.

"Yes." Professor Burkett told me to say something else if I got the chance. I later found out it was the amended title of a famous ghost story, which made it very fitting. "Oh, I'll whistle and you'll come to me, my lad."

"No!" It struggled. That vile pulsing light made me feel like puking, but I held on.

"Yes. I'll haunt you as much as I want, whenever I want, and if you don't agree I'll hold onto you until you die."

"I can't die! But you can!"

That was undoubtedly true, but at that moment I had never felt stronger. Plus, all the time Therriault was fading and he was that deadlight's toehold in our world.

I said nothing. Only clutched. And Therriault clutched me. It went on like that. I was getting cold, feet and hands losing sensation, but I held on. I meant to hold on forever if I had to. I was terrified of the thing that was inside Therriault, but it was trapped. Of course I was also trapped; that was the nature of the ritual. If I let go, it won.

At last it said, "I agree to your terms."

I loosened my grip, but only a little. "Are you lying?" A stupid question, you might say, except it wasn't.

"I can't." Sounding slightly petulant. "You know that."

"Say it again. Say you agree."

"I agree to your terms."

"You know that I can haunt you?"

"I know, but I'm not afraid of you."

Bold words, but as I'd already found out, Therriault could make as many untrue statements as he—*it*—wanted to. Statements weren't answers to questions. And anybody who has to *say* they're not afraid is lying. I didn't have to wait until later to learn that, I knew it at thirteen.

"Are you afraid of me?"

I saw that cramped expression on Therriault's face again, as if he was tasting something sour and unpleasant. Which was probably how telling the truth felt to the miserable son of a bitch.

"Yes. You're not like the others. You *see*."

"Yes what?"

"Yes I'm afraid of you!"

Sweet!

I let him go. "Get out of here, whatever you are, and go to wherever you go. Just remember if I call you, *you come*."

He whirled around, giving me one final look at the gaping hole in the left side of his head. He grabbed at the door-knob. His hand went through it and *didn't* go through it. Both at the same time. I know it's crazy, a paradox, but it happened. I saw it. The knob turned and the door opened. At the same time the overhead light blew out and glass tin-kled down from the fixture. There were a dozen or so mail-boxes in the foyer, and half of them popped open. Therriault gave me one last hateful look over his bloody shoulder, and then he was gone, leaving the front door open. I saw him go down the steps, not so much running as plunging. A guy speeding past on a bike, probably a messenger, lost his bal-ance, fell over, and sprawled in the street, cursing.

I knew the dead could impact the living, that was no sur-prise. I'd seen it, but those impacts had always been *little* things. Professor Burkett had felt his wife's kiss. Liz had felt Regis Thomas blow on her face. But the things I'd just seen—the light that blew out, the jittery, vibrating doorknob that had turned, the messenger falling off his bike—were on an entirely different level.

The thing I'm calling the deadlight almost lost its host while I was holding on, but when I let go, it did more than regain Therriault; it got stronger. That strength must have come from me, but I didn't feel any weaker (like poor Lucy Westenra while Count Dracula was using her as his personal lunch-wagon). In fact I felt better than ever, refreshed and invigorated.

It was stronger, so what? I'd owned it, had made it my bitch.

For the first time since Liz had picked me up from school that day and taken me hunting for Therriault, I felt good again. Like someone who's had a serious illness and is finally on the mend.

44

I got back home around quarter past two, a little late but not where-have-you-been-I-was-so-worried late. I had a long scrape on one arm and the knee of my pants got torn when one of the high school boys bumped me and I went down hard, but I felt pretty damned fine just the same. Valeria wasn't there, but two of her girlfriends were. One of them said Valeria liked me and the other one said I should talk to her, maybe sit with her at lunch.

God, the possibilities!

I let myself in and saw that someone—probably Mr. Provenza, the building super—had closed the mailboxes that had popped open when Therriault left. Or, to put it more accurately, when it fled the scene. Mr. Provenza had also cleaned up the broken glass, and put a sign in front of the elevator that said TEMPORARILY OUT OF ORDER. That made me remember the day Mom and I came home from school, me clutching my green turkey, and found the elevator at the Palace on Park out of order. *Fuck this elevator*, Mom had said. Then: *You didn't hear that, kiddo.*

Old days.

I took the stairs and let myself in to find Mom had dragged her home office chair up to the living room window, where she was reading and drinking coffee. "I was just about to call you," she said, and then, looking down, "Oh my God, that's a new pair of jeans!"

"Sorry," I said. "Maybe you can patch them up."

"I have many skills, but sewing isn't one of them. I'll take them to Mrs. Abelson at Dandy Cleaners. What did you have for lunch?"

"A burger. With lettuce and tomato."

"Is that true?"

"I cannot tell a lie," I said, and of course that made me think of Therriault, and I gave a little shiver.

"Let me see your arm. Come over here where I can get a good look." I came over and displayed my battle scar. "No need of a Band-Aid, I guess, but you need to put on some Neosporin."

"Okay if I watch ESPN after I do that?"

"It would be if we had electricity. Why do you think I'm reading at the window instead of at my desk?"

"Oh. That must be why the elevator isn't working."

"Your powers of deduction stun me, Holmes." This was one of my mom's literary jokes. She has dozens of them. Maybe hundreds. "It's just our building. Mr. Provenza says something blew out all the breakers. Some kind of power surge. He said he's never seen anything like it. He's going to try to get it fixed by tonight, but I've got an idea we'll be running on candles and flashlights once it gets dark."

Therriault, I thought, but of course it wasn't. It was the deadlight thing that was now inhabiting Therriault. It blew the light fixture, it opened some of the mailboxes, and it fried the circuit breakers for good measure when it left.

I went into the bathroom to get the Neosporin. It was pretty dark in there, so I flipped the light switch. Habit's a bitch, isn't it? I sat on the sofa to spread antibiotic goo on my scrape, looking at the blank TV and wondering how many circuit breakers there were in an apartment building the size of ours, and how much power it would take to cook them all.

I could whistle for that thing. And if I did, would it come to the lad named Jamie Conklin? That was a lot of power for a kid who wouldn't even be able to get a driver's license for another three years.

"Mom?"

"What?"

"Do you think I'm old enough to have a girlfriend?"

"No, dear." Without looking up from her manuscript.

"When will I be old enough?"

"How does twenty-five sound?"

She started laughing and I laughed with her. Maybe, I thought, when I was twenty-five or so I'd summon Therriault and ask him to bring me a glass of water. But on second thought, anything *it* brought might be poison. Maybe, just for shits and giggles, I'd ask it to stand on its Therriault head, do a split, maybe walk on the ceiling. Or I could let it go.

Tell it to get buzzin', cousin. Of course I didn't have to wait until I was twenty-five, I could do that anytime. Only I didn't want to. Let it be *my* prisoner for awhile. That nasty, horrible light reduced to little more than a firefly in a jar. See how it liked that.

The electricity came back on at ten o'clock, and all was right with the world.

45

On Sunday, Mom proposed a visit to Professor Burkett to see how he was doing and to retrieve the casserole dish. "Also, we could bring him some croissants from Haber's."

I said that sounded good. She gave him a call and he said he'd love to see us, so we walked to the bakery and then hailed a cab. My mother refused to use Uber. She said they weren't New York. *Taxis* were New York.

I guess the miracle of healing goes on even when you're old, because Professor Burkett was down to only one cane and moving pretty well. Not apt to be running in the NYC Marathon again (if he ever had), but he gave Mom a hug at the door and I wasn't afraid he was going to face-plant when he shook my hand. He gave me a keen look, I gave him a slight nod, and he smiled. We understood each other.

Mom bustled around, setting out the croissants and pats of butter and the tiny pots of jam that came with them. We ate in the kitchen with the mid-morning sun slanting in. It was a nice little meal. When we were done, Mom transferred the remains of the casserole (which was most of it; I guess old folks don't eat much) to a Tupperware and washed her dish. She set it to dry and then excused herself to use the bathroom.

As soon as she was gone, Professor Burkett leaned across the table. "What happened?"

"He was in the foyer when I came out of the elevator yesterday. I didn't think about it, just rushed forward and grabbed him."

"He was there? This Therriault? You saw him? *Felt* him?" Still half-convinced it was all in my mind, you know. I could see it on his face, and really, who could blame him?

"Yeah. But it's not Therriault, not anymore. The thing inside, it's a light, tried to get away but I held on. It was scary, but I knew it would be bad for me if I let go. Finally, when it saw that Therriault was fading out, it—"

"Fading out? What do you mean?"

The toilet flushed. Mom wouldn't come back until she'd washed her hands, but that wouldn't take long.

"I told it what you told me to say, Professor. That if I whistled, it had to come to me. That it was my turn to haunt *it*. It agreed. I made it say it out loud, and it did."

My mother came back before he could ask any more questions, but I could see he looked troubled and was still thinking the whole confrontation had been in my mind. I got that but I was a little pissed just the same—I mean, he *knew* stuff, about the rings and Mr. Thomas's book—but looking back on it, I understand. Belief is a high hurdle to get over and I think it's even higher for smart people. Smart people know a lot, and maybe that makes them think they know everything.

"We ought to go, Jamie," Mom said. "I've got a manuscript to finish."

"You always have a manuscript to finish," I said, which made her laugh because it was true. There were to-read stacks in both the agency office and her home office, and both of them were always piled high. "Before we go, tell the professor what happened in our building yesterday."

She turned to Professor Burkett. "That was so strange, Marty. Every circuit breaker in the building blew out. All at once! Mr. Provenza—he's the super—said there must have been some kind of power surge. He said he'd never seen anything like it."

The professor looked startled. "Only your building?"

"Just ours," she agreed. "Come on, Jamie. Let's get out of here and let Marty rest."

Going out was an almost exact replay of going in. Professor Burkett gave me a keen look and I gave him a slight nod.

We understood each other.

46

That night I got an email from him, sent from his iPad. He was the only person of my acquaintance who ever used a salutation when he sent one, and wrote actual letters instead of stuff like *How r u* and *ROFL* and *IMHO*.

Dear Jamie,

After you and your mother left this morning, I did some research concerning the discovery of the bomb at the Eastport supermarket, a thing I should have done earlier. What I found was interesting. Elizabeth Dutton did not figure prominently in any of the news stories. The Bomb Squad got most of the credit (especially the dogs, because people love dogs; I believe the mayor may have actually given a dog a medal). She was mentioned only as "a detective who received a tip from an old source." I found it peculiar that she did not take part in the press conference following the successful defusing of the bomb, and that she did not receive an official commendation. She has, however, managed to keep her job. That may have been all the reward she wanted and all her superiors felt she deserved.

Given my research on this matter, plus the strange power outage in your building at the time of your confrontation with Therriault, plus other matters of which you have made me aware, I find myself unable to disbelieve the things you've told me.

I must add a word of caution. I did not care for the look of confidence on your face when you said it was your turn to haunt it, or that you could whistle for it and it would come. Perhaps it would, BUT I URGE YOU NOT TO DO IT. Tightrope walkers sometimes fall. Lion tamers can be mauled by cats they believed to be completely tamed. Under certain conditions, even the best dog may turn and bite his master.

My advice to you, Jamie, is to leave this thing alone.

With every good wish from your friend,
Prof. Martin Burkett (Marty)

PS: I am very curious to know the exact details of your

extraordinary experience. If you can come and see me, I would listen with great interest. I am assuming you still do not want to burden your mother with the story, since it seems that matters have come to a successful conclusion.

I wrote back right away. My response was much shorter, but I made sure to compose it as he had, like a snail-mail letter.

Dear Professor Burkett,

I'd be glad to do that, but I can't until Wednesday because of a trip to the Metropolitan Museum of Art on Monday and intramural volleyball, boys against the girls, on Tuesday. If Wednesday is okay, I will come after school, like around 3:30, but I can only stay for an hour or so. I'll tell my mother I just wanted to visit you, which is true.

Yours in friendship,
James Conklin

Professor Burkett must have had his iPad in his lap (I could picture him sitting in his living room, with all its framed pictures of old times), because he replied at once.

Dear Jamie,

Wednesday will be fine. I will look for you at three-thirty and will supply raisin cookies. Would you prefer tea or a soft drink to go with them?

Yours,
Marty Burkett

I didn't bother making my reply look like a snail-mail letter, just typed *I wouldn't mind a cup of coffee*. After thinking about that, I added *It's OK with my mom*. Which wasn't a total lie, and he actually sent me an emoji in return: a thumbs-up. I thought that was pretty hip.

I did speak with Professor Burkett again, but there were no drinks or snacks. He no longer used those things, because he was dead.

47

On Tuesday morning, I got another email from him. My mother got the same one, and so did several other people.

Dear friends and associates,

I have received some bad news. David Robertson—old friend, colleague, and former department head—suffered a stroke at his retirement home on Siesta Key in Florida last evening and is now in Sarasota Memorial Hospital. He is not expected to live, or even to regain consciousness, but I have known Dave and his lovely wife Marie for over forty years and must make the trip, little as I want to, if only to offer comfort to his wife and attend the funeral, should it come to that. I will reschedule such appointments as I have upon my return.

I will be in residence at Bentley's Boutique Hotel (such a name!) in Osprey for the length of my stay, and you can reach me there, but the best way to get in touch with me is still email. As most of you know, I do not carry a personal phone. I apologize for any inconvenience.

Sincerely yours,
Prof. Martin F. Burkett (Emeritus)

"He's old school," I said to Mom as we ate our breakfast: grapefruit and yogurt for her, Cheerios for me.

She nodded. "He is, and there aren't many of his kind left. To rush to the bedside of a dying friend at his age…" She shook her head. "Remarkable. Admirable. And that email!"

"Professor Burkett doesn't write emails," I said. "He writes letters."

"True, but not what I was thinking of. Really, how many appointments and scheduled visitors do you think he has at his age?"

Well, there was one, I thought, but didn't say.

48

I don't know if the professor's old friend died or not. I only know that the professor did. He had a heart attack on the flight and was dead in his seat when the plane landed. He had another old friend who was his lawyer—he was one of the recipients of the professor's final email—and he was the one who got the call. He took charge of getting the body shipped back, but it was my mom who stepped up after that. She closed the office and made the funeral arrangements. I was proud of her for that. She cried and was sad because she had lost a friend. I was just as sad because I'd made her friend my own. With Liz gone, he'd been my only grown-up friend.

The funeral was at the Presbyterian church on Park Avenue, same as Mona Burkett's had been seven years before. My mother was outraged that the daughter—the one on the west coast—didn't attend. Later, just out of curiosity, I called up that last email from Professor Burkett and saw she hadn't been one of the recipients. The only three women who'd gotten it were my mother, Mrs. Richards (an old lady he was friendly with on the fourth floor of the Palace on Park), and Dolores Magowan, the woman Mrs. Burkett had mistakenly predicted her widower husband would soon be asking out to lunch.

I looked for the professor at the church service, thinking that if his wife had attended hers, he might attend his. He wasn't there, but this time we went to the cemetery service as well and I saw him sitting on a gravestone twenty or thirty feet away from the mourners but close enough to hear what was being said. During the prayer, I raised my hand and gave him a discreet wave. Not much more than a twiddle of the fingers, but he saw it, and smiled, and waved back. He was a regular dead person, not a monster like Kenneth Therriault, and I started to cry.

My mother put her arm around me.

49

That was on a Monday, so I never did get to the Metropolitan Museum of Art with my class. I got the day off school to go to the funeral, and when we got back, I told my mother I wanted to go for a walk. That I needed to think.

"That's fine…if you're okay. *Are* you okay, Jamie?"

"Yes," I said, and gave her a smile to prove it.

"Be back by five or I'll worry."

"I will be."

I got as far as the door before she asked me the question I'd been waiting for. "Was he there?"

I had thought about lying, like maybe that would spare her feelings, but maybe it would make her feel better, instead. "Yes. Not at the church but at the cemetery."

"How…how did he look?"

I told her he looked okay, and that was the truth. They're always wearing the clothes they had on when they died, which in Professor Burkett's case was a brown suit that was a little too big for him but still looked quite cool, in my humble opinion. I liked that he'd put on a suit for the plane ride, because it was another part of being old school. And he didn't have his cane, possibly because he wasn't holding it when he died or because he dropped it when the heart attack struck.

"Jamie? Could your old mom have a hug before you go out on your walk?"

I hugged her a long time.

50

I walked to the Palace on Park, much older and taller than the little boy who'd come from his school one fall day holding his mother's hand on one side and his green turkey on the other. Older, taller, and maybe even wiser, but still that same person. We change, and we don't. I can't explain it. It's a mystery.

I couldn't go inside the building, I had no key, but I didn't need to, because Professor Burkett was sitting on the steps in his brown traveling suit. I sat down beside him. An old lady walked by with a little fluffy dog. The dog looked at the professor. The old lady didn't.

"Hello, Professor."

"Hello, Jamie."

It had been five days since he died on the airplane, and his voice was doing that fade-out thing they do. As if he was talking to me from far away and getting farther all the time. And while he seemed as kind as ever, he also seemed sort of, I don't know, disconnected. Most of them do. Even Mrs. Burkett was that way, although she was chattier than most (and some don't talk at all, unless you ask them a question). Because they are watching the parade instead of marching in it? That's close, but still not quite right. It's as if they've got other, more important things on their minds, and for the first time I realized that my voice must be fading for him, as well. The whole world must be fading.

"Are you okay?"

"Yes."

"Did it hurt? The heart attack?"

"Yes, but it was over soon." He was looking out at the street, not at me. As if storing it up.

"Is there anything you need me to do?"

"Only one thing. Never call for Therriault. Because Therriault is gone. What would come is the thing that possessed him. I believe that in the literature, that sort of entity is called a walk-in."

"I won't, I promise. Professor, why could it even possess him in the first place? Because Therriault was evil to start with? Is that why?"

"I don't know, but it seems likely."

"Do you still want to hear what happened when I grabbed him?" I thought of his email. "The details?"

"No." This disappointed me but didn't surprise me. Dead people lose interest in the lives of the living. "Just remember what I've told you."

"I will, don't worry."

A faint shadow of irritation came into his voice. "I wonder. You were incredibly brave, but you were also incredibly lucky. You don't understand because you're just a child, but take my word for it. That thing is from outside the universe. There are horrors there that no man can conceive of. If you truck with it you risk death, or madness, or the destruction of your very soul."

I had never heard anyone talk about *trucking* with something—I suppose it was another of the professor's old-school words, like icebox for refrigerator, but I got the gist. And if he meant to scare me, he had succeeded. The destruction of my *soul*? Jesus!

"I won't," I said. "I really won't."

He didn't reply. Just looked out at the street with his hands on his knees.

"I'll miss you, professor."

"All right." His voice was growing fainter all the time. Pretty soon I wouldn't be able to hear him at all, I'd only be able to see his lips moving.

"Can I ask you one more thing?" Stupid question. When you ask, they have to answer, although you might not always like what you hear.

"Yes."

I asked my question.

51

When I got home, my mother was making salmon the way we like it, wrapped in wet paper towels and steamed in the microwave. You wouldn't think anything so easy could taste good, but it does.

"Right on time," she said. "There's a bag-salad Caesar. Will you put it together for me?"

"Okay." I got it out of the fridge—the icebox—and opened the bag.

"Don't forget to wash it. The bag says it's already been washed, but I never trust that. Use the colander."

I got the colander, dumped in the lettuce, and used the sprayer. "I went to our old building," I said. I wasn't looking at her, I was concentrating on my job.

"I kind of thought you might. Was he there?"

"Yes. I asked him why his daughter never came to visit him and didn't even come to the funeral." I turned off the water. "She's in a mental institution, Mom. He says she'll be there for the rest of her life. She killed her baby, and then tried to kill herself."

My mother was getting ready to put the salmon in the microwave, but she set it on the counter instead and plopped down on one of the stools. "Oh my God. Mona told me she was an assistant in a biology lab at Caltech. She seemed so *proud*."

"Professor Burkett said she's cata-whatsit."

"Catatonic."

"Yeah. That."

My mother was looking down at our dinner-to-be, the salmon's pink flesh kind of glimmering through its shroud of paper towels. She seemed to be thinking very deeply. Then the vertical line between her eyebrows smoothed out.

"So now we know something we probably shouldn't. It's done and can't be undone. Everybody has secrets, Jamie. You'll find that out for yourself in time."

Thanks to Liz and Kenneth Therriault, I had found that out already, and I found out my mother's secret, too.

Later.

52

Kenneth Therriault disappeared from the news, replaced by other monsters. And because he had stopped haunting me, he also disappeared from the forefront of my mind. As that fall chilled into winter, I still had a tendency to step back from the elevator doors when they opened, but by the time I turned fourteen, that little tic had disappeared.

I saw other dead people from time to time (and there were probably some I missed, since they looked like normal people unless they died of injuries or you got right up close). I'll tell you about one, although it has nothing to do with my main story. He was a little boy no older than I had been on the day I saw Mrs. Burkett. He was standing on the divider that runs down the middle of Park Avenue, dressed in red shorts and a Star Wars tee-shirt. He was paper pale. His lips were blue.

And I think he was trying to cry, although there were no tears. Because he looked vaguely familiar, I crossed the downtown side of Park and asked him what was wrong. You know, besides being dead.

"I can't find my way home!"

"Do you know your address?"

"I live at 490 Second Avenue Apartment 16B." He ran it off like a recording.

"Okay," I said, "that's pretty close. Come on, kid. I'll take you there."

It was a building called Kips Bay Court. When we got there, he just sat down on the curb. He wasn't crying anymore, and he was starting to get that drifting-away look they all get. I didn't like to leave him there, but I didn't know what else to do. Before I left, I asked him his name and he said it was Richard Scarlatti. Then I knew where I'd seen him. His picture was on NY1. Some big boys drowned him in Swan Lake, which is in Central Park. Those boys all cried like blue fuck and said they had only been goofing around. Maybe that was true. Maybe I'll understand all that stuff later, but actually I don't think so.

53

By then we were doing well enough that I could have gone to a private school. My mother showed me brochures from the Dalton School and the Friends Seminary, but I chose to stay public and go to Roosevelt, home of the Mustangs. It was okay. Those were good years for Mom and me. She landed a super-big client who wrote stories about trolls and woods elves and noble guys who went on quests. I landed a girlfriend, sort of. Mary Lou Stein was kind of a goth intellectual in spite of her girl-next-door name and a huge cinephile. We went to the Angelika just about once every week and sat in the back row reading subtitles.

One day shortly after my birthday (I'd reached the grand old age of fifteen), Mom texted me and asked if I could drop by the agency office after school instead of going straight home—not a huge deal, she said, just some news she wanted to pass on in person.

When I got there she poured me a cup of coffee—unusual but not unheard-of by then—and asked if I remembered Jesus Hernandez. I told her I did. He had been Liz's partner for a couple of years, and a couple of times Mom brought me along when she and Liz had meals with Detective Hernandez and his wife. That was quite awhile ago, but it's hard to forget a six-foot-six detective named Jesus, even if it is pronounced *Hay-soos*.

"I loved his dreads," I said. "They were cool."

"He called to tell me Liz lost her job." Mom and Liz had been quits a long time by then, but Mom still looked sad. "She finally got caught transporting drugs. Quite a lot of heroin, Jesus says."

It hit me hard. Liz hadn't been good for my mother after awhile, and she sure as shit hadn't been good for me, but it was still a bummer. I remembered her tickling me until I almost wet my pants, and sitting between her and Mom on the couch, all of us making stupid cracks about the shows, and the time she took me to the Bronx Zoo and bought me a cone of cotton candy bigger than my head. Also, don't forget that she saved fifty or maybe even a hundred lives that would have been lost if Thumper's last bomb had gone off. Her motivation might have been good or bad, but those lives were saved either way.

That overheard phrase from their last argument came to me. *Serious weight*, Mom had said. "She isn't going to jail, is she?"

Mom said, "Well, she's out on bail now, Jesus said, but in the end...I think there's a good chance she will, honey."

"Oh, fuck." I thought of Liz in an orange jumpsuit, like the women in that Netflix show my mother sometimes watched.

She took my hand. "Right right right."

54

It was two or three weeks later when Liz kidnapped me. You could say she did that the first time, with Therriault, but you could call that a "soft snatch." This time it was the real deal. She didn't force me into her car kicking and screaming, but she still forced me. Which makes it kidnapping as far as I'm concerned.

I was on the tennis team, and on my way home from a bunch of practice matches (which our coach called "heats," for some dumb reason). I had my pack on my back and my tennis duffle in one hand. I was headed for the bus stop and saw a woman leaning against a beat-up Toyota and looking at her phone. I walked past without a second glance. It never occurred to me that this scrawny chick—straw-blonde hair blowing around the collar of an unzipped duffle coat, over-sized gray sweatshirt, beat-up cowboy boots disappearing into baggy jeans—was my mom's old friend. My mom's old friend had favored tapered slacks in dark colors and low-cut silk blouses. My mom's old friend wore her hair slicked back and pulled into a short stump of ponytail. My mom's old friend had looked healthy.

"Hey, Champ, not even a howya doin for an old friend?"

I stopped and turned back. For a moment I still didn't recognize her. Her face was bony and pale. There were blemishes, untouched by makeup, dotting her forehead. All the curves I'd admired—in a little-boy way, granted—were gone. The baggy sweatshirt beneath the coat showed only a hint of what had been generous breasts. At a guess, I'd say she was forty or even fifty pounds lighter and looked twenty years older.

"Liz?"

"None other." She gave me a smile, then obscured it by wiping her nose with the heel of her hand. *Strung out*, I thought. *She's strung out*.

"How are you?"

Maybe not the wisest question, but the only one I could think of under the circumstances. And I was careful to keep what I considered to be a safe distance from her, so I could outrun her if she tried anything weird. Which seemed like a possibility, because she *looked* weird. Not like actors pretending to be drug addicts on TV but like the real ones you saw from time to time, nodding out on park benches or in the doorways of abandoned buildings. I guess New York is a lot better than it used to be, but dopers are still an occasional part of the scenery.

"How do I look?" Then she laughed, but not in a happy way. "Don't answer that. But hey, we did a mitzvah once upon a time, didn't we? I deserved more credit for that than I got, but what the hell, we saved a bunch of lives."

I thought of all I'd been through because of her. And it wasn't just because of Therriault, either. She had fucked up my mom's life, too. Liz Dutton had put us both through a bad time, and here she was again. A bad penny, turning up when you least expected it. I got mad.

"You didn't deserve *any* of the credit. I was the one who made him talk. And I paid a price for it. You don't want to know."

She cocked her head. "Sure I do. Tell me about the price you paid, Champ. A few bad dreams about the hole in his head? You want bad dreams, take a look at three crispy critters in a burned-out SUV sometime, one of them just a kid in a car seat. So what price did you pay?"

"Forget it," I said, and started walking again.

She reached out and grabbed the strap of my tennis duffle. "Not so fast. I need you again, Champ, so saddle up."

"No way. And let go of my bag."

She didn't, so I pulled. There was nothing to her and she went to her knees, letting out a small cry and losing her grip on the strap.

A man who was passing stopped and gave me the look adults give a kid when they see him doing something mean. "You don't do that to a woman, kid."

"Fuck off," Liz told him, getting to her feet. "I'm police."

"Whatever, whatever," the man said, and got walking again. He didn't look back.

"You're not police anymore," I said, "and I'm not going anywhere with you. I don't even want to talk to you, so leave me alone." Still, I felt a little bad about pulling her so hard she went to her knees. I remembered her on her knees in our apartment, too, but because she was playing Matchbox cars with me. I tried to tell myself that was in another life, but it didn't work because it wasn't another life. It was my life.

"Oh, but you *are* coming. If you don't want the whole world to know who really wrote Regis Thomas's last book, that is. The big bestseller that pulled Tee away from bankruptcy just in time? The *posthumous* bestseller?"

"You wouldn't do that." Then, as the shock of what she'd said cleared away a little: "You *can't* do that. It would be your word against Mom's. The word of a drug trafficker. Plus a junkie, from the look of you, so who'd believe you? No one!"

She had put her phone in her back pocket. Now she took it out. "Tia wasn't the only one recording that day. Listen to this."

What I heard made my stomach drop. It was my voice—much younger, but mine—telling Mom that Purity would find the key she'd been looking for under a rotted stump on the path to Roanoke Lake.

Mom: "How does she know which stump?"

Pause.

Me: "Martin Betancourt chalked a cross on it."

Mom: "What does she do with it?"

Pause.

Me: "Takes it to Hannah Royden. They go into the swamp together and find the cave."

Mom: "Hannah makes the Seeking Fire? The stuff that almost got her hung as a witch?"

Pause.

Me: "That's right. And he says George Threadgill sneaks after them. And he says that looking at Hannah makes George tumescent. What's that, Mom?"

Mom: "Never mi—"

Liz stopped the recording there. "I got a lot more. Not all of it, but an hour, at least. No doubt about it, Champ—that's you telling your mother the plot of the book *she* wrote. And *you* would be a bigger part of the story. James Conklin, Boy Medium."

I stared at her, my shoulders sagging. "Why didn't you play that for me before? When we went looking for Therriault?"

She looked at me as if I was stupid. Probably because I was. "I didn't need to. Back then you were basically a sweet kid who wanted to do the right thing. Now you're fifteen, old enough to be a pain in the ass. Which could be your right as a teenager, I guess, but that's a discussion for another day. Right now the question is this: do you get in the car and take a ride with me, or do I go to this reporter I know on the *Post* and give him a juicy scoop about the literary agent who faked her dead client's last book with the help of her ESP son?"

"Take a ride where?"

"It's a mystery tour, Champ. Get in and find out."

I didn't see any choice. "Okay, but one thing. Stop calling me Champ, like I was your pet horse."

"Okay, Champ." She smiled. "Joking, just joking. Get in, Jamie."

I got in.

55

"Which dead person am I supposed to talk to this time? Whoever it is and whatever they know, I don't think it will keep you from going to jail."

"Oh, I'm not going to jail," she said. "I don't think I'd like the food, let alone the company."

We passed a sign pointing to the Cuomo Bridge, which everybody in New York still calls the Tappan Zee, or just the Tap. I didn't like that. "Where are we going?"

"Renfield."

The only Renfield I knew was the Count's fly-eating helper in *Dracula*. "Where's that? Someplace in Tarrytown?"

"Nope. Little town just north of New Paltz. It'll take us two or three hours, so settle back and enjoy the ride."

I stared at her, more than alarmed, almost horrified. "You've got to be kidding! I'm supposed to be home for *supper*!"

"Looks like Tia's going to be eating in solitary splendor tonight." She took a small bottle of whitish-yellow powder from the pocket of her duffle coat, the kind that has a little gold spoon attached to the cap. She unscrewed it one-handed, tapped some of the powder onto the back of the hand she was using to drive, and snorted it up. She screwed the cap back on—still one-handed—and repocketed the vial. The quick dexterity of the process spoke of long practice.

She saw my expression and smiled. Her eyes had a new brightness. "Never seen anyone do that before? What a sheltered life you've led, Jamie."

I had seen kids smoke the herb, had even tried it myself, but the harder stuff? No. I'd been offered ecstasy at a school dance and turned it down.

She ran the palm of her hand up over her nose again, not a charming gesture. "I'd offer you some, I believe in sharing, but this is my own special blend: coke and heroin two-to-one, with just a dash of fentanyl. I've built up a tolerance. It would blow your head off."

Maybe she did have a tolerance, but I could tell when it hit her. She sat up straighter and talked faster, but at least she was still driving straight and keeping to the speed limit.

"This is your mother's fault, you know. For years, all I did was carry dope from Point A, which was usually the 79th Street Boat Basin or Stuart Airport, to Point B, which could be anywhere in the five boroughs. At first it was mostly cocaine, but times changed because of OxyContin. That shit hooks people fast, I mean *kabang*. When their doctors stopped supplying it, the dopers bought it on the street. Then the price went up and they realized they could get about the same high from the big white nurse, and cheaper. So they went to that. It's what the man we're going to see supplied."

"The man who's dead."

She frowned. "Don't interrupt me, kiddo. You wanted to know, I'm telling you."

The only thing I could remember wanting to know was where we were going, but I didn't say that. I was trying not to be scared. It was working a little because this was still Liz, but not very much because this didn't seem like the Liz I'd known at all.

"Don't get high on your own supply, that's what they say, that's the mantra, but after Tia kicked me out, I started chipping a little. Just to keep from being too depressed. Then I started chipping a lot. After awhile you couldn't really call it chipping at all. I was using."

"My mom kicked you out because you brought junk into the house," I said. "It was your own fault." Probably would have been smarter to keep quiet, but I couldn't help it. Her trying to blame Mom for what she'd become made me mad all over again. In any case, she paid no attention.

"I'll tell you one thing, though, Cha—Jamie. I have never used the spike." She said this with a kind of defiant pride. "Never once. Because when you snort, you've got a shot at getting clean. Shoot that stuff, and you're never coming back."

"Your nose is bleeding." Just a trickle down that little gutter between her nose and upper lip.

"Yeah? Thanks." She wiped with the heel of her palm again, then turned to me for a second. "Did I get it all?"

"Uh-huh. Now look at the road."

"Yessir, Mr. Backseat Driver, sir," she said, and for just a moment she sounded like the old Liz. It didn't break my heart, but it squeezed it a little.

We drove. The traffic wasn't too bad for a weekday afternoon. I thought about my mother. She'd still be at the agency now, but she'd be home soon. At first she wouldn't worry. Then she would worry a little. Then she'd worry a lot.

"Can I call Mom? I won't tell her where I am, just that I'm okay."

"Sure. Go ahead."

I took my phone out of my pocket and then it was gone. She grabbed it with the speed of a lizard snaring a bug. Before I had even quite realized what was happening, she had opened her window and dropped it onto the highway.

"Why did you do that?" I shouted. "That was mine!"

"I'm glad you reminded me about your phone." Now we were following signs to I-87, the Thruway. "I totally forgot. They don't call it dope for nothing, you know." And she laughed.

I punched her on the shoulder. The car swerved, then straightened. Someone gave us a honk. Liz whipped another glance at me, and she wasn't smiling now. She had the look she probably got on her face when she was reading people their rights. You know, perps. "Hit me again, Jamie, and I'll hit you back in the balls hard enough to make you puke. God knows it wouldn't be the first time someone puked in this fucking beater."

"You want to try fighting me while you're driving?"

Now the smile came back, her lips parting just enough to show the tops of her teeth. "Try me."

I didn't. I didn't try anything, including (if you're wondering) yelling for the creature inhabiting Therriault, although it was now theoretically at my command—whistle and you'll come to me, my lad, remember that? The truth is, he—or *it*—never crossed my mind. I forgot, just like Liz forgot to take my phone at first, and I didn't even have a snoutful of dope to blame. I might not have done it, anyway. Who knew if it would actually come? And if it did…well, I was scared of Liz, but more scared of the deadlight thing. *Death, madness, the destruction of your very soul*, the professor had said.

"Think about it, kiddo. If you called and said you were fine but taking a little ride with your old friend Lizzy Dutton, do you think she'd just say 'Okay, Jamie, that's fine, make her buy you dinner?' "

I said nothing.

"She'd call the cops. But that isn't the biggest thing. I should have gotten rid of your cell right away, because she can track it."

My eyes widened. "Bull*shit* she can!"

Liz nodded, smiling again, eyes on the road again as we pulled past a double-box semi. "She put a locater app on the first phone she gave you, when you were ten. I was the one who told her how to hide it, so you wouldn't find it and get all pissy about it."

"I got a new phone two years ago," I muttered. There were tears prickling the corners of my eyes, I don't know why. I felt…I don't know the word. Wait a minute, maybe I do. *Whipsawed*. That's how I felt, whipsawed.

"You think she didn't put that app on the new one?" Liz gave a harsh laugh. "Are you kidding? You're her one and only, kiddo, her little princeling. She'll still be tracking you ten years from now, when you're married and changing your first kid's diapers."

"Fucking liar," I said, but I was talking to my own lap.

She snorted some more of her special blend once we were clear of the city, the movements just as agile and practiced, but this time the car *did* swerve a little, and we got another disapproving honk. I thought of some cop lighting us up, and at first I thought that would be good, that it would end this nightmare, but maybe it wouldn't be good. In her current wired-up state, Liz might try to outrun a cop, and manage to kill us both. I thought of the Central Park man. His face and upper body had been covered with somebody's jacket so the bystanders couldn't see the worst of it, but I had seen.

Liz brightened up again. "You'd make a hell of a detective, Jamie. With your particular skill, you'd be a star. No murderer would escape you, because you could talk to the vics."

This idea had actually occurred to me once or twice. James Conklin, Detective of the Dead. Or maybe *to* the Dead. I'd never figured out which sounded better.

"Not the NYPD, though," she continued. "Fuck those assholes. Go private. I could see your name on the door." She briefly raised both hands from the wheel, as if framing it.

Another honk.

"Drive the fucking car," I said, trying not to sound alarmed. It probably didn't work, because I *was* alarmed.

"Don't worry about me, Champ. I've forgotten more about driving than you'll ever learn."

"Your nose is bleeding again," I said.

She wiped it with the heel of her palm, then wiped it on her sweatshirt. Not for the first time, by the look of it. "Septum's gone," she said. "I'm going to fix it. Once I'm clean."

After that we were quiet for awhile.

56

After we got on the Thruway, Liz helped herself to another bump of her special blend. I'd say she was starting to scare me, but we were well past that point.

"Do you want to know how we got here? Me and you, Holmes and Watson off on another adventure?"

Adventure wasn't the word I would have picked, but I didn't say so.

"I can see by your face that you don't. That's okay. Long story, not very interesting, but I'll tell you this much—no kid ever said they wanted to grow up to be a bum, a college dean, or a dirty cop. Or to pick up garbage in Westchester county, which is what my brother-in-law does these days."

She laughed, although I didn't know then what was funny about being a garbageman.

"Here's something that *might* interest you. I've moved a lot of dope from Point A to Point B and got paid for it, but the blow your mother found in my coat pocket that time was a freebie for a friend. Ironic, when you think about it. By then IAD already had their eye on me. They weren't sure, but they were getting there. I was scared to death that Tee would spill the beans. That would have been the time to get out, but by then I couldn't." She paused, considering this. "Or wouldn't. Looking back it's hard to tell which. But it makes me think of something Chet Atkins said once. You ever heard of Chet Atkins?"

I shook my head.

"How soon the great are forgotten. Google him when you get back. Excellent guitarist, up there with Clapton and Knopfler. He was talking about how shitty he was at tuning his instrument. 'By the time I realized I was no good at this part of the job, I was too rich to quit.' Same with me and my career as a transporter. Tell you one other thing, since we're just passing the time on the good old New York Thruway. You think your mother was the only one who got hurt when the economy went tits-up in '08? Not true. I had a stock portfolio—teeny-weenie, but it was mine—and that went poof."

She passed another double box, being careful to use her blinker before swinging out and then tucking back in. Considering how much dope she'd ingested, I was amazed. Also grateful. I didn't want to be with her, but even more than that I didn't want to die with her.

"But the main thing was my sister Bess. She married this guy who worked for one of the big investment companies. Probably haven't heard of Bear Stearns any more than you've heard of Chet Atkins, right?"

I didn't know whether to nod my head or shake it, so I just sat there.

"Danny—my brother-in-law, now majoring in waste management—was just entry-level at Bear when Bess married him, but he had a clear path forward. Future was so bright he had to wear shades, if I may borrow from an old song. They bought a house in Tuckahoe Village. Hefty mortgage, but everyone assured them—me included, damn my eyes—that property values out that way had nowhere to go but up. Like the stock market. They got an au pair for their kid.

They got a junior membership in the country club. Were they overextended? Fuck, yes. Was Bessie able to look down on my paltry seventy grand a year? Ten-four. But you know what my father used to say?"

How would I? I thought.

"He used to say that if you try to outrun your own shadow, you're bound to fall on your face. Danny and Bess were talking about putting in a swimming pool when the bottom fell out. Bear Stearns specialized in mortgage securities, and all at once the paper they were holding was just paper."

She brooded on this as we passed a sign that said NEW PALTZ 59 POUGHKEEPSIE 70 and RENFIELD 78. We were a little over an hour away from our final destination, and just thinking that gave me the creeps, *Final Destination* being a particularly gory horror movie me and my friends had watched. Not up there with the *Saw* flicks, but still pretty fucking grim.

"Bear Stearns? What a joke. One week their shares were selling for over a hundred and seventy dollars a pop, the next they were going for ten bucks. JP Morgan Chase picked up the pieces. Other companies took the same long walk off the same short dock. The guys at the top made it through okay, they always do. The little guys and gals, not so much. Go on YouTube, Jamie, and you can find clips of people coming out of their fancy midtown office buildings with their whole careers in cardboard boxes. Danny Miller was one of those guys. Six months after joining the Green Hills Country club, he was riding on a Greenwise garbage truck. And he was one of the lucky ones. As for their house, underwater. Know what that means?"

It so happened that I did. "They owed more on it than it was worth."

"A-plus work, Cham…Jamie. Go to the head of the class. But it was the only asset they had, not to mention a place where Bess, Danny, and my niece Francine could lay down their heads at night without getting rained on. Bess said she had friends who were sleeping in their camper. Who do you think kicked in enough so they could keep up with the payments on that four-bedroom white elephant?"

"I'm guessing you did."

"Right. Bess stopped looking down on my seventy grand a year, I can tell you that. But was I able to do it on just my salary, plus all the overtime I could glom? No way. Because I got part-time work as security in a couple of clubs? *More* no way. But I met people there, made connections, got offers. Certain lines of work are recession-proof. Funeral parlors always make out. Repo companies and bail bondsmen. Liquor stores. And the dope biz. Because, good times or bad, people are going to want to get high. And okay, I like nice things. Won't apologize for it. I find nice things a comfort, and felt like I deserved them. I was keeping a roof over my sister's family's head, after all the years Bess high-hatted me because she was prettier, smarter, went to a real college instead of a community deal. And, of course, she was *hetero*." Liz almost snarled this last.

"What happened?" I asked. "How did you lose your job?"

"IAD blindsided me with a piss test I wasn't ready for. Not that they didn't know all along, they just couldn't get rid of me right away after I pitched in with Therriault. Wouldn't have looked good. So they waited, which I suppose was smart, and then when they had me in a box—at least they thought they did—they tried to turn me. Get me to wear a wire and all that good *Serpico* shit. But here's another saying, one I didn't learn from my father: snitches wind up in ditches. And they didn't know I had an ace up my sleeve."

"What ace?" You can think I was stupid if you want, but that was actually an honest question.

"You, Jamie. You're my ace. And ever since Therriault, I knew the time would come when I'd have to play it."

57

We drove through downtown Renfield, which must have had a big population of college kids, judging from all the bars, bookstores, and fast food restaurants on its single main street. On the other side, the road turned west and began to rise into the Catskills. After three miles or so, we came to a picnic area overlooking the Wallkill River. Liz turned in and killed the engine. We were the only ones there. She took out her little bottle of special blend, seemed about to unscrew the cap, then put it away. Her duffle coat pulled open and I saw more smears of dried blood on her sweatshirt. I thought about her saying her septum was gone. Thinking about how the powder she was snorting was eating into her flesh was worse than any *Final Destination* or *Saw* movie, because it was real.

"Time to tell you why I brought you here, kiddo. You need to know what to expect, and what I expect of you. I don't think we'll part friends, but maybe we can part on relatively good terms."

I doubt that was another thing I didn't say.

"If you want to know how the dope biz works, watch *The Wire*. It's set in Baltimore instead of New York, but the dope biz doesn't change much from place to place. It's a pyramid, like any other big-money organization. You've got your junior street dealers at the bottom, and most of them *are* juniors, so when they get popped they get tried as juveniles. In family court one day, back on the street corner the next. Then you've got your senior dealers, who service the clubs— where I got recruited—and the fat cats who save money by buying in bulk."

She laughed, and I didn't get why that was funny, either.

"Go up a little and you've got your suppliers, your junior executives to keep things running smoothly, your accountants, your lawyers, and then the top boys. It's all compartmentalized, or at least it's supposed to be. The people at the bottom know who's directly above them, but that's all they know. The people in the middle know everyone below them, but still only one layer above them. I was different. Outside the pyramid. Outside the, um, hierarchy."

"Because you were a transporter. Like in that Jason Statham movie."

"Pretty much. Transporters are supposed to know only two people, the ones we receive from at Point A and the ones we turn the load over to at Point B. Those at Point B are the senior distributors who start the dope flowing down the pyramid to its final destination, the users."

Final destination. There it was again.

"Only as a cop—dirty, but still a cop—I pay attention, okay? I don't ask many questions, doing that is dangerous, but I listen. Also, I have—had, anyway—access to NYPD and DEA databases. It wasn't hard to trace the pyramid all the way to the tippy-top. There are maybe a dozen people importing three major kinds of dope into the New York and New England territories, but the one I was working for lives right here in Renfield. Lived, I should say. His name is Donald Marsden, and when he filed his taxes, he listed *developer* as his former occupation and *retired* as his current one. He's retired, all right."

Lived, I should say. Retired.

It was Kenneth Therriault all over again.

"The kid gets the picture," Liz said. "Fantastic. Mind if I smoke? I shouldn't have another bump until this is over. Then I'll treat myself to a double. Really redline the old blood pressure."

She didn't wait for me to give permission, just lit up. But at least she rolled down her window to let the smoke out. Most of it, anyway.

"Donnie Marsden was known to his colleagues—his *crew*—as Donnie Bigs, for good reason. He was one fat fuck, pardon my political incorrectness. Three hundred ain't in it, dear—try four and a quarter. He was asking for it, and he got it yesterday. Cerebral hemorrhage. Blew his brains out and didn't even need a gun."

She dragged deep and shot smoke out her window. The daylight was still strong but the shadows were getting long. Soon the light would start to fade.

"A week before he stroked out, I got word through two of my old contacts—this would be Point B guys I stayed friendly with—that Donnie received a shipment from China. *Huge* shipment, they said. Not powder, pills. Knockoff OxyContin, a lot of it for Donnie Bigs's personal sale. Maybe as a kind of bonus. That'd be my guess, anyway, because there really *is* no top of the pyramid, Jamie. Even the boss has bosses."

This made me think of something Mom and Uncle Harry used to chant sometimes. They had learned it as kids, I guess, and Uncle Harry remembered it even when all of the important stuff had blown away. *Big fleas have little fleas upon their backs to bite em, and little fleas have lesser fleas, and so on ad infinitum.* I supposed I might chant that to my own kids. If I ever had the chance to have them, that was.

"Pills, Jamie! *Pills!*" She sounded enraptured, which was mondo creepy. "Easy to transport and easier to sell! *Huge* could mean two or three thousand, maybe *ten* thousand. And Rico—one of my Point B guys—says they're forties. You know what forties go for on the street? Never mind, I know you don't. Eighty a pill. And never mind sweating out a run with heroin in plastic garbage bags, I could carry these in a fucking suitcase."

Smoke slithered out between her lips and she watched it drift away toward the guardrails with their sign reading STAY BACK FROM THE EDGE.

"We're going to get those pills, Jamie. You're going to find out where he put them. My guys asked me to cut them in if I got a line on the stuff, and of course I said yes, but this is my deal. Besides, there might not be ten thousand tabs. There might only be eight thousand. Or eight hundred."

She cocked her head, then shook it. As if arguing with herself.

"There'll be a couple thousand. A couple thousand at least,

got to be. Probably more. Donnie's executive bonus for doing a good job of supplying his New York clientele. But if you start splitting that, pretty soon you're stuck with chump change, and I'm no chump. Got a little bit of a drug problem, but that doesn't make me a chump. You know what I'll do, Jamie?"

I shook my head.

"Make it out to the west coast. Disappear from this part of the world forever. New clothes, new hair color, new me. I'll find someone out there who can broker a deal for the Oxy. I may not get eighty a pill, but I'll get a lot, because Oxy is still the gold standard, and the Chinese shit is as good as the real stuff. Then I'm going to get myself a nice new identity to go with my new hair and clothes. I'll check into a rehab and get clean. Find a job, maybe the kind where I can start making up for the past. Atonement is what the Catholics call it. How does that sound to you?"

Like a pipe dream, I thought.

It must have showed on my face, because the happy smile she'd been wearing froze. "You don't think so? Fine. Just watch me."

"I don't want to watch you," I said. "I want to get the hell away from you."

She raised a hand and I cringed back in my seat, thinking she meant to give me a swat, but she only sighed and wiped her nose with it again. "How can I blame you for that? So let's make it happen. We're going to drive up to his house—last one on Renfield Road, all by its lonesome—and you're going to ask him where those pills are currently residing. My guess would be in his personal safe. If so, you'll ask him for the combination. He'll have to tell you, because dead people can't lie."

"I can't be sure of that," I said, a lie which proved I was still alive. "It's not like I've questioned hundreds of them. Mostly I don't talk to them at all. Why would I? They're dead."

"But Therriault told you where the bomb was, even though he didn't want to."

I couldn't argue with that, but there was another possibility. "What if the guy's not there? What if he's wherever his body went? Or, I don't know, maybe he's visiting his mom and dad in Florida. Maybe once they're dead they can teleport anywhere."

I thought that might shake her, but she didn't look upset at all. "Thomas was at his place, wasn't he?"

"That doesn't mean they *all* are, Liz!"

"I'm pretty sure Marsden will be." She sounded very sure of herself. She didn't understand that dead people can be unpredictable. "Let's do this. Then I'll grant you your fondest wish. You'll never have to see me again."

She said this in a sad way, like I was supposed to feel sorry for her, but I didn't. The only thing I felt about her was scared.

58

The road ran upward in a series of lazy S-turns. At first there were some houses with mailboxes beside the road, but they were farther and farther apart. The trees began to crowd in, their shadows meeting and making it seem later than it was.

"How many do you think there are?" Liz asked.

"Huh?"

"People like you. Ones who can see the dead."

"How should I know?"

"Did you ever run into another one?"

"No, but it isn't exactly the kind of thing you talk about. Like starting a conversation with 'Hey, do you see dead people?' "

"I suppose not. But you sure didn't get it from your mother." Like she was talking about the color of my eyes or my curly hair. "What about your father?"

"I don't know who he is. Or was. Or whatever." Talking about my father made me uneasy, probably because my mother refused to.

"You never asked?"

"Sure I asked. She doesn't answer." I turned in my seat to look at her. "She never said anything about it…about him…to you?"

"I asked and got what you got. Brick wall. Not like Tee at all."

More curves, tighter now. The Wallkill was far below us, glittering in the late afternoon sunshine. Or maybe it was early evening. I'd left my watch at home on my nightstand, and the dashboard clock said 8:15, which was totally fucked up. Meanwhile the quality of the road was deteriorating. Liz's car rumbled over crumbling patches and thudded into potholes.

"Maybe she was so drunk she doesn't remember. Or maybe she got raped." Neither idea had ever crossed my mind, and

I recoiled. "Don't look so shocked. I'm only guessing. And you're old enough to at least consider what your mom might have gone through."

I didn't contradict her out loud, but in my mind I did. In fact, I thought she was full of shit. Are you ever old enough to wonder if your life is the result of blackout sex in the backseat of some stranger's car, or that your mom was hauled into an alley and raped? I really don't think so. That Liz did probably said all I needed to know about what she'd become. Maybe what she was all along.

"Maybe the talent came from your dear old Daddy-O. Too bad you can't ask him."

I thought I wouldn't ask him anything if I ran across him. I thought I would just punch him in the mouth.

"On the other hand, maybe it came from nowhere. I grew up in this little New Jersey town and there was a family down the street from us, the Joneses. Husband, wife, and five kids in this little shacky trailer. The parents were dumb as stone boats and so were four of the kids. The fifth was a fucking genius. Taught himself the guitar at six, skipped two grades, went to high school at twelve. Where did *that* come from? You tell me."

"Maybe Mrs. Jones had sex with the mailman," I said. This was a line I'd heard at school. It made Liz laugh.

"You're a hot sketch, Jamie. I wish we could still be friends."

"Then maybe you should have acted like one," I said.

59

The tar ended abruptly, but the dirt beyond was actually better: hard-packed, oiled down, smooth. There was a big orange sign that said PRIVATE ROAD NO TRESPASSING.

"What if there are guys there?" I asked. "You know, like bodyguards?"

"If there were, they really would be guarding a body. But the body's gone, and the guy he had minding the gate will also be gone. There was no one else except for the gardener and the housekeeper. If you're imagining some action movie scenario with men in black suits and sunglasses and semi-autos guarding the kingpin, forget about it. The guy at the gate was the only one who was armed, and even if Teddy still happens to be there, he knows me."

"What about Mr. Marsden's wife?"

"No wife. She left five years ago." Liz snapped her fingers. "Gone with the wind. Poof."

We swung around another turn. A mountain all shaggy with fir trees loomed ahead, blotting out the western half of the sky. The sun shone through a valley notch but would soon be gone. In front of us was a gate made out of iron stakes. Closed. There was an intercom and a keypad on one side of it. On the other, inside the gate, was a little house, presumably where the gatekeeper spent his time.

Liz stopped, turned off the car, and pocketed the keys. "Sit still, Jamie. This will be over before you know it."

Her cheeks were flushed and her eyes were bright. A trickle of blood ran from one of her nostrils and she wiped it away. She got out and went to the intercom, but the car windows were closed and I couldn't tell what she was saying. Then she went to the gatehouse side and this time I *could* hear her, because she raised her voice. "Teddy? Are you in there? It's your buddy Liz. Hoping to pay my respects, but I need to know where!"

There was no answer and no one came out. Liz walked back to the other side of the gate. She took a piece of paper from her back pocket, consulted it, then punched some numbers into the keypad. The gate trundled slowly open. She came back to the car, smiling. "Looks like we've got the place to ourselves, Jamie."

She drove through. The driveway was tar, smooth as glass. There was another S-curve, and as Liz piloted through it, electric torches lit up on either side of the driveway. Later on I found out you call those kind of lights flambeaux. Or maybe that's only for torches like the mob waves when they're storming the castle in the old *Frankenstein* movies.

"Pretty," I said.

"Yeah, but look at that fucking thing, Jamie!"

On the other side of the S, Marsden's house came into view. It was like one of those Hollywood Hills mansions you see in the movies: big and jutting out over the drop. The side facing us was all glass. I imagined Marsden drinking his morning coffee and watching the sun rise. I bet he could see all the way to Poughkeepsie, maybe even beyond. On the other hand…a view of Poughkeepsie? Maybe not one to kill for.

"The house that heroin built." Liz sounded vicious. "All

the bells and whistles, plus a Mercedes and a Boxster in the garage. The stuff I lost my job for."

I thought of saying *you had a choice*, which is what my mom always said to me when I screwed up, but kept my mouth shut. She was wired like one of Thumper's bombs, and I didn't want to set her off.

There was one more curve before we came to the paved yard in front of the house. Liz drove around it and I saw a man standing in front of the double garage where Marsden's fancy cars were (they sure hadn't taken Donnie Bigs to the morgue in his Boxster). I opened my mouth to say it must be Teddy, the gatekeeper—the guy was thin, so it sure wasn't Marsden—but then I saw his mouth was gone.

"The Boxster's in there?" I asked, hoping my voice was more or less normal. I pointed at the garage and the man standing in front of it.

She took a look. "Yup, but if you were hoping for a ride, or even a look, you're going to be disappointed. We must be about our business."

She didn't see him. Only I saw him. And given the red hole where his mouth had been, he hadn't died a natural death.

Like I said, this is a horror story.

60

Liz killed the engine and got out. She saw me still sitting in the passenger seat, my feet planted amid a bunch of snack wrappers, and gave me a shake. "Come on, Jamie. Time to do your job. Then you're free."

I got out and followed her to the front door. On the way I snuck another glance at the man in front of the double garage. He must have known I was seeing him, because he raised a hand. I checked to make sure Liz wasn't looking at me and lifted my own in return.

Slate steps led to a tall wooden door with a lion's head knocker. Liz didn't bother with that, just took the piece of paper out of her pocket and punched more numbers into a keypad. The red light on it turned green and there was a thud as the door unlocked.

Had Marsden given those numbers to a lowly transporter? I didn't think so, and I didn't think whoever she'd heard about the pills from would have known them. I didn't like that she had them, and for the first time I thought of Therriault…or the thing that now lived in what remained of him. I had bested that thing in the Ritual of Chüd, and maybe it would come if I called, always supposing it had to honor the deal we'd made. But that was yet to be proven. I would only do it as a last resort in any case, because I was terrified of it.

"Go on in." Liz had put the piece of paper in her back pocket, and the hand that had been holding it went into the pocket of her duffle coat. I took one more glance at the man—Teddy, I assumed—standing by the garage. I looked at the bloody hole where his mouth had been and thought of the smears on Liz's sweatshirt. Maybe those had come from wiping her nose.

Or not.

"I said go in." Not an invitation.

I opened the door. There was no foyer or entrance hall,

just a huge main room. In the middle was a sunken area furnished with couches and chairs. I later found out that sort of thing is called a conversation pit. There was more expensive-looking furniture placed around it (maybe so folks could spectate on the conversations going on below), a bar that looked like it was on wheels, and stuff on the walls. I say *stuff* because it didn't look like art to me, just a bunch of splats and squiggles, but the splats were framed so I guess it was art to Marsden. There was a chandelier over the conversation pit that looked like it weighed at least five hundred pounds, and I wouldn't have wanted to sit under it. Beyond the conversation pit, on the far side of the room, was a swooping double staircase. The only one remotely like it I'd seen in real life, as opposed to in the movies or on TV, was at the Apple Store on Fifth Avenue.

"Quite the joint, isn't it?" Liz said. She shut the door—*THUD*—and bammed the heel of her hand on the bank of light switches beside it. More flambeaux came on, plus the chandelier. It was a beautiful thing and cast a beautiful light, but I was in no mood to enjoy it. I was becoming more and more sure that Liz had already been here, and shot Teddy before she came to get me.

She won't have to shoot me if she doesn't know I saw him, I told myself, and although this made a degree of sense, I knew I couldn't trust logic to get me through this. She was as high as a kite, practically vibrating. I thought again of Thumper's bombs.

"You didn't ask me," I said.

"Ask you what?"

"If he's here."

"Well, is he?" She didn't ask with any real concern in her voice, more like it was for form's sake. What was up with that?

"No," I said.

She didn't seem upset like she had been when we were hunting for Therriault. "Let's check the second floor. Maybe he's in the master bedroom, recalling all the happy times he spent there boinking his whores. There were many after Madeline left. Probably before, too."

"I don't want to go up there."

"Why not? The place isn't *haunted*, Jamie."

"It is if he's up there."

She considered this, then laughed. Her hand was still in the pocket of her jacket. "I suppose you have a point, but since it's him we're looking for, go on up. *Ándale, ándale.*"

I gestured to the hall leading away from the right side of the great room. "Maybe he's in the kitchen."

"Getting himself a snack? I don't think so. I think he's upstairs. Go on."

I thought about arguing some more, or point-blank refusing, but then her hand might come out of her jacket pocket and I had a pretty good idea of what would be in it. So I started up the right-hand staircase. The rail was cloudy green glass, smooth and cool. The steps were made out of green stone. There were forty-seven steps in all, I counted, and each one was probably worth the price of a Kia.

On the wall at the top of this set of stairs was a gilt-framed mirror that had to be seven feet tall. There was one just like it on the other side. I watched myself rise into the mirror with Liz behind me, looking over my shoulder.

"Your nose," I said.

"I see it." Both of her nostrils were bleeding now. She wiped her nose, then wiped her hand on her sweatshirt. "It's stress. Stress makes it happen because all the capillaries in there are fragile. Once we find Marsden and he tells us where the pills are, the stress will be relieved."

Did it bleed when you shot Teddy? I wondered. *How stressful was that, Liz?*

The hall at the top was actually a circular balcony, almost a catwalk, with a waist-high rail. Looking over it made my stomach feel funny. If you fell—or got pushed—you'd take a short ride straight down to the middle of the conversation pit, where the colorful rug wouldn't do much to cushion you from the stone floor beneath.

"Left turn, Jamie."

Which meant away from the balcony, and that was good. We went down a long hall with all the doors on the left, so whoever was in those rooms could dig the view. The only door that was open was halfway down. It was a circular library, every shelf crammed with books. My mother would have swooned with delight. There were chairs and a sofa in front of the only wall without books. That wall was a window, of course, curved glass looking out on a landscape that was now turning purple with dusk. I could see the nest of lights that must have been the town of Renfield, and I would have given almost anything to be there.

Liz didn't ask if Marsden was in the library, either. Didn't even give it a glance. We came to the end of the hall and she used the hand not in her jacket pocket to point at the last door. "I'm pretty sure he's in there. Open it."

I did, and sure enough, Donald Marsden was there, sprawled on a bed so big it looked like a triple, maybe even a quadruple, instead of a double. He was a quadruple himself, Liz had been right about that. To my child's eyes, the bulk of him was almost hallucinatory. A good suit might have disguised at least some of his flab, but he wasn't wearing a suit. He was wearing a pair of gigantic boxer shorts and nothing else. His immense girth, jumbo man-breasts, and flabby arms were crisscrossed with shallow cuts. His full moon of a face was bruised and one eye was swollen shut. There was a weird thing stuck in his mouth that I later learned (on one of those websites you don't want your mom to know about) was a ball-gag. His wrists had been handcuffed to the top bed-posts. Liz must have only brought two pairs of cuffs, because his ankles had been duct-taped to the bottom posts. She must have used a roll for each one.

"Behold the man of the house," Liz said.

His good eye blinked. You would say I should have known from the cuffs and the duct tape. I should have known because some of the cuts were still oozing. But I didn't. I was in shock and I didn't. Not until that single blink.

"He's alive!"

"I can fix that," Liz said. She took the gun out of her coat pocket and shot him in the head.

61

Blood and brains spattered the wall behind him. I screamed and ran out of the room, down the stairs, out the door, past Teddy, and down the hill. I ran all the way to Renfield. All of this in one second. Then Liz wrapped her arms around me.

"Steady, kiddo. Stead—"

I punched her in the stomach and heard her woof out a surprised breath. Then I was whirled and my arm was twisted up behind me. It hurt like blue fuck and I screamed some more. All of a sudden my feet were no longer holding me up. She'd swept them right out from under me and I went on my knees, yelling my head off with my arm twisted up so high that my wrist was touching my shoulderblade.

"Shut up!" Her voice, little more than a growl, was in my ear. This was the woman who had once played Matchbox cars with me, both of us down on our knees while my mother stirred spaghetti sauce in the kitchen, listening to oldies on Pandora. "Quit that squalling and I'll let you go!"

I did and she did. Now I was on my hands and knees, staring down at the rug, shaking all over.

"On your feet, Jamie."

I managed to do it, but I kept looking at the rug. I didn't want to look at the fat man with the top of his head gone.

"Is he here?"

I stared at the rug and said nothing. My hair was in my eyes. My shoulder throbbed.

"*Is he here?* Look around!"

I raised my head, hearing my neck creak as I did it. Instead of looking directly at Marsden—although I could still see him, he was too big to miss—I looked at the table beside his bed. There was a cluster of pill bottles on it. There was also a fat sandwich and a bottle of spring water.

"*Is he here?*" She slapped me on the back of my head.

I scoped the room. There was nobody but us and the fat man's corpse. Now I'd seen two men shot in the head.

Therriault had been bad, but at least I hadn't had to watch him die.

"No one," I said.

"Why not? Why isn't he here?" She sounded frantic. I couldn't think much then, I was too fucking terrified. It was only later, replaying that endless five minutes in Marsden's room, that I realized she was doubting the whole thing. In spite of Regis Thomas and his book, in spite of the bomb in the supermarket, she was afraid I couldn't see dead people at all, and she'd killed the only person who knew where that stash of pills was hidden.

"I don't know. I was never where someone actually died. Maybe…maybe it takes awhile. I don't know, Liz."

"Okay," she said. "We'll wait."

"Not in here, okay? Please, Liz, not where I have to look at him."

"In the hall, then. If I let go of you, are you going to be good?"

"Yes."

"Not going to try to run?"

"No."

"You better not, I'd hate to shoot you in the foot or the leg. That'd be the end of your tennis career. Back out."

I backed out and she backed out with me, so she could block me off if I tried to make a break for it. When we were in the hall, she told me to look around again. I did. Marsden wasn't there and I told her that.

"Damn." Then: "You saw the sandwich, didn't you?"

I nodded. A sandwich and a bottle of water for a man who was bound to his jumbo bed. Bound hand and foot.

"He loved his food," Liz said. "I ate with him in a restaurant once. He should have had a shovel instead of a fork and spoon. What a pig."

"Why would you leave him a sandwich he couldn't eat?"

"I wanted him to look at it, that's why. Just look. All day, while I went to get you and bring you back. And believe me, a shot in the head is just what he deserved. Do you have any idea how many people he killed with his…his happy poison?"

Who helped him? I thought, and of course didn't say.

"How long do you think he would have lived, anyway? Two years? Five? I've been in his bathroom, Jamie. He's got a double-wide toilet seat!" She made a sound somewhere between a laugh and a snort of disgust. "Okay, let's stroll down to the balcony. We'll see if he's in the great room. Slow."

I couldn't have gone fast if I'd wanted to, because my thighs were trembling and my knees felt like jelly.

"You know how I got the gate code? Marsden's UPS man. Guy has a hell of a coke habit, I could have slept with his wife if I'd wanted to, he'd've been happy to supply her if I kept supplying him. The house code I got from Teddy."

"Before you killed him."

"What else was I supposed to do?" Like I was the dumbest kid in class. "He could identify me."

So can I, I thought, and that brought me back to the thing this lad—me—could whistle for. I'd have to do it, but I still didn't want to. Because it might not work? Yeah, but not just that. Rub a magic lamp and get a genie, okay, good for you. Rub it and summon a demon—a deadlight—and God might know what would happen, but I didn't.

We reached the balcony with its low rail and high drop. I peered over.

"Is he down there?"

"No."

The gun prodded me in the small of my back. "Are you lying?"

"No!"

She gave a harsh sigh. "This isn't the way it's supposed to go."

"I don't know how it's supposed to go, Liz. For all I know, he could be outside talking with T—" I stopped.

She took hold of my shoulder and turned me around. There was blood all over her upper lip now—her stress must have been very high—but she was smiling. "You saw Teddy?"

I dropped my eyes. Which was answer enough.

"You sly dog." She actually laughed. "We'll go out and take a look if Marsden doesn't show in here, but for the time being, let's just wait a little. We can afford to. His latest whore is visiting her relatives in Jamaica or Barbados or somewhere with palm trees, and he doesn't get company during the week, does all his business by phone these days. He was just lying there when I came in, watching that *John Law* court show on TV. Christ, I wish he'd at least been wearing some pajamas, you know?"

I said nothing.

"He told me there were no pills, but I could see on his face that he was lying, so I secured him and then cut him a little. Thought that might loosen his tongue, and you know what he did? He *laughed* at me. Said yes, okay, there was Oxy, a lot of it, but he'd never tell me where it was. 'Why should I?' he said. 'You're going to kill me anyway.' That's when the penny dropped. Couldn't believe I hadn't thought of it before. *Muy stupido.*" She hit the side of her head with the hand holding the gun.

"Me," I said. "I was the penny that dropped."

"Yes indeed. So I left him a sandwich and a bottle of water to admire and I went to New York and I got you and we drove back and nobody came and here we are, *so where the fuck is he?*"

"There," I said.

"What? *Where?*"

I pointed. She turned and of course saw nothing, but I could see for both of us. Donald Marsden, also known as Donnie Bigs, was standing in the doorway of his circular library. He was wearing nothing but his boxer shorts and the top of his head was pretty much gone and his shoulders were drenched with blood, but he was staring at me with the eye Liz hadn't punched shut in her fury and frustration.

I raised a tentative hand to him. He raised one of his in return.

62

"Ask him!" She was digging into my shoulder and breathing in my face. Neither was pleasant, but her breath was worse.

"Let go of me and I will."

I walked slowly toward Marsden. Liz followed close behind. I could feel her, *looming*.

I stopped about five feet away. "Where are the pills?"

He replied without hesitation, talking as all of them did—with the exception of Therriault, that was—as if it didn't really matter. And why would it? He didn't need pills anymore, not where he was and not where he was going. Assuming he was going anywhere.

"Some are on the table beside my bed, but most are in

the medicine cabinet. Topomax, Marinox, Inderal, Pepcid, Flomax…" Plus half a dozen more. Droning them off like a shopping list.

"What did he—"

"Be quiet," I said. For the moment I was in charge, although I knew that wouldn't last long. Would I be in charge if I called the thing inhabiting Therriault? That I didn't know. "I asked the wrong question."

I turned to look at her.

"I can ask the right one, but first you have to promise you're going to let me go once you get what you came for."

"Of course I am, Jamie," she said, and I knew she was lying. I'm not sure exactly *how* I knew, there was nothing logical about it, but it wasn't pure intuition. I think it had to do with the way her eyes shifted away from mine when she used my name.

I knew then I'd have to whistle.

Donald Marsden was still standing by the door of his library. I wondered briefly if he actually read the books in there, or if they were just for show. "She doesn't want your prescription stuff, she wants the Oxy. Where is it?"

What happened next had happened just once before. When I asked Therriault where he'd planted his last bomb. Marsden's words stopped matching the movements of his mouth, as if he was struggling against the imperative to answer. "I don't want to tell you."

Exactly what Therriault had said.

"Jamie! What—"

"Be quiet, I said! Give me a chance!" Then, to him: "Where is the Oxy?"

When pressed, Therriault had looked like he was in pain, and I think—don't know but *think*—that's when the deadlight-thing came in. Marsden didn't look to be in physical pain, but something emotional was going on there even though he was dead. He put his hands over his face like a child who's done something wrong and said, "Panic room."

"What do you mean? What's a panic room?"

"It's a place to go in case of a break-in." The emotion was gone, fast as it had come. Marsden was back to his shopping-list drone. "I have enemies. She was one. I just didn't know it."

"Ask him where it is!" Liz said.

I was pretty sure I knew that, but I asked, anyway. He pointed into the library.

"It's a secret room," I said, but since that wasn't a question, he made no response. "Is it a secret room?"

"Yes."

"Show me."

He went into the library, which was now shadowy. Dead people aren't ghosts, exactly, but as he went into that dimness, he sure looked like one. Liz had to feel around for the switch that turned on the overhead and more flambeaux, suggesting to me that she'd never spent any time in there, even though she was a reader. How many times had she actually been in this house? Maybe once or twice, maybe never. Maybe she only knew it from pictures and very careful questions to people who had been there.

Marsden pointed to a shelf of books. Because Liz couldn't see him, I copied his gesture and said, "That one."

She went to it and pulled. I might have run right then,

except she pulled me along with her. She was stoned and redlining with excitement, but she still had at least some of her cop instincts. She yanked on several shelves with her free hand, but nothing happened. She cursed and turned to me.

To forestall another shaking or arm-twisting, I asked Marsden the obvious question. "Is there a catch that opens it?"

"Yes."

"What's he saying, Jamie? Goddam it, what's he saying?"

Besides being scary as fuck, she was driving me crazy with her questions. She had forgotten to wipe her nose and now fresh blood was running over her upper lip, making her look like one of Bram Stoker's vampires. Which in my opinion she sort of was.

"Give me a chance, Liz." Then to Marsden: "Where's the catch?"

"Top shelf, on the right," Marsden said.

I told Liz. She stood on her toes, fumbled some more, and then there was a click. This time when she pulled, the bookcase swung out on hidden hinges, revealing a steel door, another keypad, and another small red light above the numbers. Liz didn't have to tell me what to ask next.

"What's the code?"

Once again he raised his hands and covered his eyes, that childish gesture that says *If I can't see you, you can't see me.* It was a sad gesture, but I couldn't afford to be touched by it, and not just because he was a drug baron whose product had undoubtedly killed hundreds, maybe even thousands of people, and hooked thousands more. I had enough problems of my own.

"What...is...the...code?" Enunciating each word, as I had with Therriault. This was different, but it was also the same.

He told me. He had to.

"73612," I said.

She punched in the numbers, still holding onto my arm. I almost expected a thump and a hiss, like an airlock opening in a science fiction movie, but the only thing that happened was the red light turning green. There was no handle or doorknob, so Liz pushed on the door and it swung open. The room inside was as black as a black cat's asshole.

"Ask him where the light switches are."

I did, and Marsden said, "There aren't any." He had dropped his hands again. His voice was already starting to fade. At that moment I thought maybe he was going so fast because he'd been murdered instead of dying a natural death or having an accident. Later on I changed my mind. I think he wanted to be gone before we found out what was in there.

"Try just stepping inside," I said.

She took a tentative step into the dark, never losing her hold on me, and overhead fluorescents came on. The room was stark. On the far side was an icebox (Professor Burkett's voice came back to me), a hotplate, and a microwave. To the left and right were shelves stacked with cheap canned food, stuff like Spam and Dinty Moore Beef Stew and King Oscar sardines. There were also pouches containing more food (later I found out those were what the army calls MREs, meals ready to eat), and sixpacks of water and beer. There was a landline telefungus on one of the lower shelves. In the middle of the room was a plain wooden table. There was a desktop computer on it, a printer, a thick folder, and a zippered shaving bag.

"Where's the Oxy?"

I asked. "He says they're in the dopp kit, whatever that is."

She seized the shaving bag, unzipped it, and turned it over. A bunch of pill bottles fell out, along with two or three small packets done up in Saran Wrap. Not exactly a treasure trove. She yelled, "What the fuck is *this*?"

I barely heard her. I had flipped open the folder beside the computer, for no other reason than it was there, and I was in shock. At first it was like I didn't even know what I was seeing, but of course I did. And I knew why Marsden hadn't wanted us to come in here, and why he could feel shame even though he was dead. It had nothing to do with drugs. I wondered if the woman I was looking at had the same ball-gag in her mouth. Poetic justice if she did.

"Liz," I said. My lips felt numb, like I'd gotten a shot of Novocain at the dentist.

"Is this all?" she was shouting. "Don't you fucking *dare* tell me this is all!" She twisted open one of the prescription bottles and dumped out the contents. There were maybe two dozen pills. "This isn't even Oxy, these are fucking *Darvons*!"

She had let go of me and I could have run right then, but I never even thought of it. Even the thought of whistling for Therriault had left my mind. "Liz," I said again.

She paid no attention. She was opening the bottles, one after the other. Different kinds of pills, but not a lot of them in any of the bottles. She was staring at some of the blue ones. "Roxies, okay, but this isn't even a *dozen*! Ask him where the rest are!"

"Liz, look at this." It was my voice, but seeming to come from far away.

"I said ask him—" She swung back and stopped, looking at what I was looking at.

It was a glossy photograph topping a thin stack of other glossy photographs. There were three people in it: two men and a woman. One of the men was Marsden. He wasn't even wearing his boxers. The other man was also naked. They were doing things to the woman with the gag in her mouth. I don't want to say, only that Marsden had a little blowtorch and the other man had one of those double-pronged meat forks.

"Shit," she whispered. "Oh, *shit*." She flipped through some more. They were unspeakable. She closed the folder. "It's her."

"Who?"

"Maddie. His wife. Guess she didn't run off after all."

Marsden was still outside in the library, but looking away from us. The back of his head was a ruin, like the left side of Therriault's had been, but I barely noticed. There are worse things than bullet wounds, a little something I found out that evening.

"They tortured her to death," I said.

"Yes, and had fun while they were doing it. Look at those big smiles. You still sorry I killed him?"

"You didn't kill him because of what he did to his wife," I said. "You didn't know about that. You killed him because of the dope."

She shrugged as if it didn't matter, and to her it probably didn't. She looked out of the panic room, where he came to look at his awful pictures, and across the library to the upstairs hall. "Is he still there?"

"Yes. In the doorway."

"At first he said there weren't any pills, but I knew he was lying. Then he said there were a lot. A *lot*!"

"Maybe he was lying when he said that. He could, because he wasn't dead yet."

"But he told you they were in the panic room! He was already dead then!"

"He didn't say how many." I asked Marsden, "That's all you've got?"

"That's all," he said. His voice was starting to drift.

"You told her you had a lot!"

He shrugged his bloody shoulders. "As long as she believed I had what she wanted, I thought she'd keep me alive."

"But that tip she heard about your getting a big private shipment—"

"Just bullshit," he said. "There's a lot of bullshit in this business. People say all sorts of shit just to hear themselves talk."

Liz shook her head when I told her what he'd said, not believing it. Not *wanting* to believe it because if she did, it meant all her west coast plans fell down. It meant she'd been conned.

"He's hiding something," she insisted. "Somehow. Somewhere. Ask him again where the rest of them are."

I opened my mouth to say that if there were more he would have told me already. Then—probably because the terrible pictures had slapped a dazed part of me awake—I had an idea. Maybe I could do some conning of my own, because she was certainly ready to be conned. If it worked, I might be able to get away from her without whistling up a demon.

She grabbed my shoulders and gave me a shake. "Ask him, I said!"

So I did. "Where's the rest of the dope, Mr. Marsden?"

"I told you, that's all there is." His voice was fading, fading. "I keep a few on hand for Maria, but she's in the Bahamas. Bimini."

"Oh, okay. That's more like it." I pointed to the shelves of canned goods. "See the cans of spaghetti on the top shelf?" There was no way she could miss them, there had to be at least thirty. Donnie Bigs must have really loved his Franco-American. "He said he hid some in those—not Oxy, they're something else."

She could have dragged me with her, but I was thinking there was a good chance she'd be too eager, and I was right. She ran to the shelves of canned goods. I waited until she was standing on her tiptoes and reaching up. Then I bolted out of the panic room and across the library. I wish I'd remembered to shut the door, but I didn't. Marsden was standing there and he looked solid, but I ran right through him. There was a moment of freezing cold, and my mouth filled with an oily taste I think was pepperoni. Then I was sprinting for the stairs.

There was a clatter of falling cans from behind me. "Get back here, Jamie! Get back!"

She came after me. I could hear her. I made it to where

those stairs swooped down, and looked over my shoulder. That was a mistake. I tripped. Out of other options, I pursed my lips to whistle, but I couldn't do anything but huff air. My mouth and lips were too dry. So I screamed instead.

"*THERRIAULT!*"

I started to crawl down the stairs headfirst with my hair in my eyes, but she grabbed my ankle.

"*THERRIAULT, HELP ME! GET HER OFF ME!*"

Suddenly everything—not just the balcony, not just the stairs, but all of the space above the great room and the conversation pit—filled with white light. I was looking back at Liz when it happened, and I squinted against the glare, all but blinded. It was coming from that tall mirror, and more was pouring out of the mirror on the other side of the balcony.

Liz's grip loosened. I grabbed one of the slate stairs and yanked on it as hard as I could. Down I went on my belly, like a kid on the world's bumpiest toboggan ride. I came to a stop about a quarter of the way down. Behind me, Liz was shrieking. I looked between my arm and my side, because of my position seeing her upside down. She was standing in front of the mirror. I don't know exactly what she saw, and that's good, because I might never have slept again. The light was enough—that brilliant no-color light that came glaring out of the mirror like a solar flare.

The deadlight.

Then I saw—I *think* I saw—a hand come out of the mirror and seize Liz by the neck. It yanked her against the glass and I heard it crack. She continued to shriek.

All the lights went out.

It was still the tag-end of dusk so it wasn't pitch dark in

the house, but it was getting close. The room below me was a well of shadows. Behind me, at the top of the curving staircase, Liz was shrieking and shrieking. I used the smooth glass railing to pull myself to my feet and managed to stumble my way down to the living room without falling.

Behind me, Liz stopped shrieking and began to laugh. I turned and saw her running down the stairs, just a dark shape laughing like the Joker in a Batman cartoon. She was going way too fast, and not looking *where* she was going. She weaved from side to side, bouncing off the railings, looking back over her shoulder at the mirror where the light was now fading away, like the filament in an old-fashioned light bulb when you turn it off.

"Liz, look out!"

I yelled that even though the only thing in the world I wanted was to get away from her. The warning was pure instinct, and it did no good. She overbalanced, fell forward, hit the stairs, tumbled, hit the stairs again, did another somersault, then slid all the way to the bottom. She went on laughing the first time she hit but stopped the second time. Like she was a radio and someone had turned her off. She lay face-up at the foot of the stairs with her head cocked, her nose bent sideways, one arm all the way up behind her to her neck, and her eyes staring off into the gloom.

"Liz?"

Nothing.

"Liz, are you okay?"

What a stupid question, and why did I care? That one I can answer. I wanted her to be alive because something was behind me. I didn't hear it but I knew it was there.

I knelt next to her and held a hand to her bloody mouth. There was no breath on my palm. Her eyes did not blink. She was dead. I got up, turned, and saw exactly what I expected: Liz standing there in her unzipped duffle coat and bloodstained sweatshirt. She wasn't looking at me. She was looking over my shoulder. She raised one of her hands and pointed, reminding me even in that terrible moment of the Ghost of Christmas Yet to Come pointing at Scrooge's tombstone.

Kenneth Therriault—what remained of him, at least—was coming down the stairs.

63

He was like a burned log with fire still inside. I don't know any other way to put it. He had turned black, but his skin was cracked in dozens of places and that brilliant deadlight shone through. It was coming out of his nose, his eyes, even his ears. When he opened his mouth, it came out of there, too.

He grinned and lifted his arms. "Let's try the ritual again and see who wins this time. I think you owe me that, since I saved you from her."

He hurried down the stairs toward me, ready for the big reunion scene. Instinct told me to turn tail and run, but something deeper told me to stand pat no matter how much I wanted to flee that oncoming horror. If I did, it would grab me from behind, wrap its charred arms around me, and that would be the end. It would win, and I would become its slave, bound to come when it called. It would possess me alive as it had possessed Therriault dead, which would be worse.

"Stop," I said, and the blackened husk of Therriault stopped at the foot of the stairs. Those outstretched arms were less than a foot from me.

"Go away. I'm done with you. Forever."

"You'll never be done with me." And then it said one more word, one that made my skin pebble with goosebumps and the hair stand up on the nape of my neck. "*Champ.*"

"Wait and see," I said. Brave words, but I couldn't keep the tremble out of my voice.

Still the arms were outstretched, the blackened hands with their brilliant cracks inches from my neck. "If you really want to get rid of me for good, take hold. We'll do the ritual again, and it will be fairer, because this time I'm ready for you."

I was weirdly tempted, don't ask me why, but a part of me that was far beyond ego and deeper than instinct prevailed. You may beat the devil once—through providence, bravery, dumbass luck, or a combination of all—but not twice. I don't think anyone but saints beat the devil twice, and maybe not even them.

"Go." It was my turn to point like Scrooge's last ghost. I pointed at the door.

The thing raised Therriault's charred and sooty lip in a sneer. "You can't send me away, Jamie. Don't you realize that by now? We're bound to one another. You didn't think of the consequences. But here we are."

I repeated my one word. It was all I could squeeze out of a throat that suddenly felt like it was the width of a pin.

Therriault's body seemed poised to close the distance between us, to leap at me and close me in its awful embrace, but it didn't. Maybe it couldn't.

Liz shrank away as it passed her by. I expected it to go right through the door—as I had passed through Marsden—but whatever that thing was, it was no ghost. Its hand grasped the knob and turned it, more skin splitting and more light shining through. The door swung open.

It turned back to me. "Oh whistle and I'll come to you, my lad."

Then it left.

64

My legs were going to give out and the stairs were close, but I wasn't going to sit on them with Liz Dutton's broken body sprawled at their foot. I staggered to the conversation pit and collapsed into one of the chairs near it. I lowered my head and sobbed. Those were tears of horror and hysteria, but I think they were also—although I can't remember for sure—tears of joy. I was alive. I was in a dark house at the end of a private road with two corpses and two leftovers (Marsden was looking down at me from the balcony), but I was alive.

"Three," I said. "Three corpses and three leftovers. Don't forget Teddy."

I started laughing, but then I thought of Liz laughing pretty much the same way just before she died and made myself stop. I tried to think what I should do. I decided the first thing was to shut that fucking front door. Having those two revenants (a word I learned, you guessed it, later) staring at me wasn't pleasant, but I was used to dead people seeing me seeing them. What I really didn't like was the thought of Therriault out there somewhere, with the deadlight shining through his decaying skin. I'd told him to go, and he went… but what if he came back?

I walked past Liz and shut the door. When I came back I asked her what I should do. I didn't expect an answer, but I got one. "Call your mother."

I thought of the landline in the panic room, but I wasn't going back up those stairs and into that room. Not for a million bucks.

"Do you have your phone, Liz?"

"Yes." Sounding disinterested, like most of them do. Not all, though; Mrs. Burkett had had enough life left in her to offer criticism about the artistic merits of my turkey. And Donnie Bigs had tried to hide his stash of torture porn.

"Where is it?"

"In my jacket pocket."

I went to her body and reached into the righthand pocket of her duffle coat. I touched the butt of the gun she'd used to end Donald Marsden's life and drew my hand back as if I'd touched something hot. I tried the other one and got her phone. I turned it on.

"What's the passcode?"

"2665."

I punched it in, touched the New York City area code and the first three digits of Mom's number, then changed my mind and made a different call.

"911, what is your emergency?"

"I'm in a house with two dead people," I said. "One was murdered and the other one fell down the stairs."

"Is this a joke, son?"

"I wish it was. The woman who fell down the stairs kidnapped me and brought me here."

"What is your location?" Now the woman on the other end sounded engaged.

"It's at the end of a private road outside of Renfield, ma'am. I don't know how many miles or if there's a street number." Then I thought of what I should have said right away. "It's Donald Marsden's house. He's the man the woman murdered. She's the one who fell down the stairs. Her name is Liz Dutton. Elizabeth."

She asked me if I was okay, then told me to sit tight, officers were on the way. I sat tight and called my mother. That was a much longer conversation, and not always too clear because both of us were blubbering. I told her everything except about the deadlight thing. She would have believed me, but one of us having nightmares was enough. I just said Liz tripped chasing me and fell and broke her neck.

During our conversation, Donald Marsden came down the stairs and stood by the wall. One dead with the top of his head gone, the other dead with her head on sideways. Quite the pair they made. I told you this was a horror story, you were warned about that, but I was able to look at them without too much distress, because the worst horror was gone. Unless I wanted it back, that was. If I did, it would come.

All I had to do was whistle.

After fifteen very long minutes, I began to hear whooping sirens in the distance. After twenty-five, red and blue lights filled the windows. There were at least half a dozen cops, a regular posse. At first they were only dark shapes filling the door, blotting out any last traces of daylight, assuming there were any left. One of them asked where the goddam light switches were. Another one said "Got 'em," then swore when nothing happened.

"Who's here?" another called. "Any persons here, identify yourselves!"

I stood up and raised my hands, although I doubted if they could see anything but a dark shape moving around. "I'm here! My hands are up! The lights went out! I'm the kid who called!"

Flashlights came on, conflicting beams that strobed around and then centered on me. One of the cops came forward. A woman. She swerved around Liz, surely without knowing why she was doing it. At first her hand was on the butt of her holstered gun, but when she saw me she let go of it. Which was a relief.

She took a knee. "Are you alone in the house, son?"

I looked at Liz. I looked at Marsden, standing well away from the woman who had killed him. Even Teddy had arrived. He stood in the doorway the cops had vacated, perhaps drawn by the commotion, maybe just on a whim. The Three Undead Stooges.

"Yes," I said. "I'm the only one here."

65

The lady cop put an arm around my shoulders and led me outside. I started shivering. She probably thought it was from the night air but of course it wasn't. She slipped off her jacket and put it over my shoulders, but that wasn't good enough. I put my arms down the too-long sleeves and hugged it against me. It was heavy with cop-things in the pockets, but that was okay with me. The weight felt good.

There were three cruisers in the courtyard, two flanking Liz's little car and one behind it. As we stood there, another car pulled in, this one an SUV with RENFIELD CHIEF OF POLICE on the side. I guessed it would be a holiday for drunks and speeders downtown, because most of the town's force had to be right here.

Another cop came out the door and joined the lady cop. "What happened in there, kid?"

Before I could answer, the lady cop put a finger over my lips. I didn't mind; it actually felt sort of good. "No questions, Dwight. This boy's in shock. He needs medical attention."

A burly man in a white shirt with a badge hung around his neck—the Chief, I assumed—had gotten out of the SUV and was in time to hear this last. "You take him, Caroline. Get him looked at. Are there confirmed dead?"

"There's a body at the foot of the stairs. Looks like a woman. I can't confirm she's deceased, but from the way her head's turned—"

"Oh, she's dead, all right," I told them, then started crying.

"Go on, Caro," the Chief said. "Don't bother going all the way to County, either. Take him to MedNow. No questions until I get there. Also until we've got an adult who's responsible for him. Get his name?"

"Not yet," Officer Caroline said. "It's been crazy. There are no lights in there."

The Chief bent toward me, hands on his upper thighs, making me feel like I was five again. "What's your handle, son?"

So much for no questions, I thought. "Jamie Conklin, and it's my mother who's coming. Her name is Tia Conklin. I already called her."

"Uh-huh." He turned to Dwight. "Why are there no lights? All the houses on the way up here had power."

"Don't know, Chief."

I said, "They went out when she was running down the stairs after me. I think it's why she fell."

I could see he wanted to ask me more, but he just told Officer Caroline to get rolling. As she eased her way out of the courtyard and started down the curving driveway, I felt in my pants pockets and found Liz's phone, although I didn't remember putting it there. "Can I call my mom again and tell her we're going to the doc-in-the-box?"

"Sure."

As I made the call, I realized that if Officer Caroline found out I was using Liz's phone, I could be in trouble. She might well ask how come I knew the dead woman's passcode, and I wouldn't be able to give a good answer. In any case, she didn't ask.

Mom said she was in an Uber (which would probably cost a small fortune, so it was good the agency was back on a profitable basis) and they were making excellent time. She asked if I was really all right. I told her I really was, and that Officer Caroline was taking me to MedNow in Renfield, but just to get checked out. She told me not to answer any questions until she got there, and I said I wouldn't.

"I'm going to call Monty Grisham," she said. "He doesn't do this kind of legal work, but he'll know someone who does."

"I don't need a lawyer, Mom." Officer Caroline gave me a quick sideways glance when I said that. "I didn't do anything."

"If Liz murdered someone and you were there, you need one. There'll be an inquest…press…I don't know what-all. This is my fault. I brought that bitch into our house." Then she spat: "Fucking *Liz!*"

"She was good at first." This was true, but all at once I felt very, very tired. "I'll see you when you get here."

I ended the call and asked Officer Caroline how long it would take us to get to the doc-in-the-box. She said twenty minutes. I looked over my shoulder, through the mesh blocking off the back seat, suddenly sure that Liz would be there. Or—so much worse—Therriault. But it was empty.

"It's just you and me, Jamie," Officer Caroline said. "Don't worry."

"I'm not," I said, but there was one thing I *did* have to worry about, and thank God I remembered, or me and Mom might have been in a heap of trouble. I put my head against the window and half-turned away from her. "Going to take a little nap."

"You do that." There was a smile in her voice.

I *did* take a little nap. But first I powered up Liz's phone, hiding it with my body, and deleted the recording she'd made of me passing on the plot of *The Secret of Roanoke* to my mom. If they took the phone and found out it wasn't mine, I'd make something up. Or just say I couldn't remember, which would be safer. But they couldn't hear that recording.

No way.

66

The Chief and two other cops turned up at the MedNow place an hour or so after Officer Caroline and I got there. Also a guy in a suit who introduced himself as the county attorney. A doctor examined me and said I was basically fine, blood pressure a little high but considering what I'd been through, that wasn't surprising. He felt sure it would be normal again by morning and pronounced me "your basic healthy teenager." I happened to be your basic healthy teenager who could see dead folks, but I didn't go into that.

Me and the cops and the county attorney went into the staff break room to wait for my mother, and as soon as she got there, the questions started. That night we stayed at the Renfield Stardust Motel, and the next morning there were more questions. My mother was the one who told them she and Elizabeth Dutton had been in a relationship that ended when Mom discovered Liz was involved in the drug trade. I was the one who told them how Liz had scooped me up after tennis practice and took me to Renfield, where she was expecting to rob a big haul of Oxy from Mr. Marsden's house. He finally told her where the drugs were, and she killed him, either because she didn't get the jackpot she was expecting or because of the other stuff she found in that room. The pictures.

"There's one thing I don't understand," Officer Caroline said as I gave her back her jacket, which I had kept wearing. Mom gave her a wary, ready-to-protect-my-cub look, but Officer Caroline didn't see it. She was looking at me. "She tied the guy up—"

"She said she *secured* him. That was the word she used. Because she used to be a cop, I guess."

"Okay, she secured him. And according to what she told you—also according to what we found upstairs—she tuned up on him a little. But not all that much."

"Would you get to the point?" Mom said. "My son has been through a terrible experience and he's exhausted."

Officer Caroline ignored her. She was looking at me, and her eyes were very bright. "She could have done a lot more, tortured him until she got what she wanted, but instead she left him, drove all the way to New York City, kidnapped you, and brought you back. Why did she do that?"

"I don't know."

"You had a two-hour ride with her, and she never said?"

"All she said was she was glad to see me." I couldn't remember if she'd actually said that or not, so I guess it was technically a lie, but it didn't feel like one. I thought of those nights on the couch, sitting between them and watching *The Big Bang Theory*, all of us laughing our heads off, and I started to cry. Which got us out of there.

Once we were in the motel with the door shut and locked, Mom said, "If they ask you again, say that maybe she was planning to take you with her when she headed west. Can you do that?"

"Yes," I said. Wondering if maybe that idea had been knocking around someplace in Liz's mind all along. It wasn't a good thing to speculate on, but better than what I *had* thought (and still do today): that she planned to kill me.

I didn't sleep in the connecting room. I slept on the couch in Mom's. I dreamed that I was walking on a lonely country road under a sickle moon. *Don't whistle, don't whistle*, I told myself, but I did. I couldn't help myself. I was whistling "Let It Be." I remember that very clearly. I hadn't gotten through more than the first six or eight notes when I heard footsteps behind me.

I woke up with my hands clapped over my mouth, as if to stifle a scream. I've woken up the same way a few times in the years since, and it's never a scream I'm afraid of. I'm afraid I'll wake up whistling and the deadlight thing will be there.

Arms outstretched to hug.

67

There are plenty of drawbacks to being a kid; check it out. Zits, the agony of choosing the right clothes to wear to school so you don't get laughed at, and the mystery of girls are only three of them. What I found out after my trip to Donald Marsden's house (my kidnapping, to be perfectly blunt) was that there are also advantages.

One of them was not having to run a gauntlet of reporters and TV cameras at the inquest, because I didn't have to testify in person. I gave a video deposition instead, with the lawyer Monty Grisham found for me on one side and my mom on the other. The press knew who I was, but my name never appeared in the media because I was that magic thing, a minor. The kids at school found out (the kids at school almost always find out everything), but nobody ragged on me. I got respect instead. I didn't have to figure out how to talk to girls, because they came up to my locker and talked to me.

Best of all, there was no trouble about my phone—which was actually Liz's phone. It no longer existed, anyway. Mom tossed it down the incinerator, bon voyage, and told me to say I'd lost it if anyone asked. No one did. As for why Liz came to New York and snatched me, the police came to the conclusion Mom had already suggested, all on their own: Liz had wanted a kid with her when she went west, maybe figuring a woman traveling with a kid would attract less attention. No one seemed to consider the possibility that I'd try to escape, or at least yell for help when we stopped for gas and grub in Pennsylvania or Indiana or Montana. Of course I wouldn't do that. I'd be a docile little kidnap victim, just like Elizabeth Smart. Because I was a kid.

The newspapers played it big for a week or so, especially the tabloids, partly because Marsden was a "drug kingpin" but mostly because of the pictures found in his panic room. And Liz came off as sort of a hero, weird but true. EX-COP DIES AFTER SLAYING TORTURE PORN DON, blared the *Daily News*. No mention that she'd lost her job as the result of an IAD investigation and a positive drug test, but the fact that she'd been instrumental in locating Thumper's last bomb before it could kill a bunch of shoppers *was* mentioned. The *Post* must have gotten a reporter inside Marsden's house ("Cockroaches get in everywhere," Mom said), or maybe they had pix of the Renfield place on file, because their headline read INSIDE DONNIE BIGS' HOUSE OF HORRORS. My mother actually laughed at that one, saying that the *Post*'s understanding of the apostrophe was a nice parallel for their grasp of American politics.

"Not Bigs-apostrophe," she said when I asked. "Bigs-apostrophe-S."

Okay, Mom. Whatever.

68

Before long, other news drove Donnie Bigs's House of Horrors from the front pages of the tabs, and my renown at school faded. It was like Liz said about Chet Atkins, how soon they forget. I found myself once more faced with the problem of talking to girls instead of waiting for them to come up to my locker, all round-eyed with mascara and pursed up with lip gloss, to talk to me. I played tennis and tried out for the class play. I ended up only getting a part with two lines, but I put my heart into them. I played video games with my friends. I took Mary Lou Stein to the movies and kissed her. She kissed me back, which was excellent.

Cue the montage, complete with flipping calendar pages. It got to be 2016, then 2017. Sometimes I dreamed I was on that country road and would wake up with my hands over my mouth thinking *Did I whistle? Oh God, did I whistle?* But those dreams came less frequently. Sometimes I saw dead folks, but not too often and they weren't scary. Once my mother asked me if I still saw them and I said hardly ever, knowing it would make her feel better. That was something I wanted, because she had been through a hard time, too, and I got that.

"Maybe you're growing out of it," she said.

"Maybe I am," I agreed.

This brings us to 2018, with our hero Jamie Conklin over six feet tall, able to grow a goatee (which my mother fucking loathed), accepted at Princeton, and almost old enough to vote. I *would* be old enough when the elections came around in November.

I was in my room, hitting the books for finals, when my phone buzzed. It was Mom, calling from the back of another Uber, this time on her way to Tenafly, where Uncle Harry was now residing.

"It's pneumonia again," she said, "and I don't think he's going to get better this time, Jamie. They told me to come, and they don't do that unless it's very serious." She paused, then said: "Mortal."

"I'll be there as fast as I can."

"You don't have to do that." The subtext being that I'd never really known him anyway, at least not when he was a smart guy building a career for himself and his sister in the world of tough New York publishing. Which can be a tough world indeed. Now that I was also working in the office— only a few hours a week, mostly filing—I knew that was true.

And it was true that I had only vague memories of a smart guy who should have stayed smart a lot longer, but it wasn't him I'd be going for.

"I'll take the bus." Which I could do with ease, because the bus was how we'd always gone to New Jersey in the days when Ubers and Lyfts were beyond our budget.

"Your tests…you have to study for your finals…"

"Books are a uniquely portable magic. I read that somewhere. I'll bring 'em. See you there."

"We may have to stay overnight," she said. "Are you sure?"

I said I was.

I don't know exactly where I was when Uncle Harry died. Maybe in New Jersey, maybe still crossing the Hudson, maybe even while I could see Yankee Stadium from my bird-beshitted bus window. All I know is that Mom was waiting for me outside the care home—his final care home—on a bench under a shade tree. She was dry-eyed, but she was smoking a cigarette and I hadn't seen her do that in a long time. She gave me a good strong hug and I gave it right back to her. I could smell her perfume, that old sweet smell of La Vie est Belle, which always took me back to my childhood. To that little boy who thought his green hand-turkey was just the cat's ass. I didn't have to ask.

"Not ten minutes before I got here," she said.

"Are you okay?"

"Yes. Sad, but also relieved that it's finally over. He lasted much longer than most people who suffer from what he had. You know what, I was sitting here thinking about three flies, six grounders. Do you know what that is?"

"I think so, yeah."

"The other boys didn't want to let me play because I was a girl, but Harry said if they wouldn't let me play, he wouldn't play, either. And he was popular. Always the most popular. So I was, as they say, the only girl in the game."

"Were you good?"

"I was terrific," she said, and laughed. Then she wiped at one of her eyes. Crying after all. "Listen, I need to talk to Mrs. Ackerman—she's the boss-lady here—and sign some papers. Then I need go down to his room and see if there's anything I need to take right away. I can't imagine there is."

I felt a stirring of alarm. "He's not still…?"

"No, honey. There's a funeral home they use here. I'll make arrangements tomorrow about getting him to New York and the…you know, final stuff." She paused. "Jamie?"

I looked at her.

"You don't…you don't see him, do you?"

I smiled. "No, Ma."

She grabbed my chin. "How many times have I told you not to call me that? Who says maa?"

"Baby sheep," I said, then added, "Yeah yeah yeah."

That made her laugh. "Wait for me, hon. This won't take long."

She went inside and I looked at Uncle Harry, who was standing not ten feet away. He'd been there all along, wearing the pajamas he'd died in.

"Hey, Uncle Harry," I said.

No reply. But he was looking at me.

"Have you still got the Alzheimer's?"

"No."

"So you're okay now?"

He looked at me with the merest glint of humor. "I suppose so, if being dead fits into your definition of okay."

"She's going to miss you, Uncle Harry."

No reply, and I didn't expect one because it wasn't a question. I did have one, though. He probably didn't know the answer, but there's an old saying that goes if you never ask, you never get.

"Do you know who my father is?"

"Yes."

"Who? Who is it?"

"I am," Uncle Harry said.

69

Almost done now (and I remember when I thought thirty pages was a lot!), but not quite, so don't give up before you check this out:

My grandparents—my *only* set of grandparents, as it turns out—died on their way to a Christmas party. A guy full of too much Christmas cheer swerved across three lanes of a four-lane highway and hit them head-on. The drunk survived, as they so often do. My uncle (also my father, as it turns out) was in New York when he got the news, making the rounds of *several* Christmas parties, schmoozing publishers, editors, and writers. His agency was brand-new then, and Uncle Harry (dear old dad!) was kind of like a guy in the deep woods, tending a tiny pile of burning twigs and hoping for a campfire.

He came home to Arcola—that's a small town in Illinois—
for the funeral. After it was over, there was a reception at
the Conklins'. Lester and Norma had been well liked, so lots
of people came. Some brought food. Some brought booze,
which serves as godfather to a great many surprise babies.
Tia Conklin, at that time not long out of college and working
at her first job in an accounting firm, drank a good deal. So
did her brother. Uh-oh, right?

After everybody goes home, Harry finds her in her room,
lying on her bed in her slip, crying her heart out. Harry lies
down beside her and takes her in his arms. Just for comfort,
you understand, but one kind of comfort leads to another.
Just that once, but once is enough, and six weeks later Harry—
back in New York—gets a phone call. Not long after that, my
pregnant mother joins the firm.

Would the Conklin Literary Agency have succeeded in that
tough, competitive field without her, or would my father/uncle's
little pile of twigs and leaves have fizzled out in a little runner
of white smoke before he could begin to add the first bigger
pieces of wood? Hard to say. When things took off, I was lying
around in a bassinet, peeing in my Pampers and going goo-goo.
But she was good at the job, that I know. If she hadn't been,
the agency would have gone under later, when the bottom fell
out of the financial markets.

Let me tell you, there are a lot of bullshit myths about
babies born of incest, especially when it comes to father–
daughter and sister–brother. Yes, there can be medical problems, and yes, the chances of those are a little higher when it
comes to incest, but the idea that the majority of those babies
are born with feeble minds, one eye, or club feet? Pure crap.

I did find out that one of the most common defects in babies from incestuous relationships is fused fingers or toes. I have scars on the insides of my second and third fingers on my left hand, from a surgical procedure to separate them when I was an infant. The first time I asked about those scars—I couldn't have been more than four or five—Mom told me the docs had done it before she brought me home from the hospital. "Easy-peasy," she said.

And of course there's that other thing I was born with, which might have something to do with the fact that once upon a time, while suffering from grief and alcohol, my parents got a little closer than a brother and sister should have done. Or maybe seeing dead people has nothing at all to do with that. Parents who can't carry a tune in a tin pail can produce a singing prodigy; illiterates can produce a great writer. Sometimes talent comes from nowhere, or so it seems.

Except, hold it, wait one.

That whole story is fiction.

I don't know how Tia and Harry became the parents of a bouncing baby boy named James Lee Conklin, because I never asked Uncle Harry for any of the details. He would have told me—the dead can't lie, as I think we have established—but I didn't want to know. After he said those two words—*I am*—I turned away and walked back into the care home to find my mother. He didn't follow, and I never saw him again. I thought he might come to his funeral, or turn up at the graveside ceremony, but he didn't.

On the way back to the city (on the bus, just like old times), Mom asked me if something was wrong. I said there wasn't, that I was just trying to get used to the idea that Uncle Harry was really gone. "It feels like when I lost one of my baby teeth," I said. "There's a hole in me and I keep feeling it."

"I know," she said, hugging me. "I feel the same way. But I'm not sad. I didn't expect to be, and I'm not. Because he's really been gone for a long time."

It was good to be hugged. I loved my mom and I love her still, but I lied to her that day, and not just by omission. It wasn't like *losing* a tooth; what I'd found out was like growing another tooth, one there wasn't room for in my mouth.

Certain things make the story I just told you seem more likely. Lester and Norma Conklin *were* killed by a drunk driver while on their way to a Christmas party. Harry *did* come back to Illinois for their funeral; I found an article in the Arcola *Record Herald* that says he gave the eulogy. Tia Conklin *did* quit her job and go to New York to help her brother in his new literary agency early the next year. And James Lee Conklin *did* make his debut nine months or so after the funeral, in Lenox Hill Hospital.

So yeah yeah yeah and right right right, it could all be just the way I told it. It has a fair amount of logic going for it. But it also could have been some other way, which I would like a lot less. The rape of a young woman who'd drunk herself unconscious, for instance, said act committed by her drunken, horny older brother. The reason I didn't ask is simple: I didn't want to know. Do I wonder if they discussed abortion? Sometimes. Am I worried that I have inherited more from my uncle/father than the dimples that show up when I smile, or the fact that I'm showing the first traces of white in my black hair at the tender age of twenty-two? To come right out and say it, am I worried that I may start to lose my mind at the still-tender age of thirty, or thirty-five, or forty? Yes. Of course I am. According to the Internet, my father–uncle suffered from EOFAD: early-onset familial Alzheimer's disease. It bides its time on genes PSEN1 and PSEN2, and so there's a test for it: spit in a test-tube and wait for your answer. I suppose I will take it.

Later.

Here's a funny thing—looking back over these pages, I see that the writing got better as I went along. Not trying to say I'm up there with Faulkner or Updike; what I *am* saying is that I improved by doing, which I suppose is the case with most things in life. I'll just have to hope I'll be better and stronger in other ways when I again meet the thing that took over Therriault. Because I will. I've not glimpsed it since that night in Marsden's house when whatever Liz saw in that mirror drove her insane, but it's still waiting. I sense that. Know it, actually, although I don't know what it is.

It doesn't matter. I won't live my life with the pending question of whether or not I'm going to lose my mind in middle age, and I won't live it with the shadow of that thing hanging over me, either. It has drained the color from too many days. The fact that I am a child of incest seems laughably unimportant compared to the black husk of Therriault with the deadlight shining out from the cracks in its skin.

I have done a lot of reading in the years since that thing asked me for a do-over contest, another Ritual of Chüd, and I've come across a lot of strange superstitions and odd legends—stuff that never made it into Regis Thomas's Roanoke books or Stoker's *Dracula*—and while there are plenty concerning the possession of the living by demons, I have never yet found one about a creature able to possess the dead. The closest I've come are stories about malevolent ghosts, and that's really not the same at all. So I have no idea what I'm dealing with. All I know is that I must deal with it. I'll whistle for it, it will come, we will join in a mutual hug instead of the ritual tongue-biting thing, and then…well. Then we'll see, won't we?

Yes we will. We'll see.

Later.

From the Author of LATER...

Don't Miss Stephen King's
JOYLAND

College student Devin Jones took the summer job at Joyland hoping to forget the girl who broke his heart. But he wound up facing something far more terrible: the legacy of a vicious murder, the fate of a dying child, and dark truths about life—and what comes after—that would change his world forever.

A riveting story about love and loss, about growing up and growing old—and about those who don't get to do either because death comes for them before their time—JOYLAND is Stephen King at the peak of his storytelling powers. With all the emotional impact of King masterpieces such as *The Green Mile* and *The Shawshank Redemption*, JOYLAND is at once a mystery, a horror story, and a bittersweet coming-of-age novel, one that will leave even the most hard-boiled reader profoundly moved.

"Immensely appealing."
— Washington Post

"Tight and engrossing…a prize worth all your tokens and skeeball tickets."
— USA Today

**Read on for a preview—
or get a copy today
from your favorite
local or online bookseller!**

♥

I had a car, but on most days in that fall of 1973 I walked to Joyland from Mrs. Shoplaw's Beachside Accommodations in the town of Heaven's Bay. It seemed like the right thing to do. The only thing, actually. By early September, Heaven Beach was almost completely deserted, which suited my mood. That fall was the most beautiful of my life. Even forty years later I can say that. And I was never so unhappy, I can say that, too. People think first love is sweet, and never sweeter than when that first bond snaps. You've heard a thousand pop and country songs that prove the point; some fool got his heart broke. Yet that first broken heart is always the most painful, the slowest to mend, and leaves the most visible scar. What's so sweet about that?

♥

Through September and right into October, the North Carolina skies were clear and the air was warm even at seven in the morning, when I left my second-floor apartment by the outside stairs. If I started with a light jacket on, I was wearing it tied around my waist before I'd finished half of the three miles between the town and the amusement park.

I'd make Betty's Bakery my first stop, grabbing a couple of still-warm croissants. My shadow would walk with me on the sand, at least twenty feet long. Hopeful gulls, smelling the croissants in their waxed paper, would circle overhead. And when I walked back, usually around five (although sometimes I stayed later—there was nothing waiting for me in Heaven's Bay, a town that mostly went sleepybye when summer was over), my shadow walked with me on the water. If the tide was in, it would waver on the surface, seeming to do a slow hula.

Although I can't be completely sure, I think the boy and the woman and their dog were there from the first time I took that walk. The shore between the town and the cheerful, blinking gimcrackery of Joyland was lined with summer homes, many of them expensive, most of them clapped shut after Labor Day. But not the biggest of them, the one that looked like a green wooden castle. A boardwalk led from its wide back patio down to where the seagrass gave way to fine white sand. At the end of the boardwalk was a picnic table shaded by a bright green beach umbrella. In its shade, the boy sat in his wheelchair, wearing a baseball cap and covered from the waist down by a blanket even in the late afternoons, when the temperature lingered in the seventies. I thought he was five or so, surely no older than seven. The dog, a Jack Russell terrier, either lay beside him or sat at his feet. The woman sat on one of the picnic table benches, sometimes reading a book, mostly just staring out at the water. She was very beautiful.

Going or coming, I always waved to them, and the boy waved back. She didn't, not at first. 1973 was the year of the OPEC oil embargo, the year Richard Nixon announced he was not a crook, the year Edward G. Robinson and Noel Coward died. It was Devin Jones's lost year. I was a twenty-one year-old virgin with literary aspirations. I possessed three pairs of bluejeans, four pairs of Jockey shorts, a clunker Ford (with a good radio), occasional suicidal ideations, and a broken heart.

Sweet, huh?

♥

The heartbreaker was Wendy Keegan, and she didn't deserve me. It's taken me most of my life to come to that conclusion, but you know the old saw; better late than never. She was from Portsmouth, New Hampshire; I was from South Berwick, Maine. That made her practically the girl next door. We had begun "going together" (as we used to say) during our freshman year at UNH—we actually met at the Freshman Mixer, and how sweet is that? Just like one of those pop songs.

We were inseparable for two years, went everywhere together and did everything together. Everything, that is, but "it." We were both work-study kids with University jobs. Hers was in the library; mine was in the Commons cafeteria. We were offered the chance to hold onto those jobs during the summer of 1972, and of course we did. The money wasn't great, but the togetherness was priceless. I assumed that would also be the deal during the summer of 1973, until Wendy announced that her friend Renee had gotten them jobs working at Filene's, in Boston.

"Where does that leave me?" I asked.

"You can always come down," she said. "I'll miss you like mad, but really, Dev, we could probably use some time apart."

A phrase that is very often a death-knell. She may have seen that idea on my face, because she stood on tiptoe and kissed me. "Absence makes the heart grow fonder," she said. "Besides, with my own place, maybe you can stay over." But she didn't quite look at me when she said that, and I never did stay over. Too many roommates, she said. Too little time. Of course such problems can be overcome, but somehow we never did, which should have told me something; in retrospect, it tells me a lot. Several times we had been very close to "it," but "it" just never quite happened. She always drew back, and I never pressed her. God help me, I was being gallant. I have wondered often since what would have changed (for good or for ill) had I not been. What I know now is that gallant young men rarely get pussy. Put it on a sampler and hang it in your kitchen.

♥

The prospect of another summer mopping cafeteria floors and loading elderly Commons dishwashers with dirty plates didn't hold much charm for me, not with Wendy seventy miles south, enjoying the bright lights of Boston, but it was steady work, which I needed, and I didn't have any other prospects. Then, in late February, one literally came down the dish-line to me on the conveyor belt.

Someone had been reading *Carolina Living* while he or she snarfed up that day's blue plate luncheon special, which happened to be Mexicali Burgers and Caramba Fries.

He or she had left the magazine on the tray, and I picked it up along with the dishes. I almost tossed it in the trash, then didn't. Free reading material was, after all, free reading material. (I was a work-study kid, remember.) I stuck it in my back pocket and forgot about it until I got back to my dorm room. There it flopped onto the floor, open to the classified section at the back, while I was changing my pants.

Whoever had been reading the magazine had circled several job possibilities...although in the end, he or she must have decided none of them was quite right; otherwise *Carolina Living* wouldn't have come riding down the conveyor belt. Near the bottom of the page was an ad that caught my eye even though it hadn't been circled. In boldface type, the first line read: WORK CLOSE TO HEAVEN! What English major could read that and not hang in for the pitch? And what glum twenty-one-year-old, beset with the growing fear that he might be losing his girlfriend, would not be attracted by the idea of working in a place called Joyland?

There was a telephone number, and on a whim, I called it. A week later, a job application landed in my dormitory mailbox. The attached letter stated that if I wanted full-time summer employment (which I did), I'd be doing many different jobs, most but not all custodial. I would have to possess a valid driver's license, and I would need to interview. I could do that on the upcoming spring break instead of going home to Maine for the week. Only I'd been planning to spend at least some of that week with Wendy. We might even get around to "it."

"Go for the interview," Wendy said when I told her. She didn't even hesitate. "It'll be an adventure."

"Being with you would be an adventure," I said.

"There'll be plenty of time for that next year." She stood on tiptoe and kissed me (she always stood on tiptoe). Was she seeing the other guy, even then? Probably not, but I'll bet she'd noticed him, because he was in her Advanced Sociology course. Renee St. Claire would have known, and probably would have told me if I'd asked—telling stuff was Renee's specialty, I bet she wore the priest out when she did the old confession bit—but some things you don't want to know. Like why the girl you loved with all your heart kept saying no to you, but tumbled into bed with the new guy at almost the first opportunity. I'm not sure anybody ever gets completely over their first love, and that still rankles. Part of me still wants to know what was *wrong* with me. What I was lacking. I'm in my sixties now, my hair is gray and I'm a prostate cancer survivor, but I still want to know why I wasn't good enough for Wendy Keegan.

♥

I took a train called the Southerner from Boston to North Carolina (not much of an adventure, but cheap), and a bus from Wilmington to Heaven's Bay. My interview was with Fred Dean, who was—among many other functions—Joyland's employment officer. After fifteen minutes of Q-and-A, plus a look at my driver's license and my Red Cross life-saving certificate, he handed me a plastic badge on a lanyard. It bore the word VISITOR, that day's date, and a cartoon picture of a grinning, blue-eyed German Shepherd who bore a passing resemblance to the famous cartoon sleuth, Scooby-Doo.

"Take a walk around," Dean said. "Ride the Carolina Spin, if you like. Most of the rides aren't up and running yet, but that one is. Tell Lane I said okay. What I gave you is a day-pass, but I want you back here by…" He looked at his watch. "Let's say one o'clock. Tell me then if you want the job. I've got five spots left, but they're all basically the same —as Happy Helpers."

"Thank you, sir."

He nodded, smiling. "Don't know how you'll feel about this place, but it suits me fine. It's a little old and a little rickety, but I find that charming. I tried Disney for a while; didn't like it. It's too…I don't know…"

"Too corporate?" I ventured.

"Exactly. Too corporate. Too buffed and shiny. So I came back to Joyland a few years ago. Haven't regretted it. We fly a bit more by the seat of our pants here—the place has a little of the old-time carny flavor. Go on, look around. See what you think. More important, see how you *feel*."

"Can I ask one question first?"

"Of course."

I fingered my day pass. "Who's the dog?"

His smile became a grin. "That's Howie the Happy Hound, Joyland's mascot. Bradley Easterbrook built Joyland, and the original Howie was his dog. Long dead now, but you'll still see a lot of him, if you work here this summer."

I did…and I didn't. An easy riddle, but the explanation will have to wait awhile.

♥

Joyland was an indie, not as big as a Six Flags park, and no-where near as big as Disney World, but it was large enough to be impressive, especially with Joyland Avenue, the main drag, and Hound Dog Way, the secondary drag, almost empty and looking eight lanes wide. I heard the whine of power-saws and saw plenty of workmen—the largest crew swarming over the Thunderball, one of Joyland's two coasters—but there were no customers, because the park didn't open until June fifteenth. A few of the food concessions were doing business to take care of the workers' lunch needs, though, and an old lady in front of a star-studded tell-your-fortune kiosk was staring at me suspiciously. With one exception, everything else was shut up tight.

The exception of the Carolina Spin. It was a hundred and seventy feet tall (this I found out later), and turning very slowly. Out in front stood a tightly muscled guy in faded jeans, balding suede boots splotched with grease, and a strap-style tee shirt. He wore a derby hat tilted on his coal-black hair. A filterless cigarette was parked behind one ear. He looked like a cartoon carnival barker from an old-time newspaper strip. There was an open toolbox and a big portable radio on an orange crate beside him. The Faces were singing "Stay with Me." The guy was bopping to the beat, hands in his back pockets, hips moving side to side. I had a thought, absurd but perfectly clear: *When I grow up, I want to look just like this guy.*

He pointed to the pass. "Freddy Dean sent you, right? Told you everything else was closed, but you could take a ride on the big wheel."

"Yes, sir."

"A ride on the Spin means you're in. He likes the chosen few to get the aerial view. You gonna take the job?"

"I think so."

He stuck out his hand. "I'm Lane Hardy. Welcome aboard, kid."

I shook with him. "Devin Jones."

"Pleased to meet you."

He started up the inclined walk leading to the gently turning ride, grabbed a long lever that looked like a stick shift, and edged it back. The wheel came to a slow stop with one of the gaily painted cabins (the image of Howie the Happy Hound on each) swaying at the passenger loading dock.

"Climb aboard, Jonesy. I'm going to send you up where the air is rare and the view is much more than fair."

I climbed into the cabin and closed the door. Lane gave it a shake to make sure it was latched, dropped the safety bar, then returned to his rudimentary controls. "Ready for takeoff, cap'n?"

"I guess so."

"Amazement awaits." He gave me a wink and advanced the control stick. The wheel began to turn again and all at once he was looking up at me. So was the old lady by the fortune-telling booth. Her neck was craned and she was shading her eyes. I waved to her. She didn't wave back.

Then I was above everything but the convoluted dips and twists of the Thunderball, rising into the chilly early spring air, and feeling—stupid but true—that I was leaving all my cares and worries down below.

Joyland wasn't a theme park, which allowed it to have a little bit of everything. There was a secondary roller coaster called the Delirium Shaker and a water slide (Captain Nemo's Splash & Crash). On the far western side of the park was a special annex for the little ones called the Wiggle-Waggle Village. There was also a concert hall where most of the acts—this I also learned later—were either B-list C&W or the kind of rockers who peaked in the fifties or sixties. I remember that Johnny Otis and Big Joe Turner did a show there together. I had to ask Brenda Rafferty, the head accountant who was also a kind of den mother to the Hollywood Girls, who they were. Bren thought I was dense; I thought she was old; we were both probably right.

Lane Hardy took me all the way to the top and then stopped the wheel. I sat in the swaying car, gripping the safety bar, and looking out at a brand-new world. To the west was the North Carolina flatland, looking incredibly green to a New England kid who was used to thinking of March as nothing but true spring's cold and muddy precursor. To the east was the ocean, a deep metallic blue until it broke in creamy-white pulses on the beach where I would tote my abused heart up and down a few months hence. Directly below me was the good-natured jumble of Joyland —the big rides and small ones, the concert hall and concessions, the souvenir shops and the Happy Hound Shuttle, which took customers to the adjacent motels and, of course, the beach. To the north was Heaven's Bay. From high above the park (upstairs, where the air is rare), the town looked like a nestle of children's blocks from which four church steeples rose at the major points of the compass.

The wheel began to move again. I came down feeling like a kid in a Rudyard Kipling story, riding on the nose of an elephant. Lane Hardy brought me to a stop, but didn't bother to unlatch the car's door for me; I was, after all, almost an employee.

"How'd you like it?"

"Great," I said.

"Yeah, it ain't bad for a grandma ride." He reset his derby so it slanted the other way and cast an appraising eye over me. "How tall are you? Six-three?"

"Six-four."

"Uh-huh. Let's see how you like ridin all six-four of you on the Spin in the middle of July, wearin the fur and singin 'Happy Birthday' to some spoiled-rotten little snothole with cotton candy in one hand and a meltin Kollie Kone in the other."

"Wearing what fur?"

But he was headed back to his machinery and didn't answer. Maybe he couldn't hear me over his radio, which was now blasting "Crocodile Rock." Or maybe he just wanted my future occupation as one of Joyland's cadre of Happy Hounds to come as a surprise.

♥

I had over an hour to kill before meeting with Fred Dean again, so I strolled up Hound Dog Way toward a lunch-wagon that looked like it was doing a pretty good business. Not everything at Joyland was canine-themed, but plenty of stuff was, including this particular eatery, which was called Pup-A-Licious. I was on a ridiculously tight budget for this little job-hunting expedition, but I thought I could afford a couple of bucks for a chili-dog and a paper cup of French fries.

When I reached the palm-reading concession, Madame Fortuna planted herself in my path. Except that's not quite right, because she was only Fortuna between May fifteenth and Labor Day. During those sixteen weeks, she dressed in long skirts, gauzy, layered blouses, and shawls decorated with various cabalistic symbols. Gold hoops hung from her ears, so heavy they dragged the lobes down, and she talked in a thick Romany accent that made her sound like a character from a 1930s fright-flick, the kind featuring mist-shrouded castles and howling wolves.

During the rest of the year she was a widow from Brooklyn who collected Hummel figures and liked movies (especially the weepy-ass kind where some chick gets cancer and dies beautifully). Today she was smartly put together in a black pantsuit and low heels. A rose-pink scarf around her throat added a touch of color. As Fortuna, she sported masses of wild gray locks, but that was a wig, and still stored under its own glass dome in her little Heaven's Bay house. Her actual hair was a cropped cap of dyed black. The *Love Story* fan from Brooklyn and Fortuna the Seer only came together in one respect: both fancied themselves psychic.

"There is a shadow over you, young man," she announced.

I looked down and saw she was absolutely right. I was standing in the shadow of the Carolina Spin. We both were.

"Not that, stupidnik. Over your future. You will have a hunger."

I had a bad one already, but a Pup-A-Licious footlong would soon take care of it. "That's very interesting, Mrs... um..."

"Rosalind Gold," she said, holding out her hand. "But you can call me Rozzie. Everyone does. But during the season..." She fell into character, which meant she sounded like Bela Lugosi with breasts. "Doorink the season, I am... *Fortuna*!"

I shook with her. If she'd been in costume as well as in

character, half a dozen gold bangles would have clattered on her wrist. "Very nice to meet you." And, trying on the same accent: "I am...*Devin!*"

She wasn't amused. "An Irish name?"

"Right."

"The Irish are full of sorrow, and many have the sight. I don't know if you do, but you will meet someone who does."

Actually, I was full of happiness...along with that surpassing desire to put a Pup-A-Licious pup, preferably loaded with chili, down my throat. This was feeling like an adventure. I told myself I'd probably feel less that way when I was swabbing out toilets at the end of a busy day, or cleaning puke from the seats of the Whirly Cups, but just then everything seemed perfect.

"Are you practicing your act?"

She drew herself up to her full height, which might have been five-two. "Is no act, my lad." She said *ect* for *act*. "Jews are the most psychically sensitive race on earth. This is a thing everyone knows." She dropped the accent. "Also, Joyland beats hanging out a palmistry shingle on Second Avenue. Sorrowful or not, I like you. You give off good vibrations."

"One of my very favorite Beach Boys songs."

"But you are on the edge of great sorrow." She paused, doing the old emphasis thing. "And, perhaps, danger."

"Do you see a beautiful woman with dark hair in my future?" Wendy was a beautiful woman with dark hair.

"No," Rozzie said, and what came next stopped me dead. "She is in your past."

Ohh-kay.

I walked around her in the direction of Pup-A-Licious, being careful not to touch her. She was a charlatan, I didn't have a single doubt about that, but touching her just then still seemed like a lousy idea.

No good. She walked with me. "In your future is a little girl and a little boy. The boy has a dog."

"A Happy Hound, I bet. Probably named Howie."

She ignored this latest attempt at levity. "The girl wears a red hat and carries a doll. One of these children has the sight. I don't know which. It is hidden from me."

I hardly heard that part of her spiel. I was thinking of the previous pronouncement, made in a flat Brooklyn accent: *She is in your past.*

Madame Fortuna got a lot of stuff wrong, I found out, but she *did* seem to have a genuine psychic touch, and on the day I interviewed for a summer at Joyland, she was hitting on all cylinders…

The Best of MWA Grand Master
LAWRENCE BLOCK!

"Block grabs you...and never lets go."
— ELMORE LEONARD

Sinner Man

Block's long-lost first crime novel, about an insurance man who reinvents himself as a mobster.

Borderline

On the border between El Paso, Texas, and Juarez, Mexico, five lives are about to collide: the gambler, the divorcee, the hitch-hiker, the redhead, and the madman who's not done killing.

Getting Off

A woman sets out to track down every man she's ever slept with —and kill them all.

Grifter's Game

A con man accidentally steals a drug lord's stash of heroin—and the man's beautiful wife. But can love survive a collaboration in homicide?

The Girl with the Deep Blue Eyes

In steamy small-town Florida, ex-cop Doak Miller falls for a femme fatale and has to figure out how to get away with murder on her behalf...

The Assignment
by **WALTER HILL**

Kidnapped and operated on by the vengeful sister of one of his victims, a professional killer emerges permanently altered—and with a thirst for revenge of his own. Inspired the movie starring Michelle Rodriguez and Sigourney Weaver.

The Girl with the Dragon Tattoo
by **STIEG LARSSON & SYLVAIN RUNBERG**

The entire saga of Lisbeth Salander, adapted in three graphic novels—plus a fourth volume, *The Girl Who Danced With Death*, telling an all-new story unavailable in any other format.

Babylon Berlin
by **VOLKER KUTSCHER**

In the years leading up to WWII, Berlin is a hotbed of crime and deception, intrigue and violence. Can one detective uncover its secrets and live to see justice done?

Ryuko, Vol. 1 & 2
by **ELDO YOSHIMIZU**

From acclaimed international artist Yoshimizu, the bloody story of a daughter of the Yakuza and her quest to learn her mother's fate and redeem her suffering.